Praise for Vicki Hinze

* * *

Their mission odds were a shade shy of impossible.

"Maggie, based on all your experience, what
are the odds GRID will attack this mall?" Justin
asked.

Maggie leaned her shoulder against the creamy
wall. "Based on all we know, *without* Special
Forces being present here, I'd have put the odds at
fifty-fifty." She paused, looked down at her feet,
then went on, dreading the words to soon leave
her mouth. "*With* Special Forces on-site tomorrow,
I believe Thomas Kunz and GRID will find the
temptation to attack irresistible."

Dear Reader,

We've heard a lot about terrorists and attacks in the past few years. They are, of course, a global concern. But for all we've heard, few talk specifically about the attacks that were prevented. And even less is said about the women and men who prevent them.

They intrigue me, these women. They live dual lives, even with loved ones. There are things they can talk about, and many more things—victories and defeats—that they can never discuss. Yet the horrors they work to prevent stand to impact us all, regardless of what nation we call home. Undoubtedly, personal sacrifices are required from these women. But how many? Of what nature? And for how long?

These are the ponderings that led me to write the WAR GAMES miniseries, and *Double Dare* specifically. Because my spouse was in Special Operations, I knew how we had worked out his special job challenges. But how would a woman handle those challenges? What other challenges would she face? Could she sustain a marriage? If it failed, what *exactly* would be the marriage's proverbial last straw? And what happens to her afterward? If she sacrificed a marriage, would she then be jaded against future relationships, or would she dare to try again? And if she did dare, then how would she go about building a new relationship, and explaining her sudden absences and odd hours, and all she couldn't discuss?

Oh, there are far many more questions than answers. And when a writer runs into that situation, she has no choice. She *has* to write the book to find out!

I hope you enjoy the journey with me in *Double Dare*.

Blessings,

Vicki Hinze

DOUBLE DARE
VICKI HINZE

Silhouette® BOMBSHELL™

Published by Silhouette Books

America's Publisher of Contemporary Romance

SILHOUETTE BOOKS

ISBN 0-373-51383-6

DOUBLE DARE

www.SilhouetteBombshell.com

Printed in U.S.A.

Books by Vicki Hinze

Silhouette Bombshell

Body Double #12
Double Vision #45
Double Dare #69

Silhouette Books

Smokescreen
*"Total Recall"

*War Games

VICKI HINZE

is the author of fourteen novels, one nonfiction book and hundreds of articles published in over forty countries. Her books have received many prestigious awards and nominations, including her selection for *Who's Who in America* (as a writer and educator) and a multiple nominee for Career Achievement Awards as the Best Series Storyteller of the Year, Best Romantic Suspense Storyteller of the Year and Best Romantic Intrigue Novel of the Year. She's credited with having cocreated the first open-ended continuity series of single-title romance novels and with being among the first writers to create and establish subgenres in military women's fiction (suspense and intrigue) and military romantic-thriller novels.

To Raymond Wayne Hinze

I don't know that I've ever deserved
a son as special as you,
But I wish every parent could feel as blessed.
I am very proud of the man you've become.
Thank you, Ray, for the privilege of being your mother.

Love,
Mom

Chapter 1

"Jingle bells. Jingle bells. Jingle all the waa-aay—"

Singing along with the radio, Captain Maggie Holt hit a pothole in the dirt path leading to her office. Her right front tire dropped a solid six inches, jolting her, jarring her teeth. "Damn."

The red Jeep absorbed the shock without a groan, but her morning's first cup of coffee splashed all over the dashboard and passenger seat. The cup hit the side of the door and fell to the floorboard, a casualty of the daily war to get to the middle-of-nowhere shack without suffering bodily injury.

Maggie grimaced, just about sick of this. Her fellow operative, Darcy Clark, had trashed a set of shocks on Wilderness Trail, as they'd come to call the overgrown path, just a few days ago. What was it going to take for the commander, Colonel Sally Drake, to insist someone fix the sorry excuse for a road?

Irritated, Maggie smoothed at a soaked spot on her pale-blue uniform shirt and cranked up the radio, sifting through the lyrics to catch up to the tune. Tapping the gas, she moved through the woods, down the narrow ruts lined with hurricane-twisted pines and thick, spiky underbrush.

"In a one horse open sleigh. Hey!" She sang along and slid a glance to the Christmas ornament on the passenger's seat beside her. Everyone in the S.A.S.S.—Secret Assignment Security Specialists—unit celebrated Christmas and had to put an ornament on the tree no later than today. Colonel Drake's orders. She'd checked and none of the unit's operatives had taken time out from work to put up a tree at home this year. Hell, some hadn't even made it home in the better part of a week. The tree was the colonel's attempt at keeping everyone grounded in life as well as in work. Not likely to happen, in Maggie's humble opinion, but an endearing goal regardless.

The sparkling silver star was coffee-soaked but unbroken. Soaked would dry and unbroken was a good thing, because Maggie was damned if she was going back to Santa Bella Mall again for anything until after New Year's. It'd taken fifteen minutes to find a parking spot, ten to get inside and pick out the ornament and yet another fifteen minutes to pay for the thing and get out again. She figured that, before leaving the store's parking lot, she had more time invested in the freaking ornament than she'd spent with her ex-husband Jack in the last week of their marriage.

And wasn't that a shameful truth to have to admit?

Letting go of the steering wheel, she checked her hand.

The imprint of the spiky star and her wedding band were still there. She'd divorced Jack's sorry ass three years ago, but she still wore the wedding band most of the time. It kept rodents at a distance—and it reminded her that she hadn't been blameless in the destruction and demise of her marriage. Equally important, seeing the ring on her finger reminded her why, as long as she remained an operative, having a relationship was about as smart as Jack's recent intermittent attempts to drink himself to death.

Tapping the remote clipped to her visor, she blew past the first gate, glimpsing signs posted on the fence every eight feet: Use Of Deadly Force Authorized.

She and the other S.A.S.S. operatives stationed here were the deadly force.

A mile in, Maggie came to the second wire fence. This one was topped with razor wire so sharp it'd cut soda cans tossed at it. A speaker was attached to the gatepost. Inside was an artillery battery; dormant but maintained and ready to be used if needed.

She tapped the remote and the brakes, stopped and waited for the gate to swing open. The remote didn't have the range here that it had at the first gate, and the gate itself was slower to open. There was a specific purpose for that. Whoever was manning the monitors inside the S.A.S.S. bunker could take a look at who was coming in and have sufficient time to react.

Maggie waved at the surveillance camera and then drove on inside, whipping down the weedy trail to the shack. She parked in her normal spot, next to Kate's yellow Hummer.

Colonel Drake and the Providence Air Force Base commander, Colonel Donald Gray, were still neck-deep in a pissing contest over authority, and he assigned everyone their offices. So Gray had strutted his stuff and dumped the S.A.S.S. unit out in the middle of an abandoned bombing range twenty miles north of the Florida base. For an office, they had a shack. For water, a well. For electricity… There was no electricity.

It had been impossible to handle S.A.S.S. operations out of the shack, which had more holes than roof and walls. And it would've been hell for the unit to actually function out of the trailer parked out back, which was where Colonel Gray believed the unit had set up operations.

Gleeful at their primitive conditions, he had been generous and given them a generator. Not one that actually had the capacity to run their equipment, of course. He wanted Colonel Drake—and anyone who worked for her—to suffer because she'd beat him out in a head-to-head competition for the S.A.S.S. command job. But neither Colonel Drake nor the unit operatives complained to the honchos higher up in the chain of command to intercede. The operatives took on this challenge just as they did any other and focused on a solution.

Captain Mark Cross had been instrumental in the entire process. He'd used his money—rumor was he had a lot of it and he must, considering the palace he'd provided them—and his talent to build the S.A.S.S. unit an underground bunker. A top-notch, technologically advanced, freaking fabulous bunker with impressive offices twice as nice as any of those assigned to the Pentagon honchos, Maggie thought.

Maggie slid out of the Jeep into the brisk air and stepped

over to the shack. A hand-carved wooden sign hung above the door and read Regret. Mark had carved it as a reminder to all who entered. If Gray thought he'd won by sticking the unit in a primitive hellhole, he'd regret it.

Across the board, everyone with access to the bunker conceded that Colonel Gray had seriously lost the office-space battle in the Gray/Drake pissing contest.

Gray thought he'd won—luckily he didn't inspect very often.

Inside the falling-down shack, thin rays of sunlight filtered through the cracks and spilled onto the dirt floor. Maggie stepped to the right and pressed a board that looked more gray and aged than those around it. A split door slid open, exposing an elevator that led down a floor to the bunker's vault.

She stepped in and pushed the button to take her down. Of course, if Gray ever found out about the offices S.A.S.S. actually had, he'd commandeer them for himself and toss the unit into some other rat's nest or swamp without power or water. To avoid that, S.A.S.S. operatives had created an early warning system signaling outsiders' arrival, practiced scrambling regularly and kept their secret to themselves. So far, Colonel Gray remained in the dark. He'd never seen anyone in the S.A.S.S. unit anywhere other than in the trailer parked out behind the shack.

When the elevator door opened, Maggie stepped out into the crisp white hallway. Private offices lined the walls. At the east end, broad doors led to the Operations Center and beyond them was Darcy's private domain.

Captain Darcy Clark had been an operative until a mission had gone south and she'd received a serious head injury. It'd taken a while and a lot of determination on Darcy's part, but she'd recovered—with a kick. Total recall. The injury had taken her out of the field, but her new gift made her a hell of an asset for assimilating intel reports from around the globe.

Yet no gift comes without costs, and Darcy's were high. Around others, she suffered serious sensory-input overload. A trip to the mall was sheer hell. More often than not, she required total isolation to function normally, which meant even within the unit, she needed a place to retreat. Mark made sure she had it in her isolated office.

The good news on Darcy was that, since she had spent some time on a mission down at the Texas/Mexico border with Customs Agent Ben Kelly, she hadn't needed as much private time as she had before. Maggie was glad for that, and hoped the trend continued. Life in isolation had been hard on Darcy.

Maggie walked past the broad screens covering the common walls, past the photos of the FBI's Most Wanted, Homeland Security's suspected terrorists and the S.A.S.S.'s watch lists. She checked the hot-spots board and was relieved to see things were relatively calm worldwide, with the exception of Iraq, which was never calm these days. *Soon,* she prayed.

She dumped her purse on her desk then headed to the kitchen, located just this side of the Operations Center.

Captain Amanda West, a S.A.S.S. senior operative, was in the adjoining common room, throwing darts at a picture of Thomas Kunz tacked to the center of the dartboard.

By presidential decree, the S.A.S.S. unit's primary assignment was to intercede, interrupt and intercept Kunz.

So far, the world's most successful black marketer of top-secret, cutting-edge technology and weapons-systems/arms sales had three darts stuck right between his eyes.

Seeing his photo raised Maggie's hackles. Kunz was German, hated America and wanted to destroy it, preferably through the destruction of its economy. Unfortunately he'd had some success and he'd been as elusive as Bin Laden. Worse for the S.A.S.S. operatives pursuing him, Kunz and GRID—Group Resources for Individual Development—his raunchy band of greedy mercenaries, would use any tactics to succeed. Their loyalty was to money *at any costs,* which often made the work for Maggie and the others opposing them disheartening and sickening. When fighting an enemy dedicated to a different ideology—even if it's twisted—it's easy to respect the dedication. But there is no respect in greed. There is only fear and destruction.

Another dart whizzed through the air and stuck in Kunz's forehead, well within Amanda's one-inch group. "Thinking this morning, huh?" Maggie asked. Amanda always threw darts at Kunz when pondering something.

"Yeah." Amanda sighed and nailed him again.

Maggie paused. "Is he up to no good on something new?"

"Kunz is always up to no good. You can take that to the bank. But we haven't heard any new intel on a specific operation yet today." Amanda hiked a shoulder. "Of course, the day is young."

It was about eight o'clock in the morning. "Then, what's on your mind?"

Amanda frowned, wrinkling the skin between her brows. "It's Mark," she confessed, talking about Captain Mark Cross, with whom she'd had a serious thing going for nearly a year.

"What's wrong with him?" Maggie liked Mark, and these days she didn't like many men, which was just one of the many undesirable emotional stages of divorce: a merciless roller coaster that included far too many downsides and even more sadness. She repeated her mantra: *one bump at a time.*

Everyone else liked Mark, too, including Kate. The Queen Grouch hated almost everyone, but she loved Mark like a brother. Both alone, a couple years ago they had become surrogate family.

"Nothing's wrong with him." Amanda stopped, her arm midair, and just stared at Maggie. "Not one single thing. Not one."

So nothing was wrong with him and apparently that was a problem. "Okay, then." Maggie couldn't begin to figure this one out. She shrugged, walked across the wide room to the kitchen counter, snatched her butterfly cup from the cabinet and poured herself some coffee. The rich, heavy steam rising from the cup smelled like roasted heaven.

Amanda followed her. "It's not natural, Maggie. There should be something wrong with him, right? I mean, all men have something wrong with them."

Amanda still hadn't adjusted to being in love. Considering the abuse her father had heaped on her in her early years, Maggie expected it'd take her a good long while to learn to trust. Men who beat the hell out of you in drunken stupors then locked you in wooden boxes and forgot you there for days don't do much to inspire warm fuzzy feelings, much less a desire for taking on the risks of love.

How horrible that must have been. Shuddering, Maggie sipped from her cup then turned around. Loving Mark had kind of sneaked up on Amanda and bitten her on the backside when she hadn't been looking. With her protective shields, that's the only way it could have happened.

"You don't want to ask me that question," Maggie said. "I'm not what you'd call objective about men right now." *Not bad, Maggie. Downright diplomatic.* That too familiar knot of sadness swelled in her stomach.

"No, I do want to ask you," Amanda insisted. "You were married. You know how the relationship changed before and after. Mark and me, we're good. I—I don't want to mess it up." Her fear of doing just that pounded off her in waves. "Don't all men have something wrong with them, Maggie?"

Damn. She really didn't want to go there, but Amanda was nothing if not persistent, and she looked so worried.

"Here's my best advice, okay? You want a man with something wrong? My ex-husband will absolutely thrill you. It'll take years to count all his faults and flaws, and you'll never understand him." All true, and yet Maggie had been in love with him—until he'd stomped on her heart.

With a little sigh, she added cream to her coffee and stirred. "But if you've got any sense, you'll forget about looking for something wrong, and just be glad that every time you look Mark's way, the glare of his faults and flaws isn't blinding you."

"I am glad. Really. I just— Oh, God. I don't know." Amanda poured herself a glass of juice and then shut the fridge door.

"You don't trust what you see or think or feel," Maggie said.

"Yeah." Amanda warmed to this.

"And you don't trust him." Again the swollen knot expanded, too familiar for comfort.

She looked poleaxed. "I should. But, damn. I just don't know. I do, but it's absolutely not normal to be perfect, Maggie."

"Oh, puhleeeze." Captain Katherine Kane sauntered in, tall and thin, her short blond curls bouncing. "You can't be serious. Mark Cross, perfect?" Kate snagged her Mickey Mouse cup then sloshed coffee into it. "Get a grip, woman, and ditch the rose-colored glasses. He's a man. I love him, but believe me, he is *not* perfect."

Amanda frowned, fingered the feather on her dart. "I'm not saying he isn't human, Kate. I'm saying—"

"Wow! You're totally freaked out." Kate leaned a hip against the kitchen counter. "Did he propose to you or something?" She took a swig of coffee.

Amanda flushed. "No."

"But you think it's coming." Kate bristled at having to fish.

"Maybe." Amanda looked up, panic riddling her eyes. "I'm thinking he might. Christmas, maybe."

"Ho, ho, ho." Maggie grinned. Just because her marriage had sucked didn't mean Amanda's and Mark's would. Truly, they were the strongest, most connected couple she'd seen in her life. If they couldn't make it, no one could.

"Maggie?" Darcy Clark, the unit's intelligence expert, called. "Telephone."

Cup in hand, Maggie slipped back to her desk, before grabbing the phone and she asked, "Who is it?"

"Karen." Darcy peeked around the wall and cringed.

"She's calling about Christmas. She and Jack want to invite you for dinner."

Karen. Maggie's former best friend.

Stiffening, she ignored the phone and hung the mostly dry star ornament on the tree next to an angel. That angel was the only thing that kept Maggie from cutting loose with a stream of curses. "Tell her thanks, but no. I'd rather be alone."

"Alone on Christmas?" Darcy blanched. "Are you serious?"

"Do I look serious?" Maggie glanced back over her shoulder. "Would you like to spend Christmas with your ex and the new woman in his life?"

"Well, no. But I don't know, being alone on Christmas really sucks, Maggie."

"I know." She'd been alone the past two years and hated it. "And I'll still take being alone over being with them."

Darcy lifted the receiver to her mouth. "Karen, Maggie can't come to the phone right now. She said to tell you she appreciates the invitation but she won't be able to make it." Darcy paused, then relayed. "Um, no, Karen. She'll be alone." Another pause and then, "Um, no, I didn't know you cried all day last year because she was by herself, but…"

Humiliated, Maggie grabbed the phone. "Karen, thanks for asking. Really. But I don't need your pity. I'm just not interested in being with you or Jack."

"But, Maggie, I just—"

"I know. You just want to ease your guilty conscience and Jack's, too. Well, sorry. I'm dealing with my own guilty conscience, and you guys just have to deal with yours on your own." Maggie put the phone down on the table and threw one of Amanda's darts. It just missed Kunz's right eye. Bastard Jack was probably drunk again, insisting Karen invite Maggie over. Anger poured acid, burning in her stomach. Karen wanted him, she got him.

"Jeez, Maggie." Amanda gave her shoulders a shake. "That's a little cold. Karen just didn't want you sad and alone on Christmas."

"Uh, no." Maggie turned to face Amanda. "Cold is me pulling a seventy-two-hour stint, working the anthrax issue after 9/11, finally hauling my exhausted ass home, and finding my beloved husband in *my* bed having sex with my most trusted, best friend. That's cold."

"I still can't believe that." Amanda set down her cup, picked up her darts. "What did you do?"

"What do you think I did?" Maggie asked, reliving the shock, the betrayal, the disbelief, the guilt and the incredible, overwhelming sadness she'd felt then and since.

"I'd have shot him right in the—"

"We know what *you'd* have done, Kate," Amanda quickly cut in.

"Neuter his faithless backside with a .38," Kate said anyway. "Hollowpoint, so it'd explode on impact."

"Of course," Amanda said calmly. "And we'd expect no less from you, Kate. But this is about Maggie, not you." Amanda looked back at Maggie. "So what did you do?"

"Booted them both out—naked, like I found them. Then I dragged the mattress and all Jack's clothes into the backyard and burned them. The next morning, I filed for divorce and took half of everything else he had."

Amanda grunted, her arms folded over her chest. "You should've gone for all of it."

"Especially since you didn't shoot him," Kate interjected, snagging a powdered-sugar doughnut from a box someone had brought in.

"You did have to buy a new bed." That, from Darcy.

Maggie had. "And a new privacy fence and a new storage shed. I didn't replace the boat."

"What happened to the boat?" Amanda asked. "I missed that."

"It was parked by the fence. The wind blew the fire and things got a little out of hand."

"Right." Kate snorted. "You're a weapons expert and you're telling me you couldn't burn a mattress and some clothes without setting a boat, fence and storage shed on fire?"

Maggie looked her right in the eye with a straight face. "Shut up, Kate."

A smile tugged at Kate's lip. "But his car was too close to the house, right?"

"Parked in the garage." Thank God, or she might have burned it, too.

"Slashed tires?" she asked.

"All four." Maggie snatched a doughnut, more to cover her disgust than because she thought she could actually swallow it. "He and Karen departed, riding on rims."

"Excellent." Kate chewed and swallowed. "You got her car, too, then?"

"Her car wasn't there." Genuinely grateful, Maggie licked frosting from her lip. "It was parked down the street at Winn-Dixie, so the neighbors wouldn't notice she was there while I wasn't."

"It survived?"

"I heard it was stripped, though that was a second-hand report, so I don't know if it's true or not." And grateful she was that at least that wasn't on her conscience, too.

"Good for you, Maggie. Victim no more." Amanda grinned. "I do understand your style of justice."

"It wasn't justice. It was temper," she confessed. "At the time, I thought he could've walked anytime without incident. All he had to say is he wanted a divorce, and it would've been bloodlessly civil. But there's no excuse for showing a spouse such a lack of respect. We reap what we sow. It's universal law—immutable." That's exactly what she'd thought, and she'd been partially right. We do reap what we sow, and boy, had she.

"I'm sure he wishes he hadn't done it," Darcy said.

"Oh, yeah." Kate snickered and brushed powdered sugar off her shirtfront. "Especially at tax time when he sees his dwindled net worth."

"I'm sure he does." Maggie had refused to claim a single dime of the loss with either the insurance company or on income taxes. Right was right, and none of it had been an accident. To avoid being charged with adultery, and Maggie naming Karen as a correspondent in the legal proceedings, Jack had opted for a quiet little irreconcilable differences divorce and had eaten the loss.

Amanda sat at the table. "So why does Karen call you to come for Christmas dinner?"

Maggie hated talking about this. But the S.A.S.S. operatives were a tight unit and few secrets survived in such a close group. Better to get it all over with now since the morning was already ruined, talking about Jack and Karen.

"Because, well, lately he's taken to drinking. A lot. When he's had too much, either he calls or he has her call. He's sorry and wants absolution or help to get his life back together." Which had to make Karen feel like dirt. She, unfortunately, was reaping, too.

"Figures." Kate plopped down at her desk. "I'd have to be drunk to call you for help, too."

"Shut up, Kate," Amanda said. "Quit needling Maggie because she's a rookie. You were one once, too, you know, and don't you see this has her upset?"

"Sorry." Kate tossed Maggie a glance.

Kate rode Maggie's back all the time, and usually she stomached it because Kate was senior and Maggie was a rookie; it was expected until someone new came into the unit and became the rookie. But today, Maggie didn't give a flying fig. She was tired of eating Kate's dirt and in no mood to let her razor-sharp remarks slide off her back. "Save it until you mean it."

Kate stilled and stared at Maggie a long second. It was hard, but Maggie was just irritated enough to stare down the devil. Staring down Kate was just a shade harder. "It's a damn shame you finally think I'm a worthy human being and it's over the one thing in my whole life I most wish I could change." Maggie debated then plunged headlong. "I did all those things to Jack and Karen—all of them. I was so angry I didn't want justice. I wanted revenge. They'd hurt me. So much I didn't know anyone could hurt that much and survive."

Maggie stepped away, turned, then faced them. "After they'd gone, I threw up. Then I stood in the yard watching the flames. I felt raw. Like someone had scraped all the skin and muscle off my bones and there was nothing left of me worth keeping."

"No, Maggie." Darcy moved toward her.

Maggie lifted a shaky staying hand, her eyes brimming with tears she hadn't cried then and couldn't cry now. "I had my revenge. But I pay for it every day of my life." She swallowed a lump in her throat. "You know what's left inside me now, Kate?"

"The satisfaction of seeing justice done?" Kate hiked a shoulder, but the glib expression on her face had turned sober.

"I wish," Maggie confessed. "God, how I wish."

"Well, what's left, then?" Kate asked.

"Shame."

Obviously Kate had no idea what to do with that, so did what she always did when something cut too close to the bone. She changed the subject. "Okay, then." Nodding, she leaned back in her chair. "So, Amanda, when Mark asks, are you going to marry him, or what?"

"Let's just wait and see if he asks." She honestly looked hopeful. "Maybe he won't. I do and don't want him to, you know?"

"Good God, you're neurotic." Kate huffed and dug into the doughnut box, this time opting for a long-john with chocolate frosting.

Maggie grabbed a dart, still unnerved by the discussion and the phone call. How Jack could put Karen through that, she had no idea, but after hearing her crying in the background on a call last Christmas, Maggie had resolved not to take another call from either of them—ever. Woman to woman, she knew the pain of betrayal, and no way was she going to be a party to inflicting it on anyone else—not even on Karen. Though she couldn't help but wonder why Karen tolerated this in Jack. It wasn't her nature...or was it? Hell, Maggie couldn't figure out herself half the time, much less Karen.

"Amanda," Darcy said. "I just can't believe it. You've been with Mark a year, for pity's sake. You still don't trust him?"

"I—I love him. Of course, I do." Her words came out in a rush.

Darcy stared at her, quiet and still. "I didn't say love, I said trust."

Amanda squirmed, then sighed.

"What woman ever truly trusts men?" Maggie spared her and tossed the dart. It stabbed Thomas Kunz right in the snoz. "We know they practice deceit for years, most of them from the cradle. By the time they become men, they're so good they believe their own lies. Women don't stand a chance. We have to doubt them."

Kate folded her arms back, behind her head. "Spoken like a bitter woman who doesn't trust men *and* doesn't trust her own judgment about them."

Bitter, yes. Because she'd allowed the worst in her to run amok. Maggie cocked her head. But how could she trust her judgment when she'd been *so* wrong about Jack? "You could be right, Kate." Bitchy to point it out, but right. "Let's just say I prefer working with women I can trust to throw their knives in my face but never stab me in the back."

Kate split her lips in a toothy grin. "Why I do believe that's one of the nicest things anyone's ever said to me."

"Considering how grumpy you are—" Amanda pulled out a file and cracked it open "—I can believe that."

Katherine Kane had more bristles than a hairbrush and

about a thimble's worth of faith in Maggie's abilities. Typical anti-rookie bias, but seeing is believing, and her lack of confidence would resolve itself soon enough. Maggie had only joined the S.A.S.S. eight months ago and had just completed her initial training.

Someone cleared her throat.

"Colonel?" Darcy said, surprised.

Everyone turned to look at the hallway door, including Maggie. Colonel Sally Drake had dyed her hair blood-red, which meant she was ticked to the gills about something, and her expression proved she'd been standing there awhile and had heard far more than she'd wanted to—especially considering there was a man standing beside her.

A sexy-as-sin, gorgeous and unfortunately familiar man who was biting back what would be, at the moment, a very unwelcome smile, considering the women had been trashing his gender. In his mid-thirties, he wore steel-gray Dockers and a dove-gray shirt and tie.

Maggie's stomach clutched. Dr. Justin Crowe, owner and chief researcher for Crowe Pharmaceuticals. Now what the hell was he doing here? And why did he have to be here *now?*

Crowe nodded in Maggie's direction. Her stomach clutched again, knocking at her backbone. She knew a great deal about him. As one of the unit's resident biological weapons experts, she monitored the bio aspects of his current Department of Defense programs. The DoD had awarded him a major contract and the brilliant doctor had successfully developed an antidote to DR-27, a black market lethal virus in Thomas Kunz's arsenal. Only God knew what Kunz would do with it. Or what U.N.-sanctioned country he'd sell it to, to use against the U.S.

Maggie's face burned hot. Crowe and Colonel Drake had just heard her sound off about Jack and Karen, and her humiliating and shameful response, and she'd be lucky if the colonel ever assigned her to any mission.

A lack of control was a detriment in a S.A.S.S. operative's line of work. She swallowed hard. What had she done? Burning beds, slashing tires, and… Oh, God. Why couldn't the floor be merciful and open up and swallow her before Colonel Drake bounced her ass right out of S.A.S.S.?

Colonel Drake spared her and abstained from formal introductions. She knew they'd be moot. "Staff meeting. Conference room in two minutes."

Justin Crowe never let his gaze wander from Maggie. The embarrassment burned down her throat to her chest and up to the tips of her ears.

"Dr. Crowe?" Colonel Drake urged him.

No response.

"Dr. Crowe?"

"Yes, Colonel?" He spared her a glance.

"The conference room is this way."

"Of course." He turned a smile on Maggie that weakened her knees, then followed Colonel Drake into the hallway.

They disappeared from sight.

"Oh, my," Darcy said. "Did you see the way he looked at you, Maggie? Give him a shot, and you just might change your attitude about men."

"Can't let that happen." Her lessons had been too painful and she'd learned them too well. Losing faith in Jack had been bad. But losing faith in herself had been worse. She'd been so caught up in her job that she hadn't loved him enough or allowed him to love her enough. In top-secret positions, that was a hazard. One person, two lives. More often than not, it just didn't work out.

In the three years since, her assignment had changed and become even more secret. The job itself hadn't changed, but she had. Now she felt the sadness and regret intimately. She stood in the bald light and saw herself and her part in her marriage breakup clearly. She now looked at men in that same light. And from the intel reports on Dr. Justin Crowe, she knew far too much about him to dare to even be interested. He was like Jack. Rich, but a man who'd been caught red-handed cheating on his former wife, Andrea. And by all investigative accounts, his ex-wife had been a decent woman whose greatest crime was that she spent too much time at her garden club.

Knowing that, Maggie falling for that killer smile or for the gorgeous man wearing it would be leaping from the proverbial hot pan straight into the fire.

She was just hoping to God their common bio-warfare expertise didn't force them to team up on any mission.

Maggie grabbed a pencil and pad from her desk and walked toward the conference room, falling into step beside Darcy. "Why is he here?" Maggie asked. Regret's location was top secret. The S.A.S.S. unit was a top-secret task force functioning under the Office of Special Investigations wing of the U.S. Air Force under Colonel Drake's command. The unit had a Pentagon liaison, General Shaw, but it answered directly to the President. At the outside, only a couple hundred people in the world knew this S.A.S.S. unit existed and less than a couple dozen knew where it was headquartered. People not in S.A.S.S. were *never* brought here—at least, they hadn't been until today.

Kate, not Darcy, answered. "Dr. Crowe is on the DR-27 antidote project, right?"

"Yes." Darcy responded before Maggie could.

"Then we've got to be in for bad news. Kunz has to be up to something godawful or Crowe wouldn't be coming to us at all, much less actually showing up here."

Darcy was the intelligence expert with total recall. If anyone in S.A.S.S. knew anything, it'd be her. Maggie looked over. "Darcy?"

"Colonel Drake will handle the briefing," she said, avoiding eye contact and sounding totally noncommittal.

Oh, boy. This wasn't good. Darcy had been in the kitchen waiting for news to come through to the colonel. It had, hence the briefing and likely Crowe's presence. And that news, whatever it was, explained why Darcy was now as pale as the whitewashed walls.

"Ten bucks says we've got a Code Three." Kate let out a frustrated sigh. "At least a Three."

A Code Three was an extremely serious situation. The mission scale ran one to five and One was eminent death to masses. Maggie's nerves began to tap dance.

"I sure as hell hope not," Amanda said from directly behind Maggie. "The last Three we had left us with two dead FBI agents and contaminations HAZMAT is still cleaning up."

Hazardous materials brought all kinds of special challenges, short- and long-term, to the table.

"Better hope again," Darcy said, clenching her jaw.

They all groaned in unison. December twenty-third and

an active Code Three mission. This briefing would formally activate S.A.S.S. to prevent a major crisis threatening the public.

Maggie grimaced, questions of where and what and how fired through her mind like rockets sucking hard on jet fuel. Since it was their S.A.S.S. unit being activated, the odds were nearly a hundred percent that the "who" was Thomas Kunz. That would be in keeping with the unit's primary mission. An icy chill shot up her spine.

"Well," Amanda whispered under her breath. "Looks like we're in for yet another merry Christmas."

"Bah humbug."

"Stop it, Kate," Maggie said, still tense and irritated and embarrassed at all Crowe and Colonel Drake had overheard, and now even more worried sick about the crisis that would be revealed in the briefing.

God, please. She silently offered up a little prayer. *Don't let this be a Christmas spent grieving and mourning, or with me hating myself. Please. I—I just can't take another one hating myself.*

She shoved at the conference room door.

Chapter 2

Due to the sensitive nature of S.A.S.S. briefings, it was critical to national security that what was said in the conference room stayed there, and extreme precautions had been taken to assure that it did.

The six-foot-thick concrete walls were copperlined to secure communications and prevent interceptions. Walls and floor were painted and tiled white, and the contents in the room were limited to a well-used conference table, six chairs, a shredder and a viewing screen on the north wall for the projector standing near it.

Darcy held the remote control and took her seat on the left of the table nearest the screen. Kate sat directly across from Darcy. The commander was already waiting in her place at the head of the table, and Amanda took the foot, which put Maggie next to Darcy—and directly across the table from Justin Crowe.

Everyone in the room except Crowe was dressed in an Air Force uniform: pale blue shirts, rank on the shoulders, and dark blue slacks. The slacks proved Kate might not have been home in days, but she was holding up on doing her laundry. Otherwise she'd be in a skirt, wearing hose, and be even more grouchy than usual. The normalcy should have been comforting. No one was dressed in covert gear or BDUs—battle dress uniforms—but the grim expressions around the table, Crowe's included, had the knots in Maggie's stomach expanding.

Increasingly uneasy, she stole a sidelong glance at Colonel Drake. Dragging a hand through her short, spiked hair, she radiated vibes of total focus and extreme intensity. Worse news was that the slide projector was loaded, she'd snagged the handheld from Darcy and now gripped it in her fist.

Maggie steeled herself. This briefing was going to be intense. Dread burrowed in, laying heavily on her chest.

"White noise, Kate," the commander ordered.

Kate reached to the wall behind her and flipped a switch that activated yet another security measure installed to prevent communication interceptions.

"Darcy." The commander nodded in her direction. "Let's do it."

"Yes, ma'am." She turned to Justin. "We all know, if only vicariously, our guest, Dr. Justin Crowe. Essential specifics are that he and his company have been awarded five defense contracts for various research and development projects, all of which are dual use." It wasn't necessary to add that dual use meant the projects had both military and civilian world applications; everyone already knew it. "A year ago," Darcy went on, "Dr. Crowe won the contract of most concern to us today. It is sensitive, a Black World operations development, and it is classified Top Secret A-4. This project concerns DR-27." Darcy looked her way. "Maggie, will you brief specifics on the virus?"

Maggie launched into it. "DR-27 is a lethal virus few in the world know exists. It originated in a lab in Germany just over a year ago. We contained it, and we've been working on an antidote to it ever since. That antidote is Dr. Crowe's sensitive contract. We believe he now has successfully developed that antidote, though it hasn't yet been field-tested." She looked at him. "Is that an accurate assessment of the current standing, Doctor?"

"Yes, it is. I can add that lab results have been impressive, but the field test isn't scheduled to occur for another two months."

Kate frowned. "Why the A-4 classification? That's extraordinarily high. I'd expect an A-1 or maybe an A-2."

"We deemed it a national security asset," he said. "Frankly, the last thing the U.S. needs its enemies to know is that there's a lethal weapon, a virus for which there is no existing antidote, on the loose and available for black market purchase through GRID."

"True." Amanda cocked her head. "But why hasn't GRID broadcast it to its potential buyers?"

"Because it lacked an accurate damage assessment projection," Darcy responded. "Kunz has made a concerted effort to secure documented proof of the virus's effects, but so far, he's failed to do it."

"So who has the proof?" Amanda asked. "I haven't seen it." She looked at Kate, who shook her head. She hadn't seen it, either.

"We have it—now," Colonel Drake said. "It was in the lab during the containment, but the text was encrypted and we've only now broken the code, which gives us the tests they took and the effects." She nodded at the screen. "Take a look at these slides. They'll show you the effects of DR-27 exposure." She hit the clicker. "These photos were taken six, twelve and twenty-four hours after exposure."

Three slides flashed across the screen. Each was of an individual ravaged and made grotesque by the virus. Torn between being sick and fighting tears, Maggie's reaction was intense and swift—and she'd seen the slides before, though she wasn't at liberty to mention it. She never got used to such images.

Kate obviously hadn't seen them. Rattled, she flinched and the color drained from her face. "Oh, God. They did this to these poor people just to test the virus? They used them as freaking lab rats?"

"They did," the colonel confirmed. "These people and many more...."

"May they burn in hell."

Colonel Drake sent Kate a cold level look. "They are."

Kate cleared her throat, turned her gaze to Darcy. "Are we sure GRID has this virus?"

"Our sources strongly suspect it does, Kate," Darcy hedged. "In the past few days, Intel has reported significant chatter from multiple sources about an impending DR-27 attack. As usual, the information hasn't been specific enough for us to act on beyond the usual awareness warnings—at least, not until this morning."

"What happened this morning?" Amanda asked.

Darcy shifted in her seat. "A few hours ago, the Terrorist Threat Integration Center alerted First Responders through Project Bioshield that a GRID 'capabilities demonstration' on DR-27 is likely to occur on Christmas Eve. If it does, they project that black market bidding for the virus will begin immediately following it."

Colonel Drake stepped in. "Homeland Security contacted General Shaw at the Pentagon and requested he activate S.A.S.S."

"Why is that?" Dr. Crowe frowned at the colonel. "Why you, out here?"

Colonel Drake hesitated a short second, clearly not eager to tell him the S.A.S.S. offices had been moved out of D.C. to avoid undue interference from those on the Hill. But she did formulate an answer.

"Our entire mission centers on GRID, Doctor. When General Shaw activated this unit, one of its first orders was to stop a potential attack and recover the DR-27."

"Tall order."

Colonel Drake held his gaze. "Yes, it was."

"I understand now." Crowe nodded. "I guess it's too much to hope that a GRID capabilities demonstration isn't exactly what it sounds like it is."

Kate groaned and slid down in her chair.

Maggie frowned at her and then at him. "Given the chance, Thomas Kunz intends to demonstrate the virus on the public, Doctor. To prove without a doubt how many it will kill, how long it'll take them to die, and how much they'll suffer in between. That's how this cold-blooded bastard works." She turned to Darcy. "Do we know where he plans to attack?"

"Indisputably, no. But Intel has generated several sixty-five-percent projections," Darcy said. "Multiple S.A.S.S. units are being activated—one to cover each high-potential, high-value target. Intel cites these specific targets key. Any of them will net Kunz maximum benefit, all he could possibly want or need from the demonstration, including more than a little drama and sensationalism."

"How many potential targets are there?" Maggie asked.

"For obvious reasons, that information is classified above our pay grades," Colonel Drake said. "They're saying several targets, so I guess that's a minimum of three. Knowing Kunz, it's likely twice that, or more."

"Where is our unit's potential target?" Amanda leaned forward in her chair.

Darcy frowned. "Santa Bella."

"The shopping mall?" Crowe's tone rippled with incredulity.

"I've reviewed Kunz's criteria and Intel's deductions," Darcy said. "Santa Bella fits both profiles so well it's scary."

The mall Maggie had sworn on the way to work not to return to until after the new year. *Damn it.* She rubbed a weary hand across her brow, still curious about the other targets. "Of course Kunz won't hit someplace like New York this time of year." Not that she would wish a strike on anyone anywhere, but New York, Wall Street, was a prime target for all threats and had been since 9/11.

"Why won't he?" Crowe asked. "It's bigger and busier."

"Money," Maggie said. "Kunz is totally into money. He won't hit a financial center for a test where anyone dying will do. Uh-uh. It'd cost him a fortune in stock losses."

"Why exactly is Intel deeming Santa Bella high-risk,

Darcy?" Amanda asked for more specifics, clearly trying to home in on the big picture.

"As I said, I've reviewed the criteria and deductions and they're solid. There are reasons, Amanda, but I'm prohibited from disclosing them unless it becomes mission essential. The Center is exercising restraint to protect embedded agents. But I am free to state the obvious. Santa Bella is the biggest mall in the South, and on Christmas Eve, about 20,000 last-minute shoppers will be rotating through, keeping the facility packed to its three-story rafters."

Twenty thousand. Oh, man. Major challenges trying to defend in that situation. Major challenges. Maggie chewed her lip, worrying. "Are post-attack projections in yet?"

"Some. Two to four thousand fatalities and a minimum additional two thousand permanently disabled. I didn't get dollar cost projections on contamination losses. Bean counters are still working them."

At this point, who cared about the property? Good God, two to four *thousand* fatalities? Maggie broke into a cold sweat. "Are the projections as dire for all potential targets?"

Darcy nodded. "I'm told some are worse."

Maggie expected it, but hearing it confirmed curdled her blood and she regretted earlier choking down that doughnut. This kind of news was best digested on an empty stomach.

Kate curled her fingers, gripping the table. "What are we likely looking at with the infiltrators?"

"We don't know." Darcy grimaced. "Intel can't project which specific GRID operatives will launch the attack, though they believe Kunz will use his own subject-matter experts and not outside forces to release the virus. For tighter control and lower odds of leaks. We have no idea how many GRID operatives will work the launch, or in what part or parts of the mall they'll cut it loose—if, of course, Santa Bella is the target."

"This is a nightmare from hell." Maggie looked at the colonel.

"It gets worse," Colonel Drake said. "We can't forget the body double factor."

"What body double factor?" Justin asked, looking baffled.

Colonel Drake responded. "A lot of high-powered, influential people hire body doubles, Dr. Crowe."

He nodded, familiar with the concept. "And that relates to this…how?"

Colonel Drake didn't dodge. "Our experience has revealed that Kunz has a number of body doubles for himself and for key business associates on high-impact, lucrative black market deals. He has a nasty habit of inserting them when he knows, or senses, we're closing in on him."

"I see." Justin leaned forward on the table, rubbed at his temples, clearly distressed by this added complication. "Is there a way to know whether we're dealing with a double or the real McCoy?"

"DNA," the colonel said. "Though we have noted a three-month absence trend."

"Three-month absence?"

The colonel's gaze slid to Amanda and she responded. "Kunz kidnaps the person he wants to double, keeps them drugged and learns all he can about them. During that time, his surgeons and shrinks are creating a body double.

One who looks, acts and learns to think like the real person. It's an intensive training program to become that person, and it's very effective."

Justin's expression sobered. He'd intuited that Amanda had been one of Kunz's victims; Maggie was certain of it.

"Anyway." The colonel resumed her briefing. "We obviously must be on our guard and expect that he's made insertions of body doubles on this mission, as well."

Maggie nodded. "He has a hundred percent track record, Colonel. Every attack, every mission…"

"How many have there been?" Justin asked, clearly stunned.

Maggie wasn't surprised. None had made the press. So far S.A.S.S. had denied Kunz success, though it'd had too many close calls to feel overly confident about it, and everyone in the know realized it was only a matter of time until he managed to pull off a success.

No one responded, and Justin caught on that he'd tread onto classified ground. "Forget I asked," he said.

Colonel Drake looked at him, but didn't acknowledge he'd spoken.

"So who would he be likely to double?" Justin asked, still seeking a firm grip on this new complication to an already complicated mission.

"Anyone in authority or with the power to countermand our actions," Maggie said. "Anyone who might be able to relay our actions and defenses to him."

Justin paled. "But that's pretty much everybody."

"Yes, it is."

"Also, if the only way we can tell they're real or a body double is through DNA or three-month absences, which they aren't damn likely to admit, then how do we cover our assets?"

Everyone looked to Colonel Drake, who lifted a hand in Maggie's direction. "Captain Holt has discussed this type of challenge with Dr. Cabot."

"Morgan Cabot," Maggie explained, "is an expert psychologist and profiler. She believes that body language or abrupt changes in behavior are our best shot at telling the difference between a person and his or her double. Facial expressions, innate reactions to others—before they've had a chance to stop and think—and sudden changes in the way they process input. For example, if someone is quiet and suddenly they're aggressive, that should elevate concern."

Amanda nodded, agreeing, then turned the topic back to the attack location. "Why doesn't Intel recommend a total shutdown on all potential locations?"

"Can't. The administration wouldn't consider it, much less go for it. Makes us appear too fearful and vulnerable, which emboldens all of those against us." Darcy blew out a slow breath. "Listen, the truth is Intel isn't certain enough that the attack will be at any of the identified targets to request Homeland Security order shutdowns."

"True," Colonel Drake cut in. "But local First Responders are on heightened alert, advisory status. They are not, at this point, activated. If at any time we discover hard evidence Santa Bella is the target and conditions warrant activation, we can call them up to assist us."

"By then," Maggie said, "it'll be too late for them to successfully intercede or be much help, Colonel. And knowing Kunz, he'll keep things ambiguous until the very end.

He always has, to prevent us from being able to go after him with full force."

Colonel Drake's level look proved she didn't like this circumstance a damn bit better than Maggie, but her hands were tied. "I'm aware of that, which is why I'm telling you, Maggie, if the rules get in the way on this mission, you break them."

Maggie frowned. Often in the S.A.S.S., rules had to be broken, but that didn't mean Maggie had to like breaking them. Actually she hated it, and the colonel well knew it. Hence, the reason for the direct order—and there was no mistaking by anyone at the table, except maybe for Crowe, that this remark had been a direct order. "Yes, ma'am."

"Right now, we work with what we've got," Colonel Drake said. "And what we've got is Intel, Homeland Security, the Pentagon and the President all stating their belief that this threat is credible. In our post-9/11 world, that compels everyone responsible for defending the public to act. The S.A.S.S. unit has been activated, and we will defend Santa Bella, whether or not it wants to be defended."

Justin Crowe frowned. "What if one of the other targets Intel identified is attacked? Will this S.A.S.S. unit then stand down?"

"No." Colonel Drake sent him a regretful look. "We can't assume Kunz and GRID intends to attack only one target. He could launch simultaneous strikes at all identified targets."

"Or none of them," Maggie said.

"Or none of them," Colonel Drake agreed. "Which is why we must be on-site and prepared to intervene if Santa Bella comes under biological attack."

Kate laced her hands atop the table. "At what point do we activate the locals?"

"Eminent threat stage."

Everyone groaned. That was far too late for any type co-ordination and effective response.

"Sorry—" Colonel Drake raised a hand "—agree or disagree, with multiple potential targets and no hard intel pointing in our direction, that's the best we can do." She let her gaze glide down the table. "Maggie, you're primary."

"But, Colonel," Kate called, no doubt to oppose Maggie being given primary rather than Kate, who also had bio-expertise and was senior in experience. "I—"

"Yes, Kate?" There was steel in Colonel Drake's eyes, and if Kate was half as smart as her dossier and records stated, she'd shut up now.

Evidently she noted it. "I, um, will be happy to provide backup, ma'am."

Naturally she wouldn't object this one time when Maggie wouldn't mind. The last person in the world Maggie wanted to work closely with was Dr. Justin Crowe. He was too disturbing. Kunz had infiltrated high-level government positions before. Crowe could be a body double. If not, then his history still proved he couldn't be trusted, and she just didn't need the challenge of a disturbing man who could be a double and couldn't be trusted added to the mountain of other challenges on this mission.

"Thank you. I'll keep that in mind," the colonel said. "Dr. Crowe will assist Maggie, of course, having developed the antidote."

"Meaning no disrespect—" Maggie looked at Crowe but

spoke to Colonel Drake "—but has Dr. Crowe's DNA been cleared as authentic?"

"I'm not a body double, Captain Holt."

"Glad to hear it, Doctor." Maggie looked to the colonel for verification. "Colonel?"

"Dr. Crowe has been cleared, Maggie," the colonel said, and sounded oddly pleased that the question had been asked. "Now, there's a meeting set up for you two with Santa Bella management." She flipped through her notes then went on. "Daniel Barone is in charge—Mall Administrator. He's your point of contact, though you'll actually work more closely with Will Stanton, Chief of Security. Maggie, you and Dr. Crowe meet with them and the store owners in an hour. Do what you can to get them to voluntarily close the mall."

"And if they refuse?" Lost revenue would play a huge part in their decision, and only someone who'd flunked Business 101 wouldn't acknowledge it.

"If they refuse, and they likely will, then draft a defensive plan and implement it. The entire unit is at your disposal for whatever you need. You've got my full support to act at will."

Maggie nodded, accepting the mission.

Colonel Drake slowly looked from person to person around the table. "This incident is now officially an active S.A.S.S. mission, Priority Code Three."

Around the table, all the operatives responded, "So acknowledged." Maggie added her voice—and so, surprisingly, did Dr. Crowe.

The status gave Maggie a lot of leeway and she feared like hell she was going to need it. "Darcy, review all employee files for any three-month absences. Flag new employees, too. Anyone hired within the last six months."

Darcy looked up at her. "Anything else?"

"Yes, please," Maggie said, letting her gaze slide to Justin. "I want a full report on Dr. Crowe for the last six months. Projects he's worked on, trips he's taken, the works. I'll also need a similar report on Barone, the mall administrator, and on the head of mall security. I want to know his credentials, as well."

"You got it."

"Dismissed." Colonel Drake stood.

Maggie looked across the table at Crowe. "Let's move, Doctor. We have less than twenty-four hours."

"Dr. Crowe," Colonel Drake said, a warning bite in her tone. "Should this crisis arise, please remember that it is not a handy field test for your antidote. If you must administer it, please do so judiciously."

"Of course," he said, not taking offense. He slid back his chair. "I'll do my best to assist with the store owners, too, Colonel. If they understand the results of exposure, surely they'll cooperate."

"Maybe," she said, though it was evident she thought their odds would leave space on a pinhead.

When Maggie and he left the conference room and entered the hallway, she spared him a glance. "I trust you'll also do your best to not get in my way."

"Your way?" The soft curve in his lips flattened into a firm line. "No problem," he said. "But do clip your claws, Captain. Otherwise, they're damned sure to get in your way."

"I beg your pardon?" She stepped into the elevator. He followed and she pushed the button to take them up.

"Look, Captain Holt," he said. "I overheard enough of your chat earlier to realize how you feel about men and why, but I haven't done a thing to you, and until I do, I think it's fair to insist you keep your bias to yourself. If Kunz attacks, our preparation will be critical. That warrants our total focus, and frankly, I don't need the distraction of your attitude."

"My attitude, Dr. Crowe, is precisely what it should be." She pulled her teeth back from her lips and lifted her Jeep keys. "Are you riding with me or following?"

"Riding," he said, though it was clear he'd sooner face the tortures of hell. "We're waiting for Captain Cross to bring a remote unit so I can get in and out of here on my own."

"Fine." She walked to the Jeep and unlocked the doors. "Then get in and buckle up."

Maggie and Justin entered Santa Bella Mall through the main entrance, then looped around Rothschild's, cutting between it and Macy's, to enter the mall's administration wing. Only one door stood open along the corridor. Customer Service. People working inside were hustling. On the other doors hung discreet signs for Security and Medical Services, and tucked in the corner was Maintenance. At the far end of the hallway, positioned dead-center was the mall's administration office.

Justin opened that door and Maggie walked through. A man nearly as tall as Justin stood waiting for them in the middle of the luxurious office, talking softly to a petite woman seated at a tidy desk. Impeccably dressed in a discreet gray suit, he glanced into a mirror hanging above a table. On it sat a large vase of sweet-smelling fresh flowers. Not a single, perfectly groomed brown hair on the man's head dared to be out of place.

He smiled, his teeth gleaming white and perfect. "You must be Captain Holt—" he extended his hand, then turned to Justin "—and Dr. Crowe." They shook. "Welcome. I am Daniel Barone, Santa Bella's administrator."

"Mr. Barone," Maggie said, half expecting him to pull out a snowy-white hanky and wipe his hand.

He turned to the woman at her desk. "This is my assistant, Linda Diel."

Maggie and Justin said hello, and Barone looked at his watch. "Excellent," he said, shifting his gaze to the door. "You're right on time."

As if on cue, a second man appeared in the doorway. This one looked like an all-American mutt in his mid-forties with silvering blond hair. He wore a security uniform. His facial features were blunt and his eyes held a healthy amount of concern. Maggie innately reacted much more positively toward him than to Barone.

"Will, come in." Barone turned to Maggie. "This is Will Stanton, my chief of security. Will, may I introduce Captain Holt and Dr. Crowe."

Will extended his beefy hand, shook warmly. "I wish I could say I'm glad to meet you, but under the circumstances..."

"I understand completely," Maggie said, sensing an earnest quality in Will Stanton that enormously appealed to her. Her father had that same steadfastness, and she had mistakenly assumed all men did—at least until Jack had proved otherwise.

Barone covertly checked his watch again. "Are the owners ready, Will?"

"Yes, sir. There's a rep from each of our 520 stores."

"I told you owners were to attend this meeting," Barone said, his tone sharp.

"Only three have sent their assistants. Unavoidable, they said."

Barone grimaced. "Well, if that's the best you can do."

"It is." Will lifted his chin.

"That's an excellent response," Maggie said. "Anything under twenty percent is considered amazingly good."

"Thanks, Captain."

"Very well." Diffused, Barone looked from Will to Maggie and softened his gaze. "The auditorium is this way." He motioned to the southeast corner of the facility. "Let's not keep the owners waiting. Time is money."

Justin rolled his eyes heavenward, and whether she trusted him or not, Maggie couldn't help but agree with him. Barone was going to be an insincere pain in the backside.

When they walked through the back of the auditorium to the stage, Maggie heard the owners grumbling and speculating. Barone hadn't given them a clue about the reason for the meeting. Nor had he told them what they could be facing. She held off a sigh by the skin of her teeth. Why wasn't she surprised that he would leave the dirty work of explaining to her?

Barone introduced Maggie and Justin to the owners, and then Maggie succinctly laid out the challenge, including the fact that Santa Bella was but one of several potential targets.

The auditorium went silent. Tension escalated. Maggie

could almost feel the owners' stomachs dropping. She spoke candidly, omitting any reference to S.A.S.S., GRID or Thomas Kunz, of course, and then turned over the mike to Dr. Crowe to explain the virus and its impact in layman's terms.

He gave them the basics, then opened the floor for what Maggie feared would be hours of questions.

Left of center and three rows from the front, a sleek woman stood up. "Cassy Brown, Celebrity." She identified herself and then her store. "What are you asking us to do, Dr. Crowe?"

Justin turned to Maggie, lifted a hand. "I'll trust Captain Holt to answer that."

Maggie stepped up to the mike. "We're asking you to close your stores for the day."

The grumbling grew deafening—and overwhelmingly negative.

"George Halstead. Halstead's, Jewelry Row." A balding man stood and shouted to be heard over the din. "Captain, I'm afraid I didn't hear you correctly. You're asking us to close our stores on one of our busiest days of the year based solely on threat of an attack that might or might not happen, and if it happens, might or might not happen here?"

One bump at a time. "That is correct. Yes, sir," Maggie said. "The threat is considered credible at the highest levels. You must understand, Mr. Halstead, that the only way we can say there will absolutely be an attack is after there is one."

A stout redhead shot out of her chair. "Forget it," she shouted. "I do a fourth of my annual business on Christmas Eve. Closing would put me out of business—and I'm not the only one."

Others stood and agreed. Far too many for Maggie to delude herself into thinking she could turn them around. "I understand the challenges. But you've been apprised of the lethal impact of this virus. If it is turned loose, you must understand your customers won't be shopping Christmas Eve or any other day. They'll be dead. So will you." She paused, let the finality of that reality sink in. "I understand your challenges, I do, but the risk to human life is—"

"Is Homeland Security telling us to close?" the same redhead asked, interrupting.

Maggie hesitated. "No," she confessed. "Due to the multiplicity of potential targets, it isn't. Not yet, anyway. But—"

"Then forget it," the redhead interrupted again. "I'm not losing my business because these crazy bastards might hit us. Everyone in the country has been expecting to get attacked ever since 9/11. So far as I'm concerned, this day is no different than any of the rest."

Maggie waited for the initial roar of agreeing voices to fade. "This threat *is* different. It's much more dangerous. We're convinced that there will be an attack."

"Yeah, but you're only sixty-five percent sure it'll be here," Halstead from Jewelry Row said. "We can't close down every single day out of fear."

He had a point, and Maggie agreed. They couldn't close indefinitely or with every potential threat, but this threat was more solid. "You're making a huge mistake. Past experience with this specific attacker proves he will do anything to achieve his objectives. Anything. To anyone."

"We've seen dozens of suicide bombers on the news. They're *all* nuts."

"Call a vote." The first woman who'd stood, Cassy Brown, said. "Simple majority rules."

Maggie didn't like it, but it was more than she had expected. "Fine. Vote. But there is a provision I'll be adding."

The auditorium again went quiet. "If you vote to open the mall on Christmas Eve, then each owner must be on-site from the time your store opens until it closes. You will not risk the lives of your employees—" she shot a look at Barone "—and protect your own by not being here. I will be all over this mall, from long before it opens until long after it closes, and I'm telling you now, when I come into your store, you'll either be there or I'll close it down."

"Can she do that?" an unseen woman yelled toward Barone.

He stood, feet apart, his arms folded in front of him, and shrugged to let the owners know his hands were tied on the matter. "She can." He solemnly nodded. "So can I, though I would never do so without a majority vote. I believe everyone should have a voice, and that voice should be heard."

Spoken like a true bull-shitting politician, Maggie thought. Shifting responsibility to the owners. Very like Kunz, in that. Suspicious, she looked over at Barone and wondered if he was a Kunz double. "I not only can, I will." Maggie absorbed the gasps, shocked stares, dragging jaws and outrage aimed in her direction. "Now go ahead, cast your votes."

It took thirty minutes, but the final tally was 501 to 19 in favor of staying open.

Justin conceded, sent Maggie a defeated look laced with sympathy and worry.

"Okay, then," Maggie said, unwilling to waste energy on regret. Facts were facts, and the sooner they were accepted, the sooner everyone moved on to working within the allotted framework toward protection. "Being open, there are preparations to make and not a lot of time to make them."

Daniel Barone interrupted with a raised index finger. "Captain Holt, I won't have a large number of security forces cut loose in this facility. That would certainly unnerve shoppers. Our primary responsibility is to make them comfortable."

So the idiot would have them dead? That was some kind of whacked logic he'd embraced. No doubt, inspired by numbers. Sales. Bottom lines.

"My primary responsibility is to keep them alive." She swallowed a grimace. "We will need some things done to better our odds of protecting everyone."

"Like what?" the redhead said. "We can't do much. We're swamped already, Captain."

"You'll have make time for these things. Mr. Stanton from Security will send out a list."

Justin stepped in. "An example of what we're asking is to remove all aerosol cans from your shelves. That's not optional," Justin said. "The most effective means of spreading the virus is through an aerosol spray. We can't risk your cans being confused with the terrorists' cans. See what I mean?"

"So what?" a man sitting beside the redhead said. "We consider any spray can the virus?"

"Once you clear your shelves, yes. That's it exactly," Justin said.

"That's unreasonable," the man said. "I own a hair salon."

Justin's jaw firmed. "Do you see any other option? Do you have another fail-proof way to differentiate the cans? Because if you're not a hundred percent accurate, everyone in this room and everyone in the mall could be dead in twenty-four hours."

Gasps and silence covered a long, still moment, then the redhead spoke up. "It's your job to protect us, damn it. You do your job."

Maggie stepped in. "We're trying to, but you refused our best advice, which was to close the mall. So it's an unreasonable expectation for you to believe we're capable of being everywhere at once—particularly when extra security forces are being denied us. We'll do all we can, of course. But you must also do your part. That's the bottom line, and all the complaining in the world won't change it."

The starch went out of the protest, and the owners fell silent. "All aerosols will be removed from store shelves," she reminded him of his place before the interruption. "Continue, please, Dr. Crowe."

Justin went on, and Maggie looked out into the crowd. The owners were paying close attention now, their body language intense and rapt, but they weren't panicked. Justin was doing a good job of empowering them with essential information. But because their panic had been postponed, they could listen.

From experience, Maggie expected that when the store owners left the auditorium and they had to start making the calls on what constituted a threat and what was innocent typical behavior, the panic would return. The fear of being wrong would bring back panic with a vengeance.

Justin talked on, gave them more information to expand their comfort zones and to give them a clearer understanding to help them better assess threats.

"The germ itself is microencapsulated," he said. "Once these minute capsules are breached, either through forceful impact or contact with water, the virus will be active and contagious."

"Do you have to touch something to get it?" an unseen man asked.

"No, you do not," Justin told him. "The virus can be ingested, breathed or absorbed through the skin. A microcapsule touching wet skin is the fastest way to absorb the infection. It causes the most fatalities because the body has less time to react to protect itself."

"So if people start to get sick, they should just come to the medical office?" The redhead spoke again.

"No." Justin cast a covert glance at Maggie and caught her subtle nod to disclose. "There's no time for that, I'm afraid," he said. "Once the virus is absorbed, there's only a *two minute* window to inject the antidote. After that, it's too late."

A solemn hush filled the auditorium.

Maggie looked from face to face. All of the owners appeared to be feeling the full weight of their decision to keep the mall open. The full weight, and the full fear. Seizing the moment, she asked, "Now that you're more fully informed, would you care to cast a second vote?"

"The vote has been had, Captain. Don't attempt to intimidate the owners into bending to your will."

"Excuse me, Mr. Barone," Maggie said, her voice formal and stiff. "Offering them an opportunity to vote is hardly telling them what to do."

Barone ignored her and addressed the owners. "You'll each receive a written list of instructions within the hour. Please comply with all of them as soon as possible and then report your compliance to Security. On behalf of management, I'm asking for complete cooperation with Captain Holt and Dr. Crowe. If this attack should happen here, we will be totally reliant on their skills and expertise to avoid catastrophe. We must help them help us."

Maggie offered Barone a nod of thanks. Maybe she'd formed a negative opinion about him too soon. He seemed to be coming through for the most part now with his support.

"Also," Barone added. "Do remember to keep this discussion confidential. Otherwise, we'll have open stores tomorrow but no shoppers. None of us can afford that. In the morning, of course, you'll have to tell your employees what to watch for—but please mention nothing before then."

Barone was accurate on this. Employees would warn family and friends, who'd warn family and friends, and the next thing the owners knew, the mall would be vacant and surrounded by reporters with camera crews. Thomas Kunz would love that. He'd see it as an opportunity to infect the press and the S.A.S.S.

The owners shuffled out of the auditorium, their expressions grim.

Barone spoke to Will Stanton. "I'm going to have to excuse myself to reassure individual owners." He shifted his gaze to her. "Captain Holt, Will is available for whatever you need." He shot a warning look at Will. "Remember our limitations." Barone strode away and was immediately engulfed by worried owners.

Barone's parting comment to Will alarmed Maggie, and

from the troubled look Justin sent her way, it hadn't sat well with him, either. Maggie turned to face Will. "What did Mr. Barone mean about 'limitations'?"

Will frowned, pulled Maggie and Justin across the thoroughfare and into a hallway between the security and medical offices. The little alcove had rest rooms on the left and right, and dead-ended at a door marked No Exit—Employees Only.

"I'm not sure what he meant," Will admitted. "But I take it he hasn't mentioned anything to you about the Winter Wonderland going on here tomorrow afternoon and night."

"What exactly is that?" Stones tumbled in Maggie's stomach.

"The owners have spent a fortune to create a snowfall in the Center Court pit tomorrow for the kids. You know, snowball fights, building snowmen—things people don't normally get to do in Florida."

"Oh, man," Justin said. "That means every kid in five counties will be here."

"That's what the owners are hoping." Will shoved a hand into his pants' pocket. "The mall has twenty-six A-stores, ones comparable to Macy's. Eight are located on each level," he explained. "The rest are smaller B-stores. Specialty shops, restaurants, that kind of thing."

Maggie nodded. "Right."

"So, as you'd expect, the A-stores have a big voice in all mall operations."

"What's your point, Will?" Maggie nudged him.

He pursed his lips, debating on what to say and, for the sake of his job, what he should leave unsaid. "Right after Mr. Barone got the first call on this situation, he set up a meeting with the twenty-six. He forgot to mention it to you. That took place at seven o'clock this morning. They agreed to extra security, provided it is requested, discreet and in no way interferes with shoppers. But they flat refused to have medical staff inside the building, with the exception of Dr. Crowe. That would be a signal something was wrong that the shoppers couldn't miss. They'd be afraid and leave, taking their money with them."

"You can't be serious, Will." Justin rounded on her. "Two minutes is all we have, Maggie. I can't inject—"

She lifted a hand, half surprised he'd used her first name but fully grasping his objection. Her own mirrored it. "We'll work around it." *One bump at a time.*

"Sorry to say I'm very serious, Dr. Crowe." Will looked even more worried than he had before the meeting. "Mr. Barone will never do anything the twenty-six don't want done. No way."

"We'll work around it," Maggie said again, fighting an internal war. The owners grasped that they could be playing Russian roulette with shoppers' lives and their own, but they couldn't close their stores forever on a maybe, especially without a Homeland Security advisory ordering, or even recommending, they close.

She made a mental note to have Darcy petition again to get a shutdown order issued. And then outrage flooded Maggie. Outrage that the owners would jeopardize other people's lives for their own money. Wasn't that what Kunz was doing that everyone found so vehemently objectionable?

Her cell phone rang. Maggie stepped away and answered it. "Holt."

"We've got another wrinkle." Colonel Drake sighed.

"From five to nine on Christmas Eve, you're going to have two groups of significant interest in the mall."

Terrific. What else? "Who?"

"For one, Special Forces members and their families."

"Oh, no." Kunz would love that. Freaking love that.

"I'm afraid so." The Colonel paused. "The mall is staying open later because the store owners are creating a Winter Wonderland in their honor. Well, theirs and the local Special Olympians."

"Oh, God, no. I just found out about the Winter Wonderland but I didn't know about the guests." Maggie's heart skipped then thudded and her muscles clenched. To GRID, the Olympians would merely be collateral damage. Targeting and killing Special Forces members—the same Special Forces that dogged GRID members and activities worldwide—would be payback. "Did you make an appeal to their commander?"

"General Foster, yes," she said. "He won't budge on a *potential* attack, even if it's a credible one."

Maggie frowned, stared at the No Exit sign on the door at the end of the hall. "Neither will the store owners. They voted to stay open."

"Well, unlike the store owners, if needed, these guys will back us up."

"Well, there is that." Unfortunately the Special Forces members would feel they had reputations to protect—as well as their families—and under no circumstances would they back down to GRID. Not on a known attack, much less on a potential one. "How did you know about them and the Olympians?" Maggie asked. "Did Darcy get in an intel update?"

"No, Maggie." Colonel Drake's voice held dread. "I read it in the newspaper."

And yet another hit. They were coming so fast and furious this situation should qualify as a slugfest. "In the newspaper?" So Kunz likely had read it, too. "Have Darcy add this new information and appeal to headquarters for a shutdown order."

"Will do. But don't expect much."

"I don't." HQ would likely see Special Forces being on-site as a plus, an enhanced shot at capturing Kunz. "But I want the request on record."

"Excellent move."

"Thanks, Colonel."

Justin smiled at Maggie for no apparent reason, and in a foul mood, she lifted her chin in his general direction and ended the call.

After updating Justin and Will, Maggie needed a minute to assimilate the new wrinkle. "Excuse me," she told Justin and Will. "I'll be right back." She took refuge in the women's rest room on the left off the little alcove.

How in hell was she going to pull off a successful defense of this place? Stepping over to the sink, she washed her hands with scalding hot water and looked into her own eyes in the mirror. She had reluctant retailers in the largest mall in the south, an unknown number of potential GRID attackers cutting loose a lethal virus on Special Forces, their families and Special Olympians and, no doubt, their families, and the general public.

She had minimal intelligence, minimal and reluctant cooperation with mall management—Barone was good for lip service and Will Stanton was hamstrung—and minimal medical backup. Local authorities couldn't be activated and called up unless Homeland Security issued an authorization, and by the time it did, the assist would be too late to be of help.

If GRID did attack and release the virus at Santa Bella, there was no way Justin Crowe could be on all three levels, vaccinating everyone within two minutes. Special Forces were medically field trained and could assist with that, but even with their assistance, the person-to-person ratio was too low to be successful with a two-minute-injection window. And the antidote hadn't yet been field tested, which meant there could be a significant number and types of unexpected reactions to it.

Feeling overwhelmed, Maggie gave herself a mental shake, dried her hands, then walked back out into the narrow hallway. Justin stood waiting for her, and if the worry lining his face accurately indicated his mind-set, he'd been doing the same analysis as she and had come to the same grim conclusion.

Their mission odds were a shade shy of impossible.

"Maggie?"

"Yes, Justin." The next thirty-six hours were going to be too intense to stand on formality.

"In your personal opinion, based on all your experience, what are the odds GRID will attack this mall?"

Maggie leaned her shoulder against the creamy wall. "Based on all we know, *without* Special Forces being present here, I'd have put the odds at about fifty-fifty." She paused, looked down at her feet, then went on, dread-

ing the words to soon leave her mouth. "*With* Special
Forces being on-site tomorrow, I believe Thomas Kunz
and GRID will find the temptation to attack Santa Bella
irresistible."

Chapter 3

Santa Bella had been designed in quadrants.

The northwest quadrant was dedicated to women, the southwest to kids. Men's stores, Jeweler's Row and specialty shops from around the world were situated north of the administration wing in the northeast quadrant. Restaurants surrounded Center Court, where events were held. There was a stage with heavy red-velvet curtains and a deep marble pit, where the snow would be located. Knowing this much was fine for general purposes, but to do her job successfully, Maggie needed specific details. She looked across the waist-high counter at the front of the security office to Will Stanton. "I'm going to need a copy of the facility's floor plan as quickly as you can get it to me. All three levels."

"Yes, ma'am, Captain Holt."

"Maggie." She smiled at him. "Otherwise, we're going to be tripping over tongues by this time tomorrow."

"Maggie," Will said with a nod. "Is there anything else you need from me right now?"

"No. I know you're eager to get that listing of items to the store owners." The sooner, the better for her, as well.

"Yes, ma'am." He shoved a gold pen into his shirt pocket. It glimmered in the light.

"Thank you." She stepped back from the counter. "We," she said, meaning she and Justin, "are going to walk the facility. Afterward, we'll likely have more recommendations to add."

"We'll plan on distributing a supplemental list, then. Doing two will allow the owners to get going on some of the recommendations now." He nodded at Justin, then turned to his office staff of three women and two men seated at their desks. "Move on it," he told them, then looked back at Maggie. "The twenty-six agreed to extra security, Maggie—if you ask for it. Overtime is authorized and backup guards are on call."

Maggie didn't miss his point. "I'm asking, Will."

Relief lashed across his face. "You got it. We have thirty men trained for inside, an additional twenty for the north and south parking garages and the open parking in between. How many do you want activated?"

"I'm assuming the mall will be open all night, setting up for this Winter Wonderland. Is that right?"

"Yes, ma'am. It'll take them at least nine hours to prepare the pit and set everything up. Harry and Phil Jensen, the owners, will have the crew start at midnight."

"Then activate all the guards," Maggie said, making the

call. "Start them at midnight and carry them through until we know we're on the other side of this tomorrow night." Maggie hitched her purse strap on her shoulder. "We're also going to need personnel records on Harry and Phil, information on their company, and background data on the snow crew."

"I'm on it." Will looked over at the woman seated at the first desk and began reeling off orders.

Maggie glanced at Justin. Often lab rats got in the field and froze, but he stood quietly and calmly watching Will. Intense, but in control. *So far, so good.* "Ready?"

He nodded. "What exactly are we looking for?"

"Two things," she said softly. "Vulnerabilities and familiarity."

He pulled a pad and pen out of his briefcase. "I'll take notes."

"Thanks." That surprised her, though it shouldn't have. Of course he would feel more comfortable doing something familiar, having a tool natural to him in his hand. "Working with Darcy has spoiled me," Maggie said for no particular reason. "No notes necessary."

"Guess I'm a poor substitute for someone with her memory skills."

And just how did he know about Darcy's special skills? Maggie didn't ask but lifted a questioning brow.

"Colonel Drake explained her gifts."

"In that case, aren't we all poor substitutes for her?" Darcy remembered everything and associated values based on educated judgment and years of experience as a top-notch operative. That was hard to beat. But equally important to Maggie, she trusted Darcy. Still, not wanting a war with Justin, Maggie toned down her response. "So far, your assistance has been helpful," she said, and meant it. "You have a calm manner, Justin. It went over well with the store owners."

They turned the corner and he looked into the window at Macy's. Giant red and gold shiny balls hung from green banners. "I'm really not the devil incarnate, Maggie."

"I never said you were." She stopped, looked down the length of the thoroughfare. Center Court's stage and pit were to her right; specialty stores, to the left. She paused, mentally moving down the corridor and counting receptacles. "First on the list for Will is to have all the trash receptacles removed."

Justin scrawled it down, his pen scratching on the page. "It's going to get really messy in here."

"No doubt it will, but trash cans are easy targets and impossible to protect, which means they have to go." She walked on, sniffing intently.

After about three minutes, Justin's curiosity got the better of him. "What are you doing?"

"Smelling. The mall is using aromatherapy to influence shoppers' buying tendencies and to create positive subliminal messages to shoppers about being in the facility," she said, flipping a finger toward his notepad. "Add a cease-and-desist to Will's list." Fragrance easily masked biological contaminates. "Also, make a note that we need to address aromatherapy with the individual owners." She waited, but he didn't write anything. She lifted a questioning eyebrow.

"Both are already on the list," he said matter-of-factly. "Picked up on them immediately, and noted them."

"Really?" she asked, suitably impressed.

"The mall thoroughfares and corridors smell like Christmas pine, and nearly every store has its own specific scent—coffee, lemon, fresh air, and even salt water, though I won't hazard a guess as to why."

"Fishing," Maggie said. "It's huge here."

"Ah, of course." Justin nodded. "All are distinct, though some of the scents are subtle. Others are blatant." He grunted. "I wonder how many times people come here and never notice that?"

"A lot, I imagine," Maggie said. "Few outside the field think in terms of fragrance masking bio-contaminates." She paused and checked the center rounds. About eight feet in diameter, they were raised beds, home to potted plants and huge palms. "All of these rounds need to be netted." They formed a line down the center of the common areas throughout all three levels.

Justin blinked hard, scribbled that down. "I missed that, damn it. It'd be ridiculously easy to drop in a vial."

They walked on, through Center Court. On the far end, near the escalator and stairs, the stage stood empty. The heavy red-velvet drapes were tied to its white-column sides with thick gold ropes. "We'll need to blockade that space under the platform." Anything could be hidden under it. She looked down the wide marble steps to the pit that would be filled with snow. About three feet deep, it was roughly the size of a basketball court.

A ruckus erupted just outside the Tot Shop. Will Stanton surfaced right in the middle of it, planting himself between two shouting men. "Just calm down," Will said, his voice carrying over to Maggie.

"We'd better see what's up," Maggie said, and walked over with Justin staying at her side.

The redhead from the auditorium meeting stood to the left of them, her round face pale. "I want him arrested. He's in my store, spraying that…that…thing."

Maggie looked at the "thing" and recognized it as an inhaler. She stepped forward. "May I see that?"

The wheezing man looked at Will, who nodded, then handed it over. "Asthma?" Maggie asked.

"Yes."

She checked the label and then passed the item back to him. "Go ahead and use your inhaler, sir."

"Sorry for the inconvenience, sir," Will said. "We've had trouble with a couple guys playing with spray paint lately."

Relief washed across the man's face. He gave himself two sprays and then stuck the inhaler back in his pocket. His breathing cleared and the liquid sound disappeared from his chest. "If you've got a problem, lady," he told the redhead, "you should ask a person before creating a ruckus." Shaking his head, he then walked away with his friend.

"I had to check," the redhead said. "It was an aerosol."

"Gladys," Will Stanton said. "Don't make my life miserable. I can't be so busy monitoring you that I miss an attacker."

"Sorry."

Maggie and Justin returned to their inspection. "Put your running shoes on," she whispered. "It's already started, but when the owners get Will's lists, they'll all be jumping at ghosts."

"Annoying but inevitable, I suppose."

"Yes," Maggie agreed. "But this time tomorrow we'll wish we had Rollerblades."

* * *

By the time Maggie and Justin had completed the vulnerability-and-familiarity inspection on each of the three levels, and on all twenty-six A-stores and the B-stores, they'd also dealt with two more aerosol alarms. The first was on Level One at Queen's In, a women's clothing store. A shopper had used a perfume atomizer, and the owner had freaked. The second alarm was at a Level Three children's furniture store, Half-Pint. A mother-to-be had tested furniture polish to make sure she wasn't allergic. The clerk had heard the spray but hadn't seen the can and panicked.

Will Stanton met up with Maggie and Justin on Level One outside 24-Karat on Jewelry Row. "How's it going?"

A woman pushed a stroller with twin infants down the corridor. "Good, Will," Maggie said. "But we've got a lot to do."

"Do we have a shot at getting it done in time?"

Maggie assessed it. "Yes, but it'll take effort and focus."

"I might have to hog-tie Gladys."

The stout redhead. Maggie smiled. "More incidents?"

"Two, so far." He grunted. "We might want to reconsider having her here tomorrow."

"Can't," Justin said. "If she's not here, her life's not at risk. There's no way she'll keep quiet about the preparations going on here."

Will listened to a quick transmission on his walkie-talkie—something mundane on Level Two—checked his watch and then looked at Maggie. "Why don't you two grab some lunch at one of the restaurants while my staff finishes getting the floor plans together."

"How much longer will it be?" Maggie pulled a mint from her purse, offered Will and Justin one.

Will declined. "We need a little while. Oversize copies. Linda Diel, Barone's assistant, arranged with a local architectural firm to run copies for us."

"Terrific," Maggie said. No sense in pushing him; the man was clearly working at this as hard as he could. "Will an hour do it?"

"Linger an extra fifteen minutes over dessert, and we should be ready for you. The firm's across town and the copying will take a little extra. I'm having them duplicate everything—fire, security—all of it. Some of the more sensitive plans are stored in the vault. We had to get access and Mr. Barone was a little reluctant, but Linda finally talked him around."

Justin grunted. "No doubt, Linda convinced him with talk of legal liability. Little else would work with him."

Will sent Justin a conspiratorial grin. "You got it in one, Doc." He shifted his weight on his feet. "Maggie, Mr. Barone wants you to sign a confidentiality agreement."

"Sorry, I can't do that," Maggie said. If GRID attacked Santa Bella, she had to share knowledge with the Threat Integration Center, First Responders and her entire chain of command. "But I will classify the plans top-secret."

"That'll be fine," Will said. "I'll explain it to Mr. Barone."

Maggie didn't envy him the task. "Thanks."

Will's walkie-talkie beeped. "Enjoy your lunch. If you need me, I'll be stomping out fires."

Maggie watched him go and then turned to Justin. "Name your poison."

Surprise widened his eyes. "What?"

"Lunch," she said, then rephrased. "Where do you want to eat lunch?"

"How about seafood at Emerald Bay?" He suggested a quiet restaurant facing the Center Court pit.

"Works for me."

Ten minutes later they were seated at a small square table draped with a snowy-white linen cloth. Maggie scanned the menu and made her selection. "Linguini with white clam sauce, a small house salad and iced tea, please. Sweet."

The thin waitress had high cheekbones and dimples. She wasn't a pretty woman, but she had an interesting face and a sunny disposition that made her beautiful. "Sir?"

"Grilled shrimp," he said. "The vegetable medley, please, and a salad with house dressing. Sweet tea."

Only in the south did one order "sweet tea" instead of iced tea and then add sugar. Two months ago Maggie had returned to her last assignment, the Biological Warfare Review Board at the Pentagon in Washington, and remembered how her request for sweet tea had raised eyebrows. In Florida, where a sweet tea order is the custom, she still forgot to order that way half the time.

Midway through their meal, general chat turned serious. "May I ask you a question?" Justin asked.

Chewing, Maggie nodded.

"When you gave me the odds of a GRID attack," he said softly so as to not be overheard, "were you being conservative or generous?"

Maggie tried not to take offense. He didn't know her. Still, she felt that knot of resentment form in her stomach. "Neither," she said, hearing disdain in her voice but unable to hide it. "I was being honest."

Astute, Justin picked up on it, and that the disdain was

aimed in his direction. He frowned. "Maggie, have I done something to offend you?"

"No." She stopped there, not eager to bring her personal bias or the sadness that rode shotgun with it out into the open. She felt and acknowledged both, true. But she didn't want to have to admit it.

His expression tightened, dragging down the corners of his mouth, and his eyes turned cold and distant. "But...."

"Isn't that sufficient?"

"Actually, no. It isn't." He dabbed at his mouth with his linen napkin. "If you have a problem with me, let's get it out in the open."

"All right." She set down her fork. "The truth is, I'm not comfortable relying on you. It's a position I'd rather not be in."

"Why?" He looked baffled. "I'm just as reliant on you—likely more reliant, considering your added areas of expertise at what we're facing—and I haven't had the privilege of reading your dossier or performance reports. I don't know nearly as much about you as you do about me." He lifted a hand. "I'm a doctor, Maggie. I'm great in the lab and on bio subjects, but I'm not in the lab right now, and I don't have the other essential skills you have."

"Bluntly put, my skills are excellent or I wouldn't be here," she said. "But it isn't your lack of field skills that bothers me, Justin." Being honest was difficult, but Maggie refused to lie to him. She brushed her shoulder-length blond hair back behind her shoulder. "This will be horribly blunt, and I have no desire to hurt you, but the truth is, I don't trust you. And I try very hard to never be in a position where I must depend on someone I don't trust."

Now he was seriously offended and challenged her. "What exactly have I done to destroy your trust?"

She shrugged.

"Then your rationale escapes me."

Why did he keep pushing her on this?

Truth dawned and reflected in his eyes. He had put the puzzle pieces into place. "Whose sins am I being punished for, Maggie? Kunz and GRID, or is this about your ex-husband?"

Shame washed through her. She couldn't meet Justin's eyes. He knew way too much about her personal situation already. The shame and sadness, the regret that she couldn't go back and change anything. Not in her marriage, or in her reaction to finding out about Jack and Karen, which was totally and completely humiliating. To be that angry, that out of control...seemed so right. Dr. Morgan Cabot said hers wasn't an uncommon reaction to discovering adultery with a friend and that Maggie should forgive herself. But she looked at the wedding band on her finger and she just couldn't do it.

Justin knew most of that, except about Morgan, of course. Why did he keep pressing her?

Her chest went tight. "I don't know whether it's fear you're a double or because of Jack," she said honestly, feeling more confused than she'd felt since having her first crush on a guy in high school. "Maybe it's neither, or maybe it's both." She risked a glance up into his eyes. "I'm not being a smart-ass, Justin. You confuse me." *You make me think and feel things I don't want to feel,* she wanted to say, but didn't. Something swelled in her throat, threatening to choke off her air. She rubbed at it, hoping it'd go away, knowing it wouldn't.

And then the reason hit her. He could hurt her. She liked him, and he could hurt her. "Do we have to get into this?"

"Considering my life and those of a hell of a lot of others could well be in your hands, damn right we have to get into this. You made a judgment call against me. I deserve to know the basis of it, Maggie. Right now, I'm not comfortable relying on you, either. But I would like to be."

Her stomach revolting, her lungs air-starved, she set down her fork and laced her hands in her lap. "I'm afraid that the problem between us just hit me." She stared at him, not quite believing what she was about to say herself. "I— I like you, Justin."

He smiled. "That's good news, not a problem."

"Oh, yes, it is. No, don't laugh. I'm serious." She wiped a damp palm on the napkin draped over her lap. "It's— it's…" At a loss for words, she waved small circles with her hand.

"It's worse," he said. "Because I like you, too."

"Oh, hell." She did *not* want to hear that. Her hand on her thigh shook. Well, okay, she did want to hear it, but she damn well shouldn't. What a mess! The timing was so wrong. Maybe she'd plead for mercy. What else was left? Shame, anger, embarrassment, humiliation, and now this?

Nothing. Nothing was left. In some way, he'd touched something inside her. She didn't like it. Okay, she did like it, but she shouldn't like it. And she didn't want to like it. Definitely, plead for mercy. "Justin, just let this go. Please. I don't want to create unnecessary tension between us, and I don't want to lie to you. Nothing will be gained by us hashing through this, so there's no need and no benefit in pursuing this discussion."

"No need?" He looked shocked. "There's every need."

Maggie stared at him a long moment. He wouldn't relent. "Okay, then. Fine. But remember that you insisted." Irritated at being shoved into a corner, she washed down her food with a long drink of cold tea, then set down her glass. Chilled drops slid down its slick side to the table. "During the course of my life, I've determined a few things to be true. One you're familiar with already. Men are very good at deceit and cannot be trusted."

"A crime committed by one man, for which you're condemning an entire gender?"

"Not only one man, Justin." She gave him a pointed look, reminding him of his own infidelity.

His face flushed, but he didn't acknowledge that he was as guilty as Jack had been. "For you, there's a lot more going on here than a lack of trust," Justin speculated. "That can be earned. But you said there were a few things. What are the others?"

Earned. Yes, maybe. But he said it as if it were as easy as picking up a Sunday paper. It wasn't. It was damned hard. She returned to her topic. "There are two," she said. "The first is that men make promises and vows to appease women—and they break them the very second women interfere with what they want to do."

"Ah, I understand now."

She drank from her glass. "What?"

"The reason Colonel Drake warned you about the rules. I thought that was odd at the time, but now I totally understand why she felt compelled to issue the order."

Irritated at being this transparent, she bristled. "It's important to follow the rules, Justin. Rules. Like promises or vows, when you break them, the result isn't a hypothetical. It's real, and too often, real people get hurt."

He had to be angry. It should be radiating from him, but not a hint of it was evident in his voice. Silky-soft and smooth, it never wavered. "And your third truth?" He encouraged her to go on.

She did, seeing no sense in not saying it all now that most of it was already on the table. "Three. It's my ironclad policy never to trust a man who cheats."

"Because you divorced one," he said.

"Yes." And it'd damn near killed her. "Your marriage is none of my business, Justin, and I'm first to admit it. But it would be foolish to ignore our histories. As you said, lives depend on the decisions and judgment calls we make."

"And personal feelings just blur the lines on rules and make things messy."

"That, too."

A muscle in his jaw ticked. The look in his eyes turned hard and cold. Still his voice stayed velvet-soft. "I'm not shocked, Maggie," he said. "Maybe a little disappointed in you, but I'm not surprised that when you look at me, all you see is a man who cheated on his wife who might also, despite Colonel Drake's vouching for me, be one of Kunz's body doubles."

"I don't think you're a double—not at the moment, anyway." Confusion inside her created chaos. Was he trying to provoke her or to make her feel guilty? She refused to feel either. Her feelings were her own, valid and forged in the agony that follows betrayal, in the pain of being tossed suddenly from the lifetime expectancy of "us" into "just me" without warning. She'd trudged through months of depression and hell, wondering if her job had been the cause of their problems. Wondering why, during a time of national crisis, it had been so easy for her husband and best friend to hurt her and lie to her. She'd suffered, and she still suffered because there were no easy answers to these questions and a million more like them that haunted her. Often, there were no answers at all.

No, Justin Crowe wasn't going to make her second-guess what she knew to be true. She'd lived the victim side of the unfaithful. She'd trusted Jack implicitly, totally and completely. And with no warning, he'd left her broken and devastated in the pile of rubble that once had been her life.

No man would ever have that power over her again. She just couldn't survive it twice.

The waitress silently poured coffee, clearly picking up on the tension at the table. She cast a covert glance at Maggie's hand, checking for a wedding band, and seemed reassured on seeing one, then left the table.

"I feel the sadness in you, Maggie." Justin added cream to his coffee. "I'm sorry you were hurt."

She swallowed hard, lifted her chin. "No, I'm sorry." She bit her lip, took responsibility. "I had no right to say any of that to you."

He rubbed the handle of his cup with his thumb. "I might have gotten more than I wanted, but at least you were honest. I can respect an honest woman."

What did he mean by that? Clearly there was a message in that comment, but exactly what was it? "Look," she said. "I really don't want a war with you. I was serious earlier. You have been helpful here, and we do have to work together. It will be so much easier if we do so on a friendly footing."

"I don't want a war, either. But let's face it, you like me and I like you." He stopped a second and sadness swept over his face. "The battle lines have been drawn. Between you and me, but even more so, between you and a man I've never met, and between me and a woman you've never met." He chewed at his lip. "For what it's worth, Maggie, I'm sad, too. I guess when we get down to it, we're both victims of our experience."

His sadness slid through her protective shield. "I guess we are." Mutual regret that they suffered hit her hard. Looking at Justin Crowe honestly, she regretted it deeply. She might even resent it.

"Under the circumstances, I feel it's only fair to tell you that I don't trust you, either, Maggie."

That shocked her. She hadn't lied, hadn't given him any reason to doubt her personal ethics or her professional abilities. So why did he feel this way? Finally, she steeled herself and worked up the courage to ask. "Why not?"

"I can't." He placed his napkin on the table and signaled for the check. "No matter how smart or capable a woman might be, I could never trust a woman who holds so much sadness and bitterness in her heart that she has no room left for understanding or compassion—or even benefit of doubt enough to suspend passing judgment on the past and consider looking at the present."

Now Maggie was offended. Enormously. "Don't judge me, Justin." She had enough trouble with judging herself.

He lifted an eyebrow. "Didn't you judge me?"

She had. But he had cheated on Andrea. Of course, Maggie acknowledged that. What sane woman wouldn't? "That's different."

"Only because you're the one doing it."

The waitress walked over and placed the check on the table.

Maggie swallowed her resentment, anger and that foolish hurt. She'd learned many things from her experience with Jack and Karen. One was that sometimes you just have to accept the inevitable. And what was inevitable here was that, while they liked each other, trust was absent.

And unfortunately, in situations such as this Priority Code Three mission, success often came down to trust, to following a hunch, to noticing some minute detail at subliminal level and having the courage to act on it.

Discriminating against your partner's judgment could mean the difference between success and failure, life and death.

But the difference wasn't simply a matter of choosing to go along; Maggie had to believe in what she was doing and in her partner. In those critical seconds where a snap judgment had to be made, Maggie wouldn't trust Justin's judgment and he wouldn't trust hers.

And that frightening truth significantly decreased their already thin odds for success.

Chapter 4

"Ah, Maggie." Will Stanton smiled, then nodded at Justin.

In the security office, they walked over to the marble counter separating the reception area from the desks, and Maggie set her purse down to give her shoulder a break. Everyone on his staff was busy either at the computer or on the phone. Some were on both. "We've got that list for you, Will."

"Great. I'm already getting in a couple confirmations from the owners off the first one we distributed. So far, mostly from the B-stores."

The smaller stores would be able to comply with the requests more quickly. The A-stores, like Macy's and Krane's, needed more time. "Excellent." Maggie motioned for Justin to pass the list over.

Daniel Barone silently entered the security office behind them. He snagged the list from Will before he had a chance to even glance at it. "Let me see that."

Barone reviewed the items, slowly and methodically, and then looked over at Maggie. "Our staff will easily be able to handle the majority of your requests, Captain. But am I reading this correctly? You want all employees to wear yellow tomorrow?"

"Actually, from the time the stores close to shoppers tonight until they close tomorrow night."

Barone's resistance was palpable. Too bad.

She dredged up a smile, already weary of fighting him on specifics, particularly regarding having medical staff on the premises.

She needed to work around him on that, and put it on her mental to-do list. One way or another, she had to have medical personnel inside the mall. Using undercover shoppers would be easiest, of course, but she'd have no way of placing them specifically and roamers would be inefficient as well as obvious. For a second she debated the value of reminding Barone that she and Justin were here to save his ass, but she might just need that leverage more later. Better save it.

His forehead wrinkled and he crooked his mouth. "Wouldn't red or green be more appropriate to the holiday?"

"To the holiday, yes, Mr. Barone. But because that's true, many nonemployees will also be wearing those colors. That renders them ineffective for our purposes."

"Valid point." He paused, thoughtfully considered the other items on the list. "Will, we can have attendants in all the rest rooms and in the store's dressing rooms, can't we?"

"It's doable, sir," he said. "Provided the stores cooperate, of course, and they've no logical reason to refuse."

"Fine." Barone read on, then came to an abrupt halt. "What's this? Prepositioning antidote?" He stared at Maggie, clearly verged on refusing.

"That's not a request." Justin jumped in. "It's a mandate, Mr. Barone."

"A mandate?" His expression turned dark.

"If anything should happen here, you don't want to have to explain on the ten o'clock news why you refused to position the antidote vials inside the facility." Justin sent Barone a sincere look. "That could open a devastating Pandora's box on legal issues and become a PR nightmare."

Justin had Barone's attention; he wasn't refusing or shouting down the roof. Maggie was grateful for both.

"It's just not worth the risk," Justin went on. "Not prepositioning the antidote could be perceived by the public as deliberate deception that resulted in reckless endangerment. God forbid anyone should die." Justin tilted his head. "I'm not sure exactly what your legal standing would be then, but considering anyone can sue for anything…" Justin lifted a hand. "We consider protecting you as much as possible from costly ramifications to be in everyone's best interests."

If Santa Bella was attacked, just opening the mall for business could be considered deliberate deception and reckless endangerment, but Maggie didn't say so. Barone already knew it. Will had mentioned that legal counsel had been at that seven o'clock meeting between Barone and the twenty-six A-stores. Of course, he'd been blunt on liability. That's why he was there.

Barone pondered a moment, then said, "Prepositioning the antidote is fine, but no medical staff. The shoppers would be unnerved and leave, and that would bankrupt at least a hundred stores."

Very nice job, Justin. Well, half a job. Maggie cleared her throat, then pushed for the second half. "If we have to administer the antidote, we have two minutes to do it. That's a reminder, Mr. Barone. We have *only* two minutes before we start seeing shoppers become corpses," she reiterated. "I've developed a plan to insert some medical professionals undercover as clerks. People who are trained to react to these types of situations. For all intents and purposes, they'll appear to be normal sales staff. But if we need them, they'll be in position, ready to help." Taking a tip from Justin and his success, she added, "For your protection, this, too, is not negotiable, Mr. Barone."

He sent her a haughty look. "Everything is negotiable, Captain Holt."

So he'd defer to Justin but not to her? When she was the one with extensive experience and expertise? Why? Was his reasoning a sexist male thing or just plain stupidity? Regardless, it was time she stopped tiptoeing and spelled out the rules. "No, Mr. Barone, everything is not negotiable."

He dropped the smile. "Without orders from Homeland Security, your recommendations are no more than suggestions, Captain Holt."

Maggie gazed up at him, looking down his nose at her. She'd expected him to be reluctant, but she couldn't have expected he'd be foolish. "Actually, Mr. Barone, I have all the authorization I need to close the mall, to insert medical personnel, or to do whatever I feel I need to do. The only criteria required to reclassify any decision I choose from a recommendation to a mandate is for me to deem it essential to national security. That is my domain, and my judgment in matters of it here are final. So you see, Mr. Barone, everything is not negotiable. Only what I deem negotiable is negotiable." *Stuff that, jerk.*

"That wasn't my understanding, Captain Holt." His jaw tightened and a muscle in his left cheek twitched.

"Your understanding was inaccurate," she said simply. "I prefer to work together to form mutual decisions rather than to dictate them. But if necessary, I will dictate them. Your goal is to protect your interests. My goal is to assure that wise choices are made for everyone involved. That's my job, and I'm paid to do it well. Lives depend on my decisions, Mr. Barone. Maybe even yours." She paused, let what she'd said sink in. When he didn't respond, she added, "Is having my undercover medical staff work as clerks acceptable to you or not?"

He shifted uneasily, folded his arms over his chest. "Provided the twenty-six agree, yes. But I insist shoppers remain oblivious to them." He looked across the counter at Will. "Have the A-stores surveyed on this right away."

"Yes, sir."

"Excellent." She turned to Will Stanton. "The new list contains things that need to be addressed before midnight when the Winter Wonderland crew arrives." *The more done that fewer knew about, the better.* "We'll take care of prepositioning the antidote and installing our additional surveillance equipment."

"What additional surveillance equipment?" Barone asked, clearly annoyed again.

"Mainly entrance cameras," Maggie said, pivoting her gaze from Will back to Barone. "I want a complete recording of everyone entering and exiting the mall tomorrow during all hours of operation. Your equipment can't handle the load, so I'm bringing in mine to supplement it."

Barone didn't like it. In fact, gauging by his bitter expression, he deeply resented it. Not, she was sure, that he minded the extra protection. It was far more likely that he resented anything associated with him being considered lacking. Maggie stiffened, preparing for round two, but for some reason, Barone held his tongue. That worried her.

Will leaned against the slick marble counter. His security badge reflected in its shiny surface. "The timing will be close, Maggie, but I think we can get it all done before Phil and Harry Jensen bring the Winter Wonderland crew in."

"If there's any doubt, we need to have the covert surveillance work done first. Then, if we run short on time, it's just the general work that will be observed." Maggie jotted a note down on her personal list. "I'll bring in a crew to install the monitors."

Barone's expression turned grimmer. Changing the topic, he passed the list to Will. "Go ahead with all of this," Barone said, as if the previous ten minutes of conversation never had taken place.

Even Will Stanton, who had enormous talent for hiding his reactions, failed to sequester his surprise. "Yes, sir."

Barone turned to look at Maggie. "I'm doing everything possible to act responsibly and reasonably, Captain Holt, but I do insist that shoppers remain unaware of anything unusual going on, and that no activity or action take place without my prior knowledge and consent."

Maggie bristled but said not a word.

Forced by her silence to further explain, Barone added, "Of course, if Santa Bella should be attacked, the situation will carry enormous legal implications. It's my job to protect the interests of owners and visitors, and I'm paid well to do it." He tossed her words back at her.

If protecting shoppers and owners was uppermost in his mind, Barone would shut down the damn mall. But Maggie had said all she could say on that matter. The owners had voted. Yet she refused to make anyone a promise she couldn't keep, so she remained quiet, letting her silence encourage Barone to continue.

A little boy about seven chased a ball into the security office and bumped into Barone's leg. Barone pulled back, caught himself, and gave the boy's shoulder a stilted pat. "Watch where you're going, son," he ordered. "And play with that ball outside."

The boy recoiled from Barone's touch, ducked out of his reach and scooped up his ball, then ran out of the office.

His expression struck Maggie as strange. It had been odd; not afraid, but more like the boy had been forced to swallow a pound of spinach.

Barone turned back to Maggie. "Remember, Captain. Prior notice on all actions or activities."

"I'll attempt to honor your request," Maggie said. But her first responsibility was to the public and she would first protect it. If Santa Bella was attacked, waiting for Barone to preapprove her actions could range from unwise to impossible.

"Captain, I'm not asking for this, I'm demanding it." Barone lifted an eyebrow. "This facility is ultimately my responsibility, and I won't accept that responsibility if you act without my knowledge. Either you consult with me prior to taking any action, or you take full responsibility for this facility. One or the other."

And with that smiling remark, Barone had set her up as his scapegoat. Unfortunately for her, there was nothing she could do about it. The bottom line was if the need arose, she'd act. "I understand your position."

He gave her a curt nod and then told Will, "I'll be in my office." Barone left without another word.

Maggie watched him go, then glanced at Will, catching him in an unguarded moment. His annoyance and dislike for Barone was written in every line on his face. "Is the copy of the plans back from the architect's office yet?"

Will reached under the counter, then passed her the tube. "Here you go." He reached again, then withdrew three large, brown manila envelopes and passed them over. "Photos of all mall employees," he said, nodding at the envelopes. "It was, um, on your list."

"Thanks, Will." Maggie gave him a smile, knowing damn well there had been no request for any of this on her list. But she did have a good idea where the requests had originated. "The mall closes to shoppers at ten tonight, right?"

"Everything except DMV Drugs. It's open until midnight."

"Terrific." Maggie nodded. "Dr. Crowe and I are going to gather equipment and coordinate some things. We'll be back in plenty of time to monitor the camera installations. Whatever comes up, just follow your instincts. If you need me before I get back, here's my cell number." She passed him a business card.

"How long will the installations take?"

Maggie thought a second. All entrances, key locations she and Justin had pinpointed as blind spots, the administration wing, which oddly had no equipment in it whatsoever… The snow crew came in at midnight… "Three hours," she estimated.

"Sounds realistic."

She had to get assistance from Providence Air Force Base to make the schedule happen. That meant requesting help from Colonel Gray, which would no doubt ignite another battle in the Gray/Drake pissing contest. Colonel Drake wouldn't appreciate needing Gray's assistance, and Maggie certainly wasn't looking forward to asking for it, but some things just couldn't be avoided.

"Before we go, Maggie," Justin said. "What do you think of Security setting up a command post on each level? We could disguise it as a customer service perk for the shoppers. Maybe offer free blood pressure checks, or something?"

Standing across from her, Will smiled. "Excellent idea, Doc. Shoppers will know these people are legitimate medical personnel."

Justin smiled. "I have my moments."

This was a good moment. A very good moment. "Will, what are our odds that Barone will authorize it?" Maggie asked.

"Give me a few minutes to see what I can do." He snagged a phone and in short order came back to the counter. "Done."

Surprised, Maggie asked, "Barone went for it?"

"Turns out, he authorized it two months ago." Will hiked

both eyebrows, looking pretty pleased with himself. "According to Linda Diel, his personal assistant, the Red Cross scheduled this event back in October."

"So Linda is helping us get medical staff into position?"

"Of course not, Doc." Will frowned. "Linda's just doing her job, tracking normal commitments."

Recognizing the twinkle in Will's eye, Maggie put a restraining hand on Justin's forearm to stop any more questions. If caught inserting this onto the mall calendar of events, Linda would be fired. "Finally, a lucky break. Thanks, Will."

He nodded. "Yes, ma'am."

Maggie led Justin out of the security office, then out of the building and into the crammed parking lot to her red Jeep. She held off making any remarks until they were seated in the car with the doors closed.

"Justin, may I offer a tip without seeming critical? I really don't want to create conflict."

"Sure. Go ahead." He pulled his seat belt across his chest and clicked it into place.

"Outside the lab, it's often wise not to ask questions you can't already answer."

"Ah, Linda Diel." He nodded. "Sorry about that. I caught on to what Will and Linda were doing, but not until after I'd opened my mouth. I'll be more careful in the future."

His response surprised Maggie. If she had offered that same advice to Jack, he would have raised hell all the way back to Regret. "Terrific," she said, embracing his moment of grace. "We don't want Barone to can her for helping us. Word gets around, and if that happened, then no one else would dare to lift a finger."

"May I ask you a question?" Justin flipped up the sun visor.

She nodded and cranked the engine, slid the gearshift into reverse and backed out of the slot. Three cars were lined up in the row behind her, waiting for her parking space.

"Why did Will give you photographs of all the mall employees? He said it was on our list, but it wasn't."

This Maggie felt pretty comfortable answering. "I'm not positive, but I'm guessing Darcy phoned him and asked for them."

"To see if GRID has anyone already working inside?"

"That and so she can review them before tomorrow."

"There are thousands of photos, and she's got a lot of other things to do."

Maggie pulled out of the parking lot and into the line of cars stopped at the red light. It'd take two, maybe three, rounds before she'd get beyond the corner and through the light. "Remember that Darcy has total recall, Justin. A glimpse will commit whatever she sees to memory. Anyway, she'll review the photos and then watch the monitors. Whatever the surveillance cameras at the mall transmit back to her, she'll assimilate. Any nonemployee spotted in yellow, or anyone involved in suspicious activity, she'll report to us immediately."

Skepticism riddled Justin's face. "But there are dozens of monitors."

"Yep."

"And she can handle all of them? At one time?"

"All of them and then some."

He let out a low whistle. "She's a hell of an asset."

"She is, and she's a good friend, too." Maggie's palms went clammy on the steering wheel. "The challenge will be for us to determine whether or not someone she singles out is harmless or a legitimate threat."

"Same problem as the owners," Justin said, making the mental leap. "You're afraid we'll be jumping at ghosts."

"I guarantee we will." Maggie pulled up to the white line and braked for the red light—first in line for the next round. Her thoughts splintered into a dozen directions, all on things that needed to be done. "The stakes are enormously high."

"At least you know the enemy," Justin said, proving he had keen insight.

Thomas Kunz. Very perceptive. "Yeah, I do." And he was a force to be reckoned with. Maggie had repeatedly studied every scrap of information available on Thomas Kunz and GRID. Dossiers, history, profiles, reports of personal encounters and even recorded impressions. Not much scared Maggie, but all she had read, all she had learned from Amanda and Kate's encounters with this man and his GRID surrogates, terrified her.

Thomas Kunz would gain the proof he needed to black market the DR-27 virus and make his billions. He would kill thousands of innocent people and not even blink. He was a monster. A soulless monster, who had no compassion and granted no mercy. Maggie let out a shuddery breath.

"Are you okay?" Justin asked.

She swallowed hard, shaking off Kunz, and then looked over at Justin. He wore his concern on his face as clearly as she did. "I'm worried, Justin."

"Of course."

Of course? Where was his mockery? The put-downs and slurs for admitting fear? Startled by the absence, she just stared at him.

"What?" He sent her a baffled, questioning look.

She tried to compose herself. "Um, nothing. It's nothing." A lie. It was something. Maybe not everything, but certainly a significant something.

He frowned. "Are you under the impression that I'm not worried?"

"No, I can see that you are."

He raked a hand through his hair. "Can you see that I'm terrified?"

Fear. He admitted feeling fear? She shouldn't do it, shouldn't whisper so much as a syllable of agreement—it would be used against her later. It always was—but at that moment, looking into his eyes, it seemed perfectly natural to be open and honest and to just speak her mind. "Me, too."

Chapter 5

In the bunker at Regret, Santa Bella's triple-decker floor plan lay spread out on the conference table. Kate, Amanda, Darcy and Colonel Drake had all studied it with Maggie and Justin. Maggie had noted every comment made and concern voiced in her notebook.

Moving beyond the floor plan, Darcy clicked off other matters of interest. "Colonel Gray is being an ass, but he's providing the equipment and manpower we need to get the surveillance equipment installed." She cast an impatient look at Colonel Drake. "Turns out he's not on the best terms with General Foster, either."

"It's not smart to tick off Special Forces or a general when you're only sporting eagles on your shoulders."

"No, ma'am, it's not," Darcy told the colonel.

Maggie sighed and stepped back from the table. Pain

shot through the small of her back, protesting her being bent over too long. She pressed a hand to it. "What about the Red Cross workers?"

"We're set there," Darcy said. "There are fifty of them."

"Divide them into three groups," Maggie said. "One for each level."

Justin rubbed at his neck. "Fifty's not enough, Maggie. Fifty Special Forces members, fifty Red Cross workers— we're not even close. Each one will have time to inject two, maybe three people—if they know what's happening and act immediately. We're going to get our asses kicked."

"We'll have all forces converge at the point of the attack," Maggie said. "We don't have to inoculate everyone in two minutes. Just those directly exposed to the active virus."

Justin stuffed his hands in his pockets. "What if GRID launches multiple attacks at Santa Bella?"

Everyone went silent. Kate and Amanda exchanged a solemn look Maggie well understood.

"If that happens," Darcy confessed, "we're screwed."

"If that happens, we're screwed *and* we're ridiculously sloppy and should all be fired immediately," Maggie said, biting into an apple. "With all we're doing—the precautions, additional manpower and surveillance equipment— we have decent odds of detection prior to any launch. We pay attention to the results of these things, and we better our odds of detecting any subsequent launches." She smiled.

"What if GRID launches multiple attacks at Santa Bella *simultaneously?*" Justin persisted.

Darcy swallowed and looked him straight in the eye. "If that happens," she repeated, "we're screwed."

"Look, Justin," Maggie said. "We can make the mall more secure, but there's no way to prevent an attack. Not with shopping bags, purses, backpacks, strollers and a million nooks and crannies in the mall. Prevention is asking the impossible."

He stepped toward her. "I don't mean to insinuate that you're not doing your job. Your foresight and thoroughness have been impressive, but—"

"But even with all we've done," she interrupted. "Even with strategic prepositioning of the antidote, med staff posing as clerks, the Red Cross assisting, all the extra security staff and cameras, and other precautions we've taken, you see more challenges."

He nodded. "Shoppers aren't just going to allow us to inject them, especially since all of you are now wearing civilian clothes. You blend in, but now it's more difficult," he said. "People resist what they don't understand, and we won't have time to explain this to them."

"He's right." Colonel Drake said. "So we do the best we can and pray we can evacuate the rest quickly enough to avoid catastrophe. *If* Kunz attacks Santa Bella."

"He's going to attack somewhere, Colonel." Amanda looked at Darcy. "Has Intel further defined the target, or are they still considering the same group equally vulnerable."

"Nothing's changed on that end. We've still got multiple possibilities and the same odds."

Colonel Drake looked at Amanda, whose eyes and expression were deadpan serious. As serious as only a woman formerly held prisoner by Kunz could be.

"I know, Amanda," the colonel said softly, covering her heart with her hand. "In here, I know. But until we have hard evidence, there's nothing more we can do at Santa Bella. Every one of the potential targets is facing the same challenges we are in their locations."

Amanda nodded, understandably bitter.

Darcy cut in. "Maggie, all the communications equipment you requested is in your Jeep. Everyone in this room will be connected. We're going satellite—no cell phones for official business—for security reasons and because some areas of the mall have six-foot-thick walls as part of the hurricane-proofing construction. Difficult for land-based communications to be failsafe."

Darcy passed out yellow jackets and everyone took one. "Wear this the entire time you're at the mall. It's Kevlar."

Bulletproof. But was it virus-proof?

Maggie shoved her arms through the sleeves and addressed the group. "Colonel Drake and Darcy will be here at Regret, handling Home Base operations and keeping us all current on intel and observations at Santa Bella. Darcy, let us know how things are going with the other potential targets, too, will you?"

"Sure." She nodded. "So far, they've been working preparations, pretty much doing what we've been doing."

"Have you reviewed all the employee photographs?"

"Yes, and I've reviewed background checks on Harry and Phil Jensen and the snow-crew members." She nodded. "We're good to go on that."

"Amanda and Kate, I want you two in Center Court." Maggie pointed on the map, just north of the stage, then dragged her fingertip down the steps into the oval pit where the Winter Wonderland would be set up. "This is our most vulnerable area for high-density foot traffic and high-value targets." Special Forces would be there.

"A million kids running around screaming all day. Great." Kate grumbled, clearly anticipating a long day of heightened tension and excited squeals. "Are you passing out aspirin?"

"Bring your own." Maggie looked over at Kate, who was far from the most patient person in the world, but who was also one of the most protective, though she'd be mortified to know anyone realized it. "I'm counting on you two to keep Center Court secure."

"Mark has volunteered to be there, too, Maggie." Amanda reached over and pinpointed the stage area. "Provided you authorize it, he'll be positioned here."

"Works for me. Thanks." Maggie gnawed on her lip with her teeth as she double-checked her thoughts. Nothing new emerged that she'd missed, so she grabbed her keys. It was time to return to Santa Bella. "Let's move."

Justin fell into step beside her. "I'm riding."

"Sure." It dawned on her that she'd just assumed he would. That knocked her back a step. "When is the antidote coming in?" she asked to regain her mental footing.

"The truck should be there in about ninety minutes." He snapped the parka closed across his chest.

Outside, the sky looked dreary, like a slate of steel-blue and gray. Fog was setting in, lying low to the weedy ground. Maggie unlocked the Jeep and got inside. "I want the vials in place before maintenance and the snow crews come in tonight."

Justin slid in, buckled up and turned to look at her. "Is there something about these crews that bothers you?"

"No, not at all." She backed away from Kate's Hummer, put the Jeep into drive and then headed down Wilderness Trail to the gates. "Darcy checked out the company and its employees. They're reputable."

"Then why must security be in place before they arrive?"

"The fewer people who know how we're posturing our defense, the lower the odds are it'll leak to the enemy."

"Ah, that makes sense. People can't tell what they don't know." Justin sat back and settled in his seat, at ease with her explanation. "I just don't have a war-footing mind."

Bizarre. Admitting a shortcoming without rancor or regret? If she hadn't seen it herself, she wouldn't have believed it. Bizarre and very unusual. "I'm sure you're a wonder in your lab and it's very well protected against security challenges and invasions."

"It is, but that's different."

"Not really." She blew past the second gate, then the first, and finally turned onto the dirt road. "That's your domain."

He paused a long second, then looked over at her. "I feel incompetent in this situation, Maggie," he admitted. "I know what I know, and I'm not minimizing that, but I also know that for this, what I know is not enough. I don't like feeling this way."

"Who does?" She glanced over, saw the earnest worry in his face and touched a hand to his sleeve. "No one ever feels competent or fully prepared in these situations. How could they? Anything can happen. We accept the fear and focus on doing what we can, on trusting the training, on having well-honed instincts, and on having the courage to act. That's the best we can do, Justin. That's the best anyone can do."

His stomach growled. "My instincts are saying I'm starving. It's been a long time since lunch."

"Me, too."

"Then let's eat."

Maggie checked her watch. It wasn't quite six. "We really should get back to Santa Bella."

"Let's eat there, then."

Maggie tightened her grip on the steering wheel. She wanted to have dinner with him, and she didn't, which made her fickle. What was it about him that got to her? "Can I ask you a question?"

"Sure." Twilight slid shadows across his face.

"Remember when you said people resist what they don't understand?"

"Yes."

"You were talking about the shoppers taking the antidote injections, but you were also talking about me, weren't you? Specifically, about me not trusting you." She risked a glance at him. "Or did I read too much into that remark?"

He tilted his head and tossed her a challenge. "I'll explain over a nice dinner."

Temptation curled inside her and she shifted on her seat. "I shouldn't take that much time. I need to oversee the security installations." Uneasy and confused, she dodged a pothole and cut sharply back onto the dirt road, her knuckles going white on the wheel, her gaze planted straight ahead. Justin Crowe confused her, intrigued and tempted her. He also charmed her, and admitted things other men had refused to admit, or admitted in anger and then resented her for knowing what they'd revealed. She thumbed the wedding band, twirling it on her finger and still found it damn difficult to remember why she shouldn't let herself fall for him.

"All right," he said, oblivious to her inner turmoil. "I'll pick up a sandwich for you."

"Why?" She didn't dare to look at him. He'd see that the thoughtfulness in that comment stunned her, and she didn't want him to see that deeply inside her. She didn't want him to see inside her at all. And why was he? Why was it even an issue and at risk? How had he done this to her?

"Because you've got to be running on fumes now," he said. "You're good at what you do. Actually, you're probably great at what you do. The things you thought to check and what you did about some of what you found makes my head swim."

"You did very well, too, Justin."

"I wasn't finished."

"Sorry."

"You're great, Maggie, but you're human, too. And if you don't eat, you won't be as efficient. Everyone needs you sharp and on top of your game."

She drove down the four-lane divided highway that led south to the mall. "So you're worried about me eating so I can better protect you." That she could deal with. That was a Jack-ism. She could do more, do better, for him.

"I'm worried you'll get busy and won't want to stop long enough to eat. I'm worried about you going hungry." Justin turned to look at her, his expression oddly hurt. "You've been explicit about how little you think of unfaithful men, Maggie. I know I rank somewhere around the bottom of the food chain, but…" His voice faded.

"But what?" She prodded him to finish his thought.

"Nothing. Never mind." He sighed and turned to look out the side window. "You've got reasons for feeling as you do. That you'd extend those feelings to me is just simply one of those things."

"One of what things?" She tapped her blinker, passed an SUV poking along, then moved back into her lane.

"Those things that just have to be accepted," he said sleepily, leaning back against the headrest.

"Which means?"

He didn't answer.

She looked over. He was sound asleep.

Justin hadn't denied cheating on Andrea, but he certainly didn't strike Maggie as a guy who broke promises and tossed away vows on a whim. Was that perception honest or a practiced facade? He seemed truly decent and caring and thoughtful—not prone to faking an image for the sake of convenience. Time would tell, of course, but that wouldn't help her much now.

For three years she'd been immune to men. Then along he came and it was as if he'd flipped her hormone switch. She noticed everything about him. Reacted strangely, intensely, to him. Temptation. It worried her most of all. Temptation made women do stupid things. Assign extreme importance to things that shouldn't be of consequence. Odd things. Fascinating things. Such as the way his hair curled around his ears and the way his lip lifted slightly more on the right than the left, giving him a crooked grin that was quite endearing. Honestly, she was attracted to him on far more than a physical level. *Knowing* he had cheated on his wife. *Knowing* she should be very cautious

about trusting him. *Knowing* that if he hadn't cheated, he
would have defended himself and not just said, "Never
mind." Wouldn't he?

Oh, hell. All the conflicts in her perceptions and emotional reaction to him proved conclusively that her judgment on men hadn't improved a bit in the three years since
Jack. It was still lacking. She'd been clueless then, and apparently she was clueless now.

She drove on, berating herself for the next twenty minutes, wondering why—how—this had happened. When
had she lost control of her emotions? Lost her memory of
how badly a charming man—even a thoughtful one—could
hurt a woman? And when had she lost her recall of just how
damn long it took to get over a man who impacted her like
this? Who was she kidding? It'd been three years since
she'd walked in on Jack and Karen, and Maggie wasn't
over it yet. It colored her view on all men, on Justin. Maybe
she never would be over it.

She swallowed a lump of panic. She'd tried. She'd spent
countless hours contemplating and researching why men
are unfaithful. She'd concluded that, in her case, a fourth
of the reason was that being unfaithful was Jack's basic nature, a fourth was her job, and the other half of the reason
was because with her job, she was never around and she
hadn't seen the warning signs until it was too late.

To be fair, for months after 9/11, she'd been lucky to
make it home two nights a week, and then it hadn't been
for more than four hours. And while Maggie couldn't just
tell the country she'd sworn to defend and protect that she
wouldn't help against terrorists because her husband was
lonely, she would take the blame for the part her career

caused in the breakdown and breakup of their marriage. But not all the blame.

What she had been doing had been important, damn it. Besides, he should've had more self-control and discipline. They both should have respected each other and their marriage more. It had been a hard time for him, but it'd been hard on her, too. Jack was Jack and he'd done what he'd done. And she'd learned an important lesson from that—and from her own reaction in burning the bed and his clothes. Be slow to do anything you can't undo.

And all that was wonderful, and the lessons learned were valuable, but none of it told her anything about Justin. Why had he been unfaithful?

She couldn't imagine. Now that she knew him personally—and far better than she had from just his dossier and reports—she had to wonder. Had he really stepped out on his wife because she spent too much time at her garden club?

That was the findings in the reports, and Maggie had totally accepted them before getting to know Justin. But now… Well, now they seemed inappropriate, like a shallow and fickle conclusion, and not at all like Justin.

She tapped on her blinker to make a right at the corner. Then again, disagreeing with the conclusions was a judgment call. And her judgment was conclusively flawed.

Maggie cranked up the heater a notch. Someone else's bottom line might be different, but Maggie's personal bottom line was that there was no justifiable reason for running around on your spouse.

Her curiosity about Justin burned deeper, more compelling, and finally, pulling into an open parking slot in the mall parking lot, Maggie gave in to it. She reached over and stroked his arm. "Justin."

He came fully awake.

"We're here."

He sucked in a deep breath and his stomach growled.

She grinned. "Is that invitation for dinner still open?"

He smiled. "Of course."

"You're on, then." If there was a reason for infidelity, she wanted to know it. Not for a second did she believe it might apply to Jack. But it could apply to Justin...

Maybe.

Or maybe not.

Well, that was what she wanted to know—and she intended to find out.

Shown to their table inside Emerald Bay, Justin held out Maggie's chair and seated her. When he sat, she chuckled. "Do you realize we automatically came back here?" It was an elegant little restaurant, sleek and simple and by far the quietest place in Santa Bella.

"A reprieve from noise and tension?" he suggested, unfolding his napkin and placing it on his lap.

"Maybe." Probably. They both were ready to treasure the last bit of calmness they'd see for a while.

Justin reached inside his parka pocket, pulled out a small green box and passed it to her. "Darcy said to be sure to give you this, and to watch you put it on."

"Uh-huh." Maggie took the box, pulled the little gold halo lapel pin inside it out and attached it to her jacket front.

"I think she was afraid with so much on your mind, the

pin would be forgotten." He smiled. "Is it a good-luck charm?"

"Yes, it is." Maggie lied with a straight face. The halo was a camera that would transmit visual data to Darcy, giving her a real-time video stream of all Maggie was seeing. "Thanks for the reminder." She fished her earpiece out of her fanny pack. "Time for these, too."

Justin inserted his earpiece without questioning her and then clipped the mike to his collar. "Do we run a test or something?"

"Not necessary." Darcy's voice came through loud and clear. "I've got you."

Justin looked at the halo pin on Maggie's chest. "Not to be rude, Darcy, but do you have to join us for dinner?"

She giggled. "No, actually I don't. Why don't I take half an hour and grab dinner? That'll give you two total privacy."

"Thanks, Darcy," Justin said, his face flushing. "No offense intended."

"None taken, Dr. Crowe. Enjoy, enjoy."

Recognizing that lilt in her voice—Darcy definitely considered Justin's interest in Maggie personal—Maggie could have smacked her. And she wasn't buying that total privacy bit, either. More likely, it was a white lie to appease Justin. And it'd worked; he clearly believed her.

A gentle-looking waitress who seriously needed to gain a few pounds arrived with menus. "Would you like cocktails?"

"Better not," Maggie said. "Raspberry tea, please."

Justin grunted. "Is that good? I've never tried it."

"It's my addiction," Maggie said.

"Who could resist an endorsement like that?" He nodded to the waitress. "Two, please."

Maggie felt disproportionately pleased. Justin might not trust her judgment, but he was acting on her tea endorsement. Of course, that meant nothing. The stakes weren't significant. At worse, he'd hate it and order something else to drink. Still, he had asked her opinion and risked it....

"Are you ready to order or do you need a few minutes?"

"I'm ready," Maggie said. "Crab cakes and rosemary potatoes, and a small salad with house dressing."

Justin started to say something, stopped suddenly and obviously ordered something else entirely. "Fried shrimp, fried oysters and French fries."

Maggie's stomach flipped over. "Your arteries are going to hate you."

He shrugged. "I figured..." He glanced from the waitress to Maggie. "Considering..."

He had a point. This could be their last decent meal. "Cancel my order," she told the waitress. "I want a hamburger with everything on it, and do you have seasoned fries?"

"Waffle or wedge," she said. "We have both."

"Wedge." Maggie's mouth watered.

The waitress departed and Justin smiled at Maggie. "I think I've corrupted you."

"Not at all." She denied it. Maggie loved burgers and fries every bit as much as raspberry tea, but these days, she tended to watch her carb intake.

Soon their food arrived and they ate heartily.

When they were half done, a little boy with brown hair and bright eyes ran up to the table with his arms spread wide. "Dr. J., Dr. J.!"

Already grinning, Justin put down his fork, spun away from the table and opened his arms.

A huge grin split the boy's face and he hurled himself at Justin. "I knew it was you. I knew."

Justin caught the boy in a bear hug. "Rusty!"

"Rusty?" The boy pulled back. "No, Dr. J. It's me, Simon."

Justin laughed, deep and hard. "So it is." He patted the boy on the back. "I was just teasing."

"Oh." Relief swelled and shone on the boy's face.

"Are you here alone?"

He squirmed around and settled on Justin's lap. "Nope. My mom's over there." Simon tossed a thumb backward. "We're eating out tonight 'cuz Dad's working late."

"Boy, I'll bet he's sorry he's missing this."

"Mom says he's gonna be."

Maggie covered her smile with a hand to her mouth and Justin ruffled Simon's shoulder. "I'm glad to see you, Simon."

"Who is that lady?" Simon looked shyly at Maggie.

"She's my good friend, Maggie." Justin looked at her, his eyes shining. "Maggie, this is my good friend, Simon. He's in the first grade now and rides the big school bus."

"Wow," she said, suitably impressed.

"The little kids ride in the van. Dr. J. watched me at the bus stop until the bus came. Not now. When I was little."

"His parents had to leave early for work one day," Justin explained.

"Ah, I see." Maggie offered him her hand. "I'm very pleased to meet you, Simon."

"Thank you." He glanced back to his mother's table,

then held up a just-a-second finger. Simon told Justin all about first grade, about his teacher, Mrs. Sandlin, about the class bully, Jason Cray, and about soccer practice.

Maggie sat back and watched the interaction between them, feeling a mix of surprise and envy and maybe just a little admiration for Justin for taking such an interest in a neighbor's child.

Something niggled at her. At first it twitched, soft and subtle, a gentle nudging, and then it grew more intense until she became consciously aware and couldn't ignore it.

The niggle took form. A memory of Barone interacting with the little boy who'd chased the ball into the security office and bumped into Barone's leg. He'd ducked to get away, out of Barone's reach.

An amazingly different reaction than Simon's to Justin. Though, to be fair, Simon knew Justin and the child with Barone had been a stranger. Yet Maggie couldn't honestly say that if the boy had known Barone, his reaction to the man would have been any different.

That explained the niggle, but there was something more. Something in this that she was missing. Something significant…

The recoil.

She pegged it. The child had actually recoiled from Barone's touch. Why?

At most he should have been wary of a stranger and backed off, but he hadn't. He'd recoiled, and that was an entirely different innate reaction. That one, according to Dr. Morgan Cabot, an expert on body language, was important to note.

In Maggie's study under Morgan, recoil signified hatred, disgust or fear. The child hadn't known Barone, so hatred and disgust were out. That left fear. What had triggered such a strong reaction in the boy? It didn't make sense.

Oh, hell, Maggie. What's the big deal?

Maybe nothing. But she couldn't discount his reaction because it may be something. Kids were notoriously great judges of character. If she'd remembered that, she could have saved herself some serious misery with Jack. In her old neighborhood, Chris and Jay Simms' kids, Candace and Craig, sure hadn't trusted Jack. Kids seemed to have this built-in radar that cuts right through bull and anything fake. In no time flat, they see the truth. Facts were facts and research backed them up. Kids are seldom wrong. So what did it mean? Was Barone a body double or just a lousy man?

"I gotta go now, Dr. J." Simon crawled down from Justin's lap.

"See ya." Justin waved.

"See ya." Simon returned to his mother.

"He's a nice boy."

"He is," Justin said, his eyes shining. "His grandfather was murdered. Simon was with him when it happened. For a while, he had trouble being alone. That's why I waited with him for the bus. He thought I could protect him from anything."

"His knight in shining armor."

Justin looked at Maggie and raw pain burned in his eyes. "Sometimes the world makes me sick, Maggie."

"Me, too." A knot lodged in her throat. "But then something happens to make me glad I'm in it. Something like Simon being so happy to see you and jumping into your arms."

The pain dulled and softened, and Justin nodded. "Yeah."

They finished their meal, paid the check and then stepped out into the mall.

Maggie examined her communications equipment, including the walkie-talkie hooked to her belt. Everything was functioning properly. "Well, we had dinner, but I still haven't heard what you have to say about cheating."

"No, you haven't." He didn't sound upset or eager. "We got a little sidetracked."

They had, but Maggie still wanted to know and gave him a friendly shove. "I was hoping for some insight into that, Justin."

He stopped walking, faced her and clasped her hand in both of his. "I'm encouraged."

"By what?"

"You're at least giving me a temporary reprieve from being considered scum."

She grunted. "Reprieves mean nothing." Not with her flawed judgment.

His expression sobered. "Maybe not to you, but this one means a great deal to me."

Her breathing shallowed and her chest went tight. "Why?"

"You know why, Maggie." He dragged his lower lip with his teeth. "You knew why the first time I looked at you. How could you not know?"

Maggie had no idea what to say.

"I knew it. I knew it, Maggie. Oh, God, I'm good." Darcy's voice chimed in her ear. "He's crazy about you."

Maggie watched for Justin's reaction, mortified that he'd heard Darcy, but apparently she had transmitted to

Maggie privately. Which meant Maggie might just let the woman live.

He dragged a gentle fingertip down her cheek. "Maggie, do us both a favor, okay?"

"What favor?" Her voice sounded a little shaky. She resisted the urge to clear her throat and settled for a swallow.

"Don't judge me by other people's actions or opinions," he whispered, his eyes earnest and clear, his voice sincere and genuine. "Just get to know me—give me that much of a chance—and develop your own opinion."

"Sound advice, Maggie," Darcy said. "I'd listen to him on that one."

"Here, here." Kate chimed in unexpectedly, obviously also monitoring the private channel.

"Totally reasonable." Amanda added her two cents. "I'd go for it, Maggie."

Maggie wanted to scream. So far the only one who *hadn't* weighed in was Colonel Drake.

Before Maggie could collect herself enough to respond, Darcy's voice came through, this time, on the general frequency.

"Unauthorized entry. Level One, Door Three. Repeat. Unauthorized entry. Level One, Door Three."

Maggie turned and ran.

Chapter 6

Darcy continued transmitting on the general frequency. "Adult male. Forty-five, 5'11", 185 pounds. Brown hair and full beard. Black leather jacket, jeans and white sneakers. Suspect entered the mall carrying a handled Krane's shopping bag. He's now ditched the bag. Repeat. He's now ditched the bag."

"Where, Darcy?" Maggie asked, cutting through groups of shoppers to get to the site, feeling as worried as Justin looked. "Amanda, Kate, Mark, hold your positions." Maggie snapped the release on the walkie-talkie attached to her belt. It was dedicated to communicating with Will. No one else was on that frequency. "Will, rally the troops. Level One, Door Three. Unauthorized entry. Suspect ditched a handled Krane's shopping bag. We need to recover it and tag him. Do not, repeat, do not, touch the bag. Just secure the area surrounding it."

"On it, Maggie," Will said, then relayed the transmission to his team.

Justin caught up, fell into step at Maggie's side.

"Suspect has moved off the screen," Darcy said. "Be advised that Base has lost visual contact and is faxing still photo to Security office, FBI, Providence police and Okaloosa County Sheriff's office now…"

"Go right," Justin told Maggie, then headed left.

"Follow the bag. Will's scrambled a team," she said to Justin, then went back to Darcy. "We're going to need HAZMAT in here to recover the bag. Where is it now?"

"Northwest side of the round, directly across from So Secret."

Maggie relayed that to Will, then sidestepped a bunch of teen girls strolling.

Within two minutes Will Stanton radioed back. "I've got the bag, Maggie. It's empty."

"Don't touch it," Maggie reminded him, and picked up her pace. "It could be contaminated."

"Roger on that."

Finally, Maggie and Justin worked their way through the crowds and met up with Will. Half his security force was gathered, forming a human barricade around the bag. Shoppers slowed down, craned their necks to see what was going on. Maggie grimaced. If Barone saw this, he'd have a cow.

Justin pulled a check on the bag. "No scent, film or residue," he told Maggie. "Disband your men, Will, before Barone notices. I'll monitor it until HAZMAT arrives."

"Yes, sir." He issued the order.

Maggie stepped closer, ran her own visual and found surprisingly little.

"There's no apparent evidence," Justin said, still squatting near the bag. "But we'd better treat it as contaminated."

"Definitely," Maggie agreed.

"Base concurs," Darcy said. "HAZMAT team is inbound, Dr. Crowe. ETA, two minutes."

With an estimated time of arrival at two minutes, the hazardous materials team had to have been prepositioned on the premises outside. Darcy and Colonel Drake had picked up on Maggie's nonorder and arranged it so she wouldn't have to seek Barone's permission. *Bless 'em.*

Maggie finished her check of the bag and reached the same conclusion as Justin. Judy Meyer, a woman on Will's staff, quietly steered shoppers around the bag, unobtrusively giving it a lot of space.

The HAZMAT team of five men arrived, wearing street clothes and clear gloves rather than protective gear. They worked quickly and efficiently. Following cautionary procedure, they enclosed the shopping bag in a transportation safe hatch to remove it from the mall.

One of the team members peeled off from the group and walked over to Maggie and Justin. "Captain Holt?"

She nodded.

"I'm Matt Elden," he said. Sweat beaded at his brow and tension lined his pudgy face. "There isn't a field test available for DR-27."

"I'm aware of that, Dr. Elden." Maggie spoke softly. "So what's your plan?" They could have a mobile lab, but they really needed the full spectrum of lab equipment to get definitive answers quickly. Regardless, this was his decision and he had full authority on it.

"We alerted the lab at Providence Air Force Base. They'll work it, and get the results to you as soon as possible."

Colonel Gray's domain. Damn. Colonel Drake wasn't going to like that. "I appreciate it."

"Yes, ma'am." Elden walked out the same way his team had departed.

As he cleared the exit, Darcy again sounded an alarm. "Unauthorized entry. Level One, Door Four. Repeat. Unauthorized entry. Level One, Door Four."

Maggie relayed the information to Will, then responded to Darcy. "Same guy?"

"No, Maggie. Suspect is female. Mid-thirties, 5'4", 140 pounds. Very bad and obvious red wig, black slacks, aqua top. She entered the facility carrying a handled Krane's shopping bag and has just entered the arcade..." Darcy paused, then went on, her words rushed and urgent. "Suspect ditched the bag inside the arcade."

Which was full of kids.

Running in that direction, Maggie told Will, "Secure the bag and keep a visual on the woman. Do not intercept."

"Was that an order *not* to intercept her?" he asked. "Please verify, Maggie."

"That's correct. I want her followed." It was a long shot but the woman could lead them to Kunz's base of operations.

"Suspect is heading east," Darcy said. "She's passing the knife shop, heading toward Door Five."

Maggie rounded the corner and saw the sign for the knife shop up ahead, but she didn't see any sign of a woman in an aqua top or one wearing a red wig. "Darcy, is your external tag in place?"

"Ready and waiting for her to step outside, Maggie."

"The bag is secure," Justin said. "Same as the last one, Maggie. No scent, film or residue. Not even a crinkle. It looks unused."

"Recall HAZMAT," Maggie ordered.

Short minutes later Justin's voice rang out. "HAZ-MAT is back on-site," he informed them. "Elden's safe-hatching the bag now. Estimated time of departure, two minutes."

"Suspect is in the north parking garage," Darcy's voice sounded through Maggie's earpiece. "She's just entered a white, 2004 Honda Civic. Rental Tag," she added, then reeled off the number.

Maggie spoke into the walkie-talkie. "Will, who's handling that tag on the suspect in the parking garage?"

"Local police."

"Do you have a visual?"

"Stand by, Maggie." A pause, then Will added, "I have a visual now, yes."

"Can you verify the identity of the officer?"

"I can, Maggie. Worked with him many times."

"Okay, thanks." She had to check. Kunz was too good at making substitutions, though never this soon into a mission, to not check. She headed back toward Center Court.

Justin caught up to her. "HAZMAT's departed with the second bag."

"Good."

"Did they get her?"

Maggie nodded. "Local police are following her now."

"Aren't you going to pick her up and interrogate her?"

"No, S.A.S.S. doesn't handle overt aspects on missions."

"Ah, the unit secrecy thing."

Maggie nodded, amused at watching him assimilate and put the pieces together and into place.

"Do you think maybe she'll go back to their operations base, and we can stop this thing before it really starts?" He brushed a strand of hair back from Maggie's face. "Wouldn't that be great?"

Surprised by his touch, she stilled, her throat thick. Something hitched in her chest, left her a little breathless, which was ridiculous. It was an innocent touch. No more than that. "We can hope, but—"

"You doubt it."

"Let's just say that would be extremely atypical for Thomas Kunz. He never makes anything simple."

"The man likes complexity, eh?"

"Historically, yes," Maggie said. "His operations are always complex and multilayered—and dangerous and destructive."

"Unfortunate." Justin looked deeply into her eyes and his voice went soft. "And you have to deal with him all the time."

"We all do. Sometimes the world sucks," she said, repeating what he'd said about Simon witnessing his grandfather's murder.

"Yeah, but then something good happens." He looked her directly in the eye.

"Yeah."

"Maggie," Darcy interrupted. "Security just sent us an update on the first bagger."

"Go ahead," Maggie said, reluctantly shifting her attention.

"They've got his photo circulating and locals have issued an APB on him, but my guess is he's long gone."

"Figures. Keep me posted."

* * *

Thirty minutes later at Providence, the lab called Maggie and reported its findings.

"That's right, Captain Holt. Nothing. Not even finger or palm prints on the handle grips. As best we can tell, totally unused."

"Both bags?" Disappointment arrowed through her, but no surprise. Clear gloves. That was the only explanation.

"Yes, ma'am."

"Thanks." Maggie closed her flip-phone, stuffed it back into her purse, and walked down to Center Court. The stores would be closing soon, and the Winter Wonderland crew would be coming in.

The reprieve from the shoppers and false alarms would be welcome. They'd had twenty-seven tonight alone. The day's tally was over seventy, which was making Will and his staff totally nuts. Maggie had warned him that false alarms could anesthetize his staff. They needed to guard against it, remain diligent and not relax. She hoped they took what she said to heart.

All of the surveillance cameras were now in place and operational. The trash receptacles had been removed and put in storage. The rounds had been netted and the aromatherapy had been nixed. *So far, so good*.

But it was still early.

Darcy radioed Maggie on a private frequency. "More chatter from multiple sources has been feeding through Intel into the Threat Integration Center. Nothing any more specific than what we have, but new sources reporting the same thing on the same potential targets."

Kunz was definitely going to hit someone. Somewhere.

"Thanks." Maggie rubbed at her neck, let her gaze drift down the steps into the pit.

"Maggie?" Darcy asked.

"Go ahead."

"Providence police are reporting that the female shopper, Suspect Number Two, is about to cross the state line into Georgia. Do you want our guys to ask the state police in Georgia to intercept her?"

"Thank them for the offer, but we need the FBI on her, in case she's involved in an attack. Felony charges. Have them pick up the tag, and see where she goes."

"Truthfully, I doubt she's going anywhere of interest," Kate said.

"So do I, Kate," Maggie said. "But I don't know it. Until I know it, we've got no choice but to follow her."

"She's made a U-turn, Maggie." Darcy relayed from the police. "She's heading back south."

"Did she cross the line into Georgia?"

"No, she didn't."

That limited their options. "Does she know she's being tailed?"

A moment lapsed while Darcy relayed the question, then she answered. "No evidence of it. They've switched off teams three times."

"Let's stick with observation, then," Maggie decided, hoping she wasn't making a colossal mistake. There had to be a reason for these abandoned bags. Kunz never did anything without a reason.

"Damn it," Darcy said. "Unauthorized entry. Level One, Door One. Male. Twenty-five, 5'10", 165 pounds. Blond ponytail, navy sweater, gray slacks. Suspect entered the fa-

cility with—you guessed it—a handled Krane's shopping
bag and ditched it immediately near the Tot Shop. Repeat.
Unauthorized entry. Level One, Door One…"

Maggie took off in a full run toward the main entrance,
wishing already she had those Rollerblades.

There were no further incidents before the mall closed
to shoppers for the night.

Justin oversaw the prepositioning of the boxes of antidote vials at strategic locations on all three levels of the
mall, and ordered the undercover medical personnel manning them to never leave their stations unguarded.

Will Stanton had all his security forces assembled in the
administrator's auditorium, briefing them on things to
watch for, to guard against and procedures to follow in case
various abnormalities occurred.

Daniel Barone walked the premises with Maggie. Now
that the mall was empty of shoppers, their footsteps echoed on the tile. She gave him an update on everything
done, or about to be done, in the way of extra personnel,
cameras and observation stations.

"What about the woman?" he asked.

"What woman?" Maggie hadn't briefed him on the
shopper who'd been tracked to just this side of the state
line, back to the mall, then to a hotel three blocks away.

"The female shopper with the Krane's bag?"

Will Stanton? Had he told Barone? "Dead end," she
said, more from instinct than because she had reason to
withhold specifics. Though it broke her rule to ask a question she couldn't already answer, she had to do it. "How
did you know about her?"

"I know everything that goes on in my facility, Captain."

"Mr. Barone, I don't wish to be rude, but I don't have the time or patience for glib responses. How did you know about the shopper?"

"A security staff member told me, which you should have done yourself, Captain."

"Had it been significant, I would have," she countered.

"I'll judge what is significant."

"Uh, no. No, you won't. Because if I briefed you on all I know that's insignificant, it'll take roughly three weeks of daily, sixteen-hour briefings." She looked him over, wordlessly saying he wasn't up to the work. "Which member of Will's staff informed you of the shopper?"

He paused, then grunted. "Unfortunately, I don't recall." He shrugged. "I've spoken to a number of people who've mentioned it and I'm no longer certain who first spoke of it."

"Understandable," she said, knowing he was lying through his teeth to protect his source. "Once the first male bagger disappeared off the monitor, he wasn't seen again."

"And the third male?"

"Under surveillance by authorities outside the facility."

"Maggie?" Justin's voice came in through her earpiece. "When you have a second, I need you up on Level Three."

"On my way." She smiled at Barone. "Sorry, you'll have to excuse me. Duty calls."

He nodded and silently walked back toward his office in the administration wing.

That silence bothered her. It didn't seem to fit Barone's need to micromanage every detail. If running true to form, wouldn't he be scouting the facility, offering reassurance, soothing jittery nerves, insinuating himself?

He would.

Maggie made a decision. "Darcy, put someone on Barone. Dr. Cabot's watch signs are evident."

"Should I pull Kate or—"

"No. No, low visibility." Maggie remembered a woman on Will's staff that appeared about as threatening as a marshmallow. "Judy Meyer," Maggie said. Barone would ignore her.

"I'll notify Will."

"Don't be specific. Just say I need to borrow her for a bit."

"Right."

Maggie took the escalator, headed up to Level Three. Between the second and third floors, she followed an internal nudge, unclipped her walkie-talkie and paged Will.

"Yes, ma'am."

"Will, did you mention the female shopper we tagged to Barone?"

"No, ma'am. But he caught a member of my staff, and he told him."

Unfortunate. Why, Maggie wasn't yet sure. But her instincts had warned her several times to be wary of Barone, and they were honed. Confident the truth would reveal itself eventually, she paid attention. "So Barone knows we're watching her?"

"No, ma'am," Will said. "Actually, he doesn't. I didn't share that information with my staff."

Good. Good. "I'd rather you not." Would Will agree without her giving him specific reasons?

He hesitated a second, then came back. "Let's keep it simple, Maggie. Barone's a hell of a manager. No one denies it. But if we let him, he'll drive us crazy on every detail. I vote we don't. His intentions might be good, but his tactics could sidetrack us. We can't afford to get bogged down. We could miss something important. With that in mind, I'm making a little policy adjustment. If you want something passed on, you say so. Otherwise, what I'm told is for my ears only."

Strong instincts. "Reasonable policy, Will." She had to admit that his positive comments about Barone's skills as a manager helped to ease her mind about the man, yet her wariness on possibly dealing with a double persisted. Will Stanton had proven he had a keen sense about people, and he clearly had the ability to cull the unessential so it didn't cloud the necessary. She was lucky to have him on her team.

"Maggie," he said, again stilted and hesitant. "People entering the mall with these empty bags are really bothering me. I've run Security at Santa Bella for over five years, and I can't say I've never seen people come into the mall with empty bags, but seeing three back-to-back and abandoned in one day like we saw today…"

"With the holidays, the stores are busier than usual." She looked down over the escalator rail. Nothing snagged her attention.

"True." He conceded, but let out a frustrated sigh that crackled static through the walkie-talkie. "Still, it just doesn't sit right."

"I know what you mean." She had the same feeling. A little whisper, as persistent as an itch, nagged at her. But she couldn't yet make out the words. Diversionary tactics? Signals? Warnings? Target area alerts?

"I'm not sure if the terrorists are testing us to see what we pick up, or just distracting us."

"Could be either or neither, Will. We just have to follow through and narrow the possibilities with what happens. We can't risk letting anything pass, and we're not distracted. That's the good news." They were hyperalert and intensely aware. It was the best they could do.

"Right," he agreed. "Every staff member on duty knows that one screw-up and this could be our last night alive—and a lot of others could die with us," he said.

Heaviness settled on Maggie's shoulders, spreading through her chest. "Make sure they keep remembering that, Will. If they attack Santa Bella, they will be seeking high casualties. Factoring that in, everything we do is our best defense weapon."

"You got it."

On Level Three, Maggie stepped off the escalator. Justin stood halfway down the thoroughfare near a round.

"No net," he said as she approached. "All the rounds have been netted, except this one."

She brought up Will on the walkie-talkie and disclosed the problem.

"That's not possible. I checked them all myself not more than an hour ago. That round was netted, Maggie."

This wasn't good news. "Well, it's not netted now."

"Do you want me to send someone from Maintenance up to take care of it?"

"No." Maggie absorbed Justin's surprised look and held his gaze. "Send a security staff member instead. One you can spare awhile to stand watch."

"I'm on it."

"Maggie, what are you doing?" Justin asked.

She stepped close, looked up at him. "Trust me. I want

to see why the net was removed, and hopefully who re-moved it."

"I see now," he said in a quiet voice.

She turned away. Considering it was her job and not per-sonal, he should have known she'd have a valid reason for her actions.

"It's hard to give what you don't receive, Maggie."

Touché. She looked back at him over her shoulder. "If trusting was easy, it'd have no value."

A thin man about thirty with teen-acne scars pitting his face joined them. "Captain, I'm Donald Freeman. Chief Stanton said I should report to you for further instructions."

"The netting has been removed from this flower round by parties unknown, Donald. We need to know who did it, and why." Maggie looked around for a good observation post. "See that alcove?"

"Between Grimes and Stokes?"

"Yes." She read the signs on the store windows. "I want you to post watch from there and if anyone comes to this round, or appears to be putting something in it, report it to me immediately."

"Yes, ma'am."

"Donald, I mean anyone," she reiterated. When he sent her a blank look, she added, "That includes your cowork-ers, your boss, and even Mr. Barone. Are you clear?"

"Absolutely clear." Stern-faced, he lumbered over to the alcove.

"This round being tampered with worries me." Justin looked at Maggie. "The implication is unnerving."

It was. "Darcy?" she said.

"Yeah, Maggie?"

"Call in Colonel Drake."

Moments later Darcy said, "She's here with me now."

"Colonel, this internal tampering has me leaning toward Kunz having GRID members or some mall or store employee on his payroll." That missing net was an indicator too significant to ignore.

"I agree, Maggie."

"What's the latest intel on the other potential targets?"

"Mandatory status reports only, Maggie. No unusual activity recorded at any of the other facilities."

A cold chill swept through her. It appeared Kunz had selected his target.

Santa Bella.

Maggie coordinated with the owners, checked the facility inside and out, made sure the cameras were working and the scent-emitters were not. Darcy assisted her, matching names to key personnel still in the facility, making preparations for the big sales day tomorrow.

At 2:00 a.m., Justin radioed her from Level One. "Maggie?"

"Yes?" She was tired, but not exhausted. Adrenaline had kicked in on the concern about Barone and Kunz having an insider working here. It was still pumping through her veins at warp speed.

"Can you meet me on Level One at Center Court?"

"Sure." Up on Level Three, she judged the distance between the stairs, elevator and escalator for the quickest way down. The stairs won.

On Level One, Justin was sitting at a table under the overhang, near the counter where people ordered food. He hadn't yet seen her and she had the rare privilege of observing him unguarded. His head back, his chin up, he stretched, rustling his parka. A slow burn heated low in her belly. Very attractive man.

He caught sight of her and for a swift second delight shone in his eyes, then his protective shields slid back into place.

Phil, Harry and the snow crew were building the snow base inside the pit. The echoes of hammering and voices carried over to her. "What's up?"

"I thought you could use a cup of coffee." He stood, waited until she was seated, then sat back down. "With cream."

"You constantly surprise me, Justin." Across the pit, Amanda stood watching the crew. Mark was to her right, Kate to her left. All four sides of Center Court were covered. In Maggie's opinion, this area ranked the most vulnerable to attack in the entire facility. And Darcy considered the snow crew high-risk because time had precluded her from investigating and verifying anything beyond the topical in their background checks. "I can't believe you remembered how I like my coffee."

"It's a curse," Justin said, trying to sound serious. His smile betrayed him.

She curled her fingers around her cup. "It's charming."

Justin looked pleased, but shifted the subject. "This entire experience has been illuminating in so many ways. You're very good at your job, Maggie. You probably already know that, but it's something that should be said now and then, so you don't forget it."

"Thank you." She blew at the steaming cup and took a sip. The warmth felt great on her throat. A little curl of pleasure unfurled in her stomach. Justin might not trust her, but he still thought well of her, thought she was making a difference, and what she was doing mattered. That, and the way he was looking at her, made her feel special.

In the past three years she'd felt many things—sad reigning overall—but she hadn't once felt special. It felt... good.

She twisted the wedding band on her finger, doing her damnedest to remember all the reasons feeling special was a bad thing. But, boy, it was hard remembering that the goodness wouldn't last.

"What kind of special training did you have to have for your kind of work?"

She looked at him across the table, pain shooting through the arch of her foot. Rubbing at it, she silently swore she'd put in at least twenty miles today, walking the facility. "Oh, lots and lots of different kinds."

"Sorry." He dropped his gaze. "I shouldn't have asked that. Classified information isn't a novel concept to me."

"It's okay." The difference in his and Jack's attitudes toward her was stark. She shouldn't compare the men, or even their reactions or attitudes, but how could she not? She was human. One supposedly had loved her. The other, well, who knew if it was or ever could be love? It could be lust with a kick. But he considered her special. And both men had strayed from women to whom they were committed. Naturally, Maggie had to compare them. "No harm done."

But it was definitely time to shift away from anything personal. She was reacting to him as a woman, and there just wasn't a place for that pleasant distraction during this mission. "So, are you all set?"

"Yes, we are. Everything is in place, according to the plan."

Stubble shadowed his chin and dark circles smudged the skin under his eyes. "You look so tired. You should try to get a few hours' sleep before the mall opens."

"I know. I look like hell, while you—" he paused and let his gaze drift over her face "—look as fresh as you did when I first saw you this morning."

She wasn't, but she was used to going for long stretches of time without sleep. In her training, she routinely was forced to stay sharp for a week on ten-minute power naps. "It's the training," she confessed.

He laced his hands atop the table, studied his knuckles. "I don't want to sleep, Maggie." He lifted his gaze.

It locked with hers and she saw the truth in his eyes. If this should be his last night, he didn't want to waste it sleeping. Maggie understood completely. There'd be nothing but rest if they failed. Eternal rest. "What do you want to do?"

Slowly, he blinked, shuttering his eyes, and his expression sobered. "When we have some privacy, ask me that question again."

Her stomach fluttered and her voice went thick. "I think I should take offense to that."

"Fool." That came from Darcy.

"Huge fool," Amanda chimed in.

"Assumptive fool," Kate said. "Make him get specific."

Heat swam up Maggie's neck to her face and she flushed more with each of their comments. Fortunately they remembered to listen on the general frequency but to respond on a private one. Justin couldn't hear them. Thank heaven for that or Maggie would have been mortified—and doing bodily injury. It was bad enough that she couldn't tell them to butt out without revealing to Justin they were there and listening.

He dragged a thumb around the rim of his cup. "I didn't mean to offend you, Maggie, and I didn't mean sex."

"Oh, shoot." Darcy sighed her disappointment.

"Damn." Amanda sounded exasperated.

"Well, why not?" Kate complained. "He's not blind. We've seen the way he looks at you. He's definitely attracted, so what's up? Why not sex? Ask him, Maggie. I mean it. Ask him, or I will."

Leave it to Kate. The woman lived to push Maggie's buttons. She wanted to spit nails. Or laugh. If she'd been on the team and this was happening to anyone else, Maggie would be in stitches. Instead she was just shy of outraged. "Then what did you mean?"

He reached across the table and cupped her face in his hand. "Later," he said, standing and grabbing his coffee. "We'll revisit the subject when the entire S.A.S.S. team isn't listening in."

"Oh, my God. You heard them?" Maggie wanted to die. To slide through the floor and just die.

Kate howled.

Amanda and Darcy laughed so hard Maggie swore they were going to be too hoarse to talk.

Maggie could have shot the whole damn bunch of them with a clean conscience. "Go ahead. Have a great time, guys. But remember, I'm armed, I'm tense, and I know where you all live."

"No, Maggie." Justin clasped her hand. "I didn't hear anything. I just can't imagine them not listening."

Relief washed through her. "Well, you're right. They're listening, sticking in their noses, and making smart-ass comments."

"In my favor, I hope."

Maggie wiggled her brows at him, but didn't answer.

Chapter 7

"It's beautiful."

"It is." Maggie agreed with Amanda's opinion. The winter wonderland, complete with snow-draped trees and bushes and five-foot statues of fur-wrapped reindeer and a sleigh, set a magical scene that older shoppers could dream by and younger ones could create lifelong memories. Huge banners had been hung high around the perimeter of the pit that read Happy Holidays, North Pole, Frosty's Playground and Winter Wonderland. The snow crew had gone, except for the co-owners, Harry and Phil Jensen, who would be in the mall through closing at 9:00 p.m., monitoring the scene and eliminating any minor challenges that happened to come up. At closing, the crew would return to break down the scene and return the pit to its normal condition.

Maggie double-checked her watch. "Heads up, people. In exactly four minutes, the kids will be pouring in."

Then, the real danger began.

Amanda stood at Maggie's side, her arms folded over her chest. "He's going to do it, Maggie." She didn't look at Maggie, and her voice stayed soft, but that only exaggerated the forceful impact of her message.

Thomas Kunz would do it. He'd kill thousands and maim thousands more, all for the sake of his black market sales and his damn capabilities demonstration.

"I know."

And she prayed she'd be smart enough to stop him.

She'd spent the past few hours running a personal check on the A-stores and then the B-stores with Will Stanton. All employees were in yellow. All aerosol cans were absent from the shelves, including from DMV Drugs, though due to medical necessity, they remained under the pharmacist's control rather than sealed and stored like the others.

Maggie had done everything she'd known to do to prepare. She'd issued and seen her every order carried out, solicited advice from Justin—and been slightly dazed by his acumen and insights—and Will and the other S.A.S.S. operatives, and followed their recommendations. Now, D-day had arrived, and in less than a minute the mall would officially open for Christmas Eve traffic.

"Hey, Maggie. Do you have a minute?" Justin's asked.

He sounded calm, but his stomach had to be as knotted up as hers.

There were no typical premission shenanigans to

counter high stress levels, and she wished for just one but didn't dare to indulge. She squeezed her eyes shut and shook off thinking about stress. It just added more. "What's up?"

"I want to show you something up on Level Two."

No teasing in his tone, and his words sounded clipped; the calm was forced. "Priority code?" She had designated codes on a scale of one to five. One was imminent danger. Five was an FYI footnote.

"Code Two, Maggie."

A chill raced up her backbone. "I'm on my way."

"Southeast end," he said. "Directly above Wee Beaux."

That store overlooked Center Court and was open up through Level Two. "Thirty seconds out," she added, giving him her estimated time of arrival.

She took the stairs two at a time. Just as she hit the Level Two landing, the bell rang, signaling the official opening of the shopping mall for business.

Maggie walked from the stair landing over a span of bridge to the thoroughfare that circled the Center Court opening below. A glass-wall banister rimmed the perimeter. In the center opening, about four feet above the Level Two floor, a dome ceiling had been installed that was viewable from below.

The upper side of the dome also created a "short-stack" level: a squat floor between Levels Two and Three. The short-stack had a dual purpose. It provided a wall-to-wall floor for Level Three and a storage facility for the stores inside the short-stack, which was closed to the public.

During the night, Justin told her that he had squatted and ducked his way through every inch of the short-stack, looking for bio-hazards as well as helping to install additional surveillance equipment that gave Darcy a bird's-eye view of Center Court and access into the administration wing downstairs.

Daniel Barone would have strenuously objected, of course, since monitoring the entrance to his offices was involved. Linda Diel was proving valuable, but Maggie was definitely uneasy about Barone. She didn't ask or inform him about the installation specifics. The choice had been a simple one. She either told him, protecting his sensibilities and forfeiting her gains on observing Center Court, or not. She'd chosen not.

Justin met Maggie just off the bridge. "You okay? You look harried."

"Belly knots," she admitted far too easily, and pressed a hand to her stomach.

"Ah," he said. "Kate called it premission jitters."

"She's tougher."

"I don't know about that." He led Maggie to the glass-wall banister. "Look up. Tell me what you see."

She cranked back her neck and checked out the inside of the dome. "Light fixtures, sprinkler heads, beams, decorative trim...."

"Look right there."

She followed his fingertip to three beams left of center. "It looks like a little window." The glass appeared tinted to match the wall surrounding it. She tracked the small window's opening, imagining a trajectory beam down to the floor. It hit dead center in the pit.

The butterflies in her stomach turned to fire-breathing, acid-pumping dragons. "What in hell is that?" She spared

Justin a glance. "There are no windows in the short-stack, Justin."

"I thought I might have missed one," he said. "But I went back and double-checked."

"And?" Maggie looked from the window to him.

"You're right. There are no windows in the short-stack."

Maggie unclipped her walkie-talkie, her blood thrumming, her pulse thumping in her temples. "Will, I need you on Level Two."

"Give me five, Maggie," he radioed back. "I'm down on One, pulling a spot check on the auto center."

"Now, Will." She was reluctant to attach a priority code to this without knowing what she was looking at, but she needed the window identified now and the mystery settled.

"On my way."

"Darcy?" Maggie stepped back from the banister, rubbed at a tight muscle at the base of her neck.

"Yeah, Maggie?"

"From the plans, what am I seeing here?" The number of shoppers coming to Level Two wasn't quickly multiplying. Maggie was glad about that. A family of four walked past. They were all wearing reindeer antler headbands.

"I've triple-checked the plans, Maggie, and there's not a damn thing reflected on them. I have no idea."

Staring up at the little window, Justin frowned. "If it's not on the plans, then it had to be added after the facility was built. The question is when."

"Yeah." Maggie looked over, her worry evident in her expression and her voice. "When? Why? And most importantly, by whom?"

* * *

"No. It's new."

Will Stanton looked down from the domed ceiling at Maggie. "Definitely new."

"How new?" she asked. "Do you have any way to date it?"

"What I know and what I can prove are two different things." He thought a second. "We had a display of quilts from around the world here a month ago," he finally said, pulling his walkie-talkie up to his mouth. "Linda, do you read me?"

A short pause and then Barone's assistant, Linda Diel responded. "I sure do, Will. What can I do for you?"

"Will you pull the photos on the quilt displays from the tour? Marty, you pick them up from Linda and bring them up to me."

"Two minutes," Linda said. "Q.T.?"

Keep it quiet. Obviously, quiet from Barone. Maggie didn't look over or comment, but eagerly awaited his response. Will wasn't one to talk bad about anyone but he had good instincts, and Maggie was curious to see if his instincts, too, had been alerted on Barone.

"Q.T."

A little thread of vindication wound through Maggie. Will, too, had doubts about Barone that extended beyond his being a micromanager trying to cover his ass at the expense of exposing anyone else's. Had something specific triggered doubts in Will? Or had he just suddenly realized that several little, inconsequential things had accumulated and combined into general doubts that were just there?

Minutes later Marty came up the stairs and handed the photos to Will, then rushed back down to finish a spot check he'd been doing at Krane's department store.

Will shuffled through the pictures until he came to one of special interest to him. "Here we go. See?" He passed the photo to Maggie. "No window."

"Okay, so you can prove it wasn't there a month ago. When do you think it was installed?"

The look in his eyes turned sober. "Within the last forty-eight hours."

Surprise rippled over the radio.

"I find that difficult to believe," Kate said. "Hell, we've been all over this place. We would have noticed someone installing a freaking window."

"We haven't been on-site for forty-eight hours," Justin countered.

True, but the tight timing bothered Maggie, too. "Why forty-eight hours, Will?"

"I pulled a facility check and documented my findings," he said. "I didn't find a window there, then."

"Did you submit that report to anyone?"

"No, I held it," he said. "Normally, I'd submit it by e-mail to Mr. Barone or give Linda a hard copy, but this time, I didn't."

His tone warned Maggie he didn't want to openly state why. She gave him that one, though it created a challenge for her. "So we can't prove the report was done when you say it was done."

"The computer records when I created the report, but that's it." Will gave her a little shrug. "I do a lot of those type reports to back up my memory. I can't very well vouch for what I did or didn't know without a record. But I usually only forward the reports to Mr. Barone or Linda if something odd that they need to know turns up during the inspection."

"That's conclusive enough for me," Maggie said. "Forty-eight hours." She mentally measured the distance from the banister to the window, then headed up to Level Three to reexamine the short-stack.

Justin followed her.

Maggie stopped at the door, leading into the short-stack. A keypad lock secured it. "Darcy, I need the code."

She relayed it. "Two, three, one, seven, nine, eight."

Maggie keyed in the series of numbers. A faint tone beeped, signaling the acceptance of each number—until the last one.

"The final eight didn't hold, Darcy." Maggie's nerves stretched taut. "No beep."

"Are you sure you got it right—231798?"

"That was it, yes."

"Try it again."

Maggie did. It still didn't go through. "Hung up again on the final eight."

"Darcy can't be wrong, Maggie." Justin stepped to Maggie's side. "She has perfect recall."

Maggie glared over at him, irritated and more than a little worried. "Yes, I know."

"So what happened? Did you push the wrong number?"

"No, Justin," Maggie said slowly. "It means someone's changed the code." She held up a fingertip, warning him to back off. "Darcy, run the sequence to verify—"

"I'm on it," she said before Maggie could finish issuing the order. "Computer program says it's accurate and it is the same numerical sequence that successfully opened the short-stack for you, Justin and Will Stanton."

"Any odds that Will changed it?" Justin asked.

"No," Maggie said. "He doesn't have the authority."

"Who does?" Justin asked, sounding as if he feared he already knew.

Maggie frowned and confirmed it. "Barone. Which means he's got some explaining to do." She reached for her walkie-talkie clip.

"Maggie, wait," Darcy said. "Give me just a second to double-check something."

Maggie waited, her nerves raw and sizzling, her stomach curling over on itself. This window/code change wasn't just a wrinkle in their defense. It was a freaking groove.

"Barone hasn't been up there."

Justin muttered something under his breath that Maggie didn't catch. "Can he change the sequencing by remote?" Maggie asked Darcy.

"No, he can't. The system isn't configured to allow him remote access."

"Who has been up here with access to the code and the ability to reprogram?"

"No one."

Justin and Maggie's gazes locked and her stomach sank. "That's not possible, Darcy."

"Maybe not, but it's fact. Colonel Drake has been reviewing the tapes and verified. No one has been up there since Dr. Crowe was there and ran his double-check, Maggie. Not a soul has entered the short-stack since then."

Maggie spun through a series of possibilities that could have happened, only none of them proved any more probable than a remote shift of the code sequence. Out of ideas, she put the question to the group. "Any ideas, guys? What else could have happened?"

Kate intervened. "Sounds like an automatic rotator, Maggie."

Justin hiked his shoulders, perplexed, so Maggie explained. "A rotator will automatically change the code to a new sequence after it's been used a set number of times. Though honestly we've seen them used more on explosives devices, which is Kate's specialty, than on security system locks."

"The colonel recommends you verify with Barone or Stanton."

"Stand by." Maggie pulled out the walkie-talkie. "Will, I need you on…" She hesitated and then stopped and regrouped. "Level Three, Will, at Escalator Three," she said, sending him to the other end of the building.

Justin didn't question her tactics. "Do I stay here or go with you?"

"Stay put. Anyone tries to get in, hold them, and let me know."

He nodded, worry deepening the lines alongside his mouth.

Maggie took off in a sprint down the thoroughfare, checking the rounds as she passed them. All were still netted. When she got to Escalator Three, Will hadn't yet gotten there. A few shoppers straggled through this sector of the level, but for the most part, they hadn't yet made it up to Level Three in any significant numbers. Furniture was up here, and traditionally it didn't sell well during the holiday season.

The elevator whirred softly and she stepped to the round

and nodded at Donald Freeman, standing in the alcove between the Grimes and Stokes stores. "Tell me you haven't been up here all this time without a break, Donald."

"Oh, no, ma'am." He smiled at her. "Judy Meyer took a shift, then Cynthia Pratt did one. I just took back over from her."

Judy Meyer? She was supposed to be observing Barone. "Anything to report?"

"Not a thing, so far, ma'am." He straightened his shoulders. "But I'm not slacking."

Maggie smiled, liking him. "I'm counting on that." She walked on. "Darcy, what happened to Judy Meyer being on Barone?"

"Relieved. He asked her what the hell she was doing following him. Franklin Walker replaced her."

Will stepped out of the elevator nearest the escalator. He'd put on a fresh uniform shirt and shaved. "Maggie, what's up?"

Smelling his cologne, she walked with him out of earshot. "Do any of the security codes change by automatic rotator?"

"Not so far as I know."

"Is there a way to change the codes without going to the keypads on the individual locks?"

A tiny piece of tissue stuck to Will's cheek where he'd nicked himself shaving. "You can change most of them through the master system lockbox."

That had to be what happened, then. "Take me to it."

Worry flickered across his face. "What's going on, Maggie?"

"I'll explain on the way. I need to get to that lockbox."

"It's down on Level One." He took her down the service elevator to Level One, then to the security office. They rounded the marble counter and walked past the desks to the very back, far right corner.

Will stopped in front of a door with a keypad lock and punched in his code. The door didn't open.

"What the hell?" He tried it again.

Still nothing.

"You're going to have to go to Barone," Darcy said.

Maggie cursed. "Try it one more time, Will." She really didn't want to go to Barone. He'd have her answering questions, or trying to, for the next hour.

Will tried his code a third time. The faint beep sounded on all the numbers except the last. "No luck."

Damn it. That was it, then. She had no choice. Thumbing the catch, she unhooked the walkie-talkie and depressed the transmit button. "Linda?"

"Linda Diel."

"Would you ask Mr. Barone to come to the security office please?"

"Of course, Captain Holt."

Maggie didn't want Will and Barone in the same room, not until she found out the truth. "Will, go up and relieve Dr. Crowe and send him down here. If anything biological is involved, I'm going to need him."

"Will do, Maggie." He took off, and a scant four minutes later, Justin arrived.

"Will says you need me down here," he said to Maggie.

"I wanted Will and Barone separated, and you down here," she corrected him. "Something is definitely amiss and if it's bio, you're my man."

His eyes sparkled. "Absolutely."

Barone took a very long additional three minutes to walk the two doors down. Adding insult to injury, he looked well rested, groomed to perfection, and irritated at being summoned. "What is your problem, Captain Holt?"

Major shift. His responsibility had become her problem. Very interesting. Morgan's warnings about sudden behavioral shifts again ran through Maggie's mind and the "he could be one of Kunz's doubles" alarm sounded in her mind. She played a hunch. "The rotator on the security system has changed all the codes. I need the new ones."

"I beg your pardon?"

"I need the new security codes," she repeated, not risking a look at Justin. "The rotator has changed them."

Barone gave her a tight smile. "Captain, you're mistaken."

"Oh, did you change them, then?"

"No, I did not." He walked around her to the lockbox door. "Nothing has been done to change the security codes and there is no automatic rotator on Santa Bella's system. You're mistaken."

He looked and sounded sincere. Maggie didn't trust him, or fully trust her judgment about him, but the possibility of him offering a resolution to the problem had come to a deadend. "Kate, I need gear."

"I'm grabbing it now," she answered into Maggie's earpiece. "Give me two minutes."

"Captain Holt?" Barone crossed his arms. "Would you please explain what you've done to my security system?"

"I haven't done anything to it, Mr. Barone," she said. "But it appears that someone has changed all of your security codes."

Shock too raw not to be genuine registered on his face. "That's impossible. How could this happen and we not know it?"

"I can't yet answer that," Maggie said.

His voice turned angry, doubtful. "You must be mistaken, Captain."

Arguing with him would be futile. "Fine, Mr. Barone." She motioned to the lockbox door. "Would you open this please?"

He shot her a frosty glare laced with disdain, then shouldered her out of his way and coded the lock.

Nothing happened.

He tried again.

Still nothing happened.

Stepping back, he turned his temper on Will, just as Maggie feared he would. "Will Stanton must have done this. Where is he?"

"No," Maggie said sharply, her jaw and voice tight. "We know for fact Will has done nothing."

"Then what's happened?" Barone shouted. "I demand an explanation."

Thank God Will couldn't hear the conversation or else he'd be ticked off enough to tell Barone to shove the job and walk out. Barone could go, but Maggie needed Will. She stepped closer to Barone, bent on cooling things down. "We're attempting to determine that now, Mr. Barone. We'll report our findings to you as soon as possible. Now, if you'll excuse us, we'll get back to the investigation."

Kate came in swinging her gear pack and pushed Barone aside. "Move over, please. I need room to maneuver."

Barone automatically backed up, but he ignored Maggie's dismissal.

Kate dropped the gear bag. "You need help?"

"I think I can manage." Maggie nodded. "If not, I'll yell."

"Okay, then. I'll be back at Center Court."

"Thanks." Maggie watched her go, and then went to work on the lock.

Through her earpiece, she heard Kate radio Darcy. "Find something for Barone to do to get him out of their way, will you?"

"Send him to me," Amanda suggested. "The kids are having a great time in the snow. Maybe he'll get whacked with a stray snowball or something."

"We can but hope," Justin whispered.

Maggie hid a smile behind her hand. "Mr. Barone," Maggie said. "My associate at Center Court, Captain West, would like to consult with you on something."

"Of course." He stared at Maggie. "I expect a full report on this—and a satisfactory explanation. Security of this facility is Will Stanton's responsibility."

True to form, Barone shifted blame, covering his ass. Disgusting slug.

Justin looked as if he'd like to knock Barone down a notch or two just for general principles, but he bit his tongue and ignored Barone's crisp nod.

When Barone walked out, Kate grunted, the sound carrying through the earpiece. "That man's underwear must be too tight."

Maggie looked back at Justin and grinned.

"Miracles do happen," Justin said. "Maggie's showing me her teeth, and she's not snarling."

"Impossible." Darcy sounded adamant, then ruined it by laughing.

Maggie pulled out something sharp and pointed it at Justin. "Not one more word or I'll sic Kate on you. All I have to do is mention Aruba."

"What happened in Aruba?" Justin asked.

"Absolutely nothing," Kate said, her disgust evident.

Darcy filled Justin in. "Kate and Nathan's romantic vacation got preempted by Kunz's goons planting explosives on a federal installation."

Justin sighed, watching Maggie work. "Bet the goons regretted it."

"Oh, yeah," Darcy said.

Her tone had Justin speculating. "She shot them didn't she?" he asked no one in particular. "Never mind. Stupid question. Of course, she shot them."

"Shut up, Justin," Maggie muttered. "I'm focusing."

"I knew it," he muttered. "She shot the goons for screwing up her vacation."

"Crowe." Kate practically growled. "Drop Aruba. Final warning."

The door popped open.

Darcy let out a swooshed breath.

"Whoa, baby!" Maggie threw up her arms. "Stand back."

A full brick of C-4 explosives.

"Colonel, give notice up the chain of command and to the Threat Integration Center. Alert the local First Responders, Darcy."

"I don't have visual. What is it?" Colonel Drake asked. "What did you find?"

Maggie shook. "Enough C-4 to blow up the facility and leave one hell of a crater." She moved around the edge of the doorway, fully into the lockbox. "And a triggering device. Kate, I know you're hovering outside the security office door, just in case I needed you. Come take a look at this."

Bio and weaponry systems, not explosives, was Maggie's area of expertise. Kate had the fix on explosives and triggering devices.

Kate stepped into the lockbox and followed Maggie's lead. "It's set to trigger when someone opens the short-stack door, Colonel," Kate said.

"Can you disarm it?" Darcy asked. "Or do I need to bring in a bomb squad?"

"It's rudimentary," Kate said. "If you like, I can have it disarmed in two, maybe three minutes."

"Thanks," Maggie said. "Go ahead." She turned her attention to Darcy. "I want this area cleared and a disposal team on standby. As soon as Kate clears the device, I want these explosives out of the facility."

"HAZMAT is en route now. Judy Meyer's vacating the admin wing."

Security and Matt Elden's HAZMAT team were getting a real workout on this mission.

"Watch for a backup trigger, Kate," Maggie reminded her.

"Definitely," Amanda added. "Remember, this is Kunz."

"Oh, yeah. And he loves redundancies." Kate grimaced and kept working. "I'm all over it."

Maggie heard a strange sound and looked over at Justin. He was green around the gills. She moved over, clasped his arm. "Justin, are you all right?"

"Uh, yeah. Yeah." He gave himself a shake. "It's just— damn, Maggie. You expect C-4 on a battlefield, not at the shopping mall. Maybe for you it's typical, but for me... The man who'd do this is crazy."

"Oh, no, Justin. No," Maggie assured him. "Thomas Kunz is many things, but he's not crazy." She knew what he meant about the shock of it, too. "It isn't typical for S.A.S.S., either. It's just that we've come to know to expect the worst from him, and he always delivers it."

Maggie rubbed circles on Justin's shoulder and dropped her voice. "Breathe slow and deep, okay? You're hyperventilating."

"Oh, hell." He grumbled and groused. "This is humiliating."

Maggie found this side of him totally endearing. "If you weren't worried, I'd be checking your pulse. But don't worry about this device." Maggie nodded toward the lockbox. "Kate is hands-down the best there is at explosive devices."

"Piece of cake, Justin." Kate stuck a wire between her teeth and pinched another with a red-handled set of needle-nose pliers.

"Humiliating," he muttered.

"No, it's charming." Maggie looked at Justin, surprised by the words coming out of her own mouth, surprised by his obviously pleased reaction, and seriously surprised—and worried—about the bonding going on between them. Amazing for that to happen—especially here and now, under these conditions—but moments of high intensity often brought out the most intense emotions.

And why that reassured her when it should scare her to death, Maggie couldn't say. But it did. Morgan had been right. She'd said the human spirit and connections binding people were stronger than any crisis. Still, the comfort that came with knowing it was nothing short of a miracle.

Had Justin picked up on that? She looked up at him.

"Justin?" Her voice faded. She had no idea how to put her feelings into words.

"Yes, Maggie?" His voice sounded thick.

He'd picked up on it. Definitely. Yet Maggie lost her nerve in wanting to share it openly with him. "Never mind."

"Me, too," he said in a quiet voice she had to strain to hear.

Her heart lurched, then went tight and pounded. Terrified by the intensity, she didn't even consider saying more.

Justin went on, clearly troubled on Maggie's behalf. "You awe me, Maggie."

She had to make herself look at him, knowing the pain clouding her heart would show in her eyes. "No. No, I don't. I can't." Her voice weakened to a thread of sound. "Not after what I've done. Who I am."

Talk and radio transmissions stopped on a dime. The S.A.S.S. members were a tight unit, close and surrogate family, forced together not by blood relation but by the work's secretive nature. The unit members held few secrets from each other, and yet until this moment, none of them had realized the depth of Maggie's shame. None of them had known that she feared herself for what she'd destroyed with that fire. And what she had destroyed was her own sense of worth as a human being.

"No, Maggie," Justin said. Pain, raw and familiar, flashed over his face. He knew her revelation had rattled her and everyone else, hitting too close, and he wanted to ease the tension and make her comfortable. "You're a far better woman than you think."

"I'm not." She looked up at him, the truth in her eyes. "I'm far worse than you think."

"You're wrong," he said. "And that's a promise."

"It's out!" Kate announced. "Good damn thing no one opened that door."

"Wouldn't that have been suicide?" Justin asked, trying to refocus.

"Yes," Kate said with a shrug. "It's happened before."

Now the horror in that response was genuine, and Maggie waited, but none of the other S.A.S.S. members acknowledged it, so she responded to Justin. "Actually, it would have been a homicide bomber who also killed himself, and it's a frequent occurrence in and outside groups of extremists."

Anger and bitterness seeped into Justin's voice. "What kind of man arranges suicide and mass murder for a capabilities demonstration?"

Maggie felt an odd hitch in her chest. Desperation. Greed. Extreme beliefs. Could be a lot of things, or nothing at all. It could be a guy, or a woman who's just tired of getting kicked around by life and wants it over. And Thomas Kunz knew how to find that person and use him. "Determined minds have spent years trying to figure that out, but there is no answer, Justin, and you'll just make yourself nuts trying to come up with one that makes sense. It doesn't make sense. That's the answer. You have to accept it and let it go."

"Done." Kate stood, shoved her tools back into her pack. "Two redundancies," she said, then fed Darcy the specifics on what had been used and how.

"Darcy," Maggie said, when Kate finished. "Reset the codes so I can get in to take a look at that window and get Matt Elden in here."

Linda Diel came into the security office, looking harried. "Has anyone seen Mr. Barone?"

Maggie stilled.

"He left me a few minutes ago," Amanda said.

"Did you page him?" Maggie asked.

She nodded. "I'll try again."

"Can I do anything for you?" Maggie asked.

Linda nearly choked. "No. Um, no. I need him." She blew out a deep breath. "I'll…I'll try to page him again."

Odd reaction. Linda seemed frazzled, and that had to be uncommon for her. Maggie couldn't imagine her working so closely with Barone if she rattled easily. He was cool and collected, and he'd never tolerate an assistant who was anything else. "Why didn't you evacuate?"

"I was in the rest room and didn't know I was supposed to until the admin wing was already sealed off."

After Linda left, Maggie stepped out of the office into the corridor and walked down a little way to assure she wasn't overheard by anyone.

"Darcy, check with Franklin and get a location on Barone."

"Right away, Maggie."

"Will, heads up," she said into the walkie-talkie, watching two women go into Macy's. A cloud of their perfume lingered, scenting the air with ginger and gardenia. "Barone's not answering his page. If he comes up there, you keep him away from that door."

"No problem, Maggie."

Justin came out into the corridor, switched frequencies and then ran a check on his antidote stations, reassuring himself the undercover medical personnel had the antidote vials secured.

The sound-off ran down without incident. That took a

frantic edge off the tension, but that brick of C-4 worried the spit out of Maggie. "Darcy, I want a full search of the facility."

"What are we looking for?"

"C-4."

Moments later Darcy issued the order. And moments after that, Will sent out word to his security staff.

Santa Bella was under attack. Running true to form, Kunz was going about it so cleverly that Maggie knew it but still couldn't call the alarm as a GRID attack and just shut the damn mall down, and Barone wouldn't do it. Still, she intended to press him hard.

She found him in his office, playing solitaire on his computer. Hadn't Linda checked for him here?

"Mr. Barone."

"Yes?"

Disgusted that he'd screw off while his facility was under attack put a razor's edge on her voice. "You are aware that C-4 was found attached to the security system."

"Linda informed me, of course."

"I can't prove the terrorists have launched a bio-attack, but this facility is most definitely under attack. Since the attacker is as yet unknown, locals have authority. But I'm strongly advising you to close down the facility."

He stared at her a long second. "No."

"Mr. Barone, you seem oblivious to the severity of the dangers here." That, or he was working for Thomas Kunz.

"Oblivious? No, not at all." He rocked back in his chair. "If the attack were under way, Captain, then you'd close the facility. You wouldn't need me to do it."

Her authority applied only to GRID. She couldn't close

the mall otherwise—not at this point. She'd need national security approval from up the chain of command, and they weren't likely to give it when the man behind the administrator's desk wouldn't agree to shut down his own facility. "If the device had detonated, this facility would be rubble and everyone in it would be dead. You do understand that."

"Yes, of course," he said. "I view this as a bomb threat. It was successfully resolved and now it's over, Captain. The danger has passed. Why close now?"

"There could be other devices on the premises."

He turned back to his game. "If you find one, then come talk to me."

"Fine," she said sharply. "Your choice, your responsibility."

"*My* choice, *your* responsibility." The bastard smiled.

Fuming, she walked out and down the corridor toward the security office, taking solace where she could until she could put the puzzle pieces together. One piece was that the antidote was in place and no challenges to their possession of it had been launched.

Kate came out of the security office and intercepted Maggie. A frown wrinkled her forehead and she stepped to Maggie's side, making sure no one else was within earshot. "This job wasn't up to Kunz's standards, Maggie. His people know what they're doing. Even with the dual redundancies, this job was simplistic—not at all Kunz's style, and definitely not up to the caliber of anything we've ever seen from him or GRID."

Seeing the direction Kate was going with this, Maggie took in a resigned breath and confessed her deduction. "I know. I'm thinking the same thing, Kate," Maggie confessed.

"*What* are you thinking?" Darcy cut in.

"Yeah, what?" Amanda and Mark asked simultaneously.

Only Justin didn't ask. Maggie gave him points for restraint and had the sneaking suspicion the reason he didn't ask was he had already come to the same conclusion.

"Well?" Darcy nudged her.

Maggie looked at Kate and saw the worry she felt reflected in Kate's eyes. "I'm thinking this facility is under attack by two separate entities."

Chapter 8

"Go to Code Red, S.A.S.S. protocol immediately."

Colonel Drake's voice came through crisp and clear and in total control. Maggie changed frequencies and awaited further contact.

A moment later it came from the colonel. "This task force is now operating under S.A.S.S. protocol for emergency management of potential disaster due to unnatural causes by terrorists, domestic and/or foreign."

"Acknowledgment of priority status Code Two is hereby given. Colonel Sally Drake, Commander."

"Acknowledgment given. Primary, Captain Maggie Holt."

"Acknowledgment given. Secondary, Captain Katherine Kane."

"Acknowledgment given. Home Base Intel and Operations Officer, Captain Darcy Clark."

Amanda and Mark gave their acknowledgments, and then Darcy added, "The CAT has been activated." She used the acronym for the catastrophe response team. "Notification has been made to General Shaw, the Pentagon, the liaison to S.A.S.S., Terrorist Threat Integration Center, First Responders, Mayor Lewis and Providence Air Force Base. FEMA is on standby. FBI regional, district and field offices are now on elevated alert."

Colonel Drake spoke again. "Tape and backup DVD recordings are operational and will remain functioning. Participants of record are all included in secure satellite transmission."

Darcy took over again. "Maggie, who do you think is launching the second attack?"

"Suspect unknown at this time." She left the security corridor and walked toward the stairs. The answer to that question well might be in the short-stack, near the window. "We're acting on reports of a Kunz/GRID capabilities demonstration, which at the Santa Bella location would involve high-value, Special Forces targets. Cause for confidence that a second attacker is involved is rooted in an attempted explosion attached to Santa Bella's lockbox and security system. Key findings are based on previous Kunz/GRID experience deduction. Apparatus detonation device was deemed substandard. Explosives charge was grossly excessive. Wiring and redundancies were simplistic and inconsistent with historical GRID methodologies. Frankly, anyone with Internet access could have rigged the device. Odds that it was done by a professional are slim to none. Although, getting one's hands on that much C-4 required connections and substantial funds. Santa Bella

Administrator, Daniel Barone, has refused a specific advisory post-discovery of the C-4 device to close the facility. Should we discover secondary devices, he'll consider the request. Until then, he views the incident as a bomb threat that was successfully resolved."

"Second is in total agreement with Primary on all findings," Kate said, backing Maggie's accounting and conclusion.

Topping the stairs, Maggie saw Justin standing alone near the banister. "Colonel, permission requested to abandon Code Red protocol and return to general frequency to check the short-stack and the window."

"Granted." Colonel Drake then informed the group. "The FBI just reported our bag lady has departed her hotel room. They're tailing her now."

Terrific. Maggie reached for her walkie-talkie. "Will?"

"Yes, Maggie."

"Do you have that new code for me yet?"

"Four, four, nine, nine, one, three."

"Where's Barone?"

"Still in his office, according to Linda, and not to be disturbed," Will said. "She found him there right after asking us about him. She just missed seeing him go in."

After Maggie had talked with him. At least he was present and accounted for, and apparently he hadn't been missing at all. "Why didn't he answer Linda's page?"

"He says the battery died in his walkie-talkie and he wasn't yet aware of it," Will said.

Gauging by his tone, Will figured Barone had turned off the walkie-talkie so he couldn't be summoned. He had shifted responsibility to Maggie, and he meant to stay as blind on everything that happened subsequent to that as possible.

"Maggie?"

The man was a coward. Maggie grunted, turned toward Justin. "Yes?"

Concern shone in his eyes. "I'm coming with you into the short-stack."

"No, I need you at the door." She pulled her flashlight out of her fanny pack. "I want to know for fact that no one has followed me in."

He nodded, seemingly pleased that she was willing to depend on him. "Count your steps," he suggested. "It helped keep me oriented to where I was while in there. It's so damn dark, you can't see two feet in front of your face."

Maggie had made her way through dense woods, across the desert after a sandstorm had totally altered the landscape, through mazes of caves and swamps and other equally challenging places. She could surely deal with whatever the short-stack threw her way. But Justin's trying to help make her job easier touched her. In many ways, he was proving he was an endearing and thoughtful man. With mixed emotions about that, she hesitated and let them settle. Gratitude proved strongest. She smiled and touched his arm. "Thanks for the tip. I'll do that."

"Adorable," Darcy said. "He's a good man, Maggie, and he's definitely into you. You should keep him."

"Captain Clark." Maggie saw red. "You're on S.A.S.S. frequency being taped, I would remind you."

"No, I'm not. Not at the moment anyway. Colonel Drake abandoned protocol across the board to check out the short-stack."

Maggie hadn't realized the colonel had taken the abandon request system-wide. What TV remote hogs did with channel surfing, Darcy did with radio frequencies. Maggie should have known she'd never mix business and pleasure on a Code Red tape. That kind of chatter was frequently used as stress-busters, but it was never recorded.

"So?" Darcy prodded. "What are you going to do with him?"

"Nothing." Justin terrified her. What woman in her position with her history in her job—and in her right mind—wouldn't be terrified?

"Damn it, Maggie. He's a rare find."

Maggie ignored her, keyed in the code, then opened the door. "I'm going in." She stepped inside.

Bare-bulb lights were on, but positioned about sixteen feet apart. The light cast was sparse and dim, and long shadows stretched between, keeping vast spaces pitch-dark. She clicked on her flashlight and blew out a hollow breath. At least there weren't nine million boxes in here to trip over. Small bundles and wooden pallets of sealed boxes were neatly stacked and positioned under signs with store names posted above them. A large section on the east side had been dedicated to housekeeping equipment. The door closed behind her.

"Are you alone inside?"

Maggie swept the four walls, spinning in a slow circle. "Yes, I'm alone, Darcy."

"I guess you didn't hear me before. I said Justin's a rare find."

What did Maggie say to that? She mentally counted steps, trying to estimate when she was three beams left of center. The silence in the short-stack was deafening. Maggie went to a private frequency. "I heard you. I didn't want to respond."

"Come on, Maggie—"

"But since you're going to be so damn persistent about butting into my business, I will answer you."

"Oh, good."

"Yeah, I can't wait to hear this," Amanda said.

"She won't do it," Kate chimed in. "Giving a guy a chance after the Jack affair? No way."

"Do you want to know what I think, or just speculate among yourselves?"

"Sorry," Darcy said. "Go ahead, Maggie."

"Okay. Fine. Justin has many admirable qualities. I'm seeing that more all the time," she said, and meant it. "He's often quite charming." True. Very true. More often than not, he was charming. Or endearing. Or both. "But, don't you guys get it? I messed up. I can't risk that again. It wouldn't be right or fair. The shame of what I did haunts me. I won't risk being in that position again. For me, or for Justin, or anyone else—ever."

Oh, God. Why had she said all that? Why did she do it? She should have just kept her mouth shut. "That's all I have to say about this—and I don't want to hear any more." She sucked in a steadying breath. "And I mean it."

Maggie scraped her back against the rough outer wall, which had to be a false wall, built to conceal the real outer wall for two reasons. It was straight, not curved. If it were the true outer wall it'd be curved like the dome. And there was no window.

"You need to accept that you went too far, though Kate

and I disagree that you did," Amanda said. "Forgive your-self, and press on."

"Yeah, and I can't believe you're holding that affair against Justin," Darcy said, bringing it up again anyway. "Are you serious about that?"

"What?" Maggie couldn't believe her ears. What was wrong with these people? She moved down the wall, shin-ing the light on the joint where wall and floor met, watch-ing for a telltale crack.

"I think she's serious," Amanda piped in. "So what is she serious about, exactly?"

"Pay attention, Amanda. That Justin cheated on An-drea," Darcy repeated. "I can't believe she's holding that against him."

How could Darcy *not* hold it against him? Riled, Mag-gie got snippy. "Do I need to be here for this conversation?"

"Uh, yeah, you do," Kate said in a totally snotty tone. "I know you're not a total loser or a freaking coward, so why are you marking Justin as a jerk for that? Inquiring minds want to know—and I'll warn you, Maggie. What I think of your judgment is riding on this."

Stunned, Maggie groaned. "You're defending him, too?" She couldn't believe it. He'd gotten to the Queen Grouch? "Not fifteen minutes ago, you were issuing him a final warning about Aruba."

"So what? He's got a great ass, he remembered how you like your coffee and—"

"Oh," Amanda interrupted. "He worried she'd be hun-gry, too."

"Yeah," Kate said. "I forgot that one. And I like the way he looks at you all dopey-eyed."

"Oh, God." Maggie groaned. "Deliver me."

"For pity's sake, lighten up, Maggie," Amanda said. "Far be it from us to interfere…."

Maggie stepped around a stack of boxes and guffawed. "Oh, right. Right."

"Okay," Amanda conceded. "So maybe we are interfering a tiny bit by asking questions, but we're concerned you're going to do something totally stupid and regret it forever."

"And we'll have to listen to you bitch," Kate tossed in.

"Darn it," Amanda said. "Be gentle, Kate."

"I was being gentle."

"Subtle as a sledge." Darcy added her unsolicited opinion.

"Whatever." Kate sniffed, affronted. "I was honest."

"Be that as it may…" Amanda resumed spokesman control, her voice not registering so much as a ruffle. "You might want to reconsider your position on that little indiscretion of his, Maggie."

She cut down the aisle and wound between two waist-high stacks of boxes, sidestepping the edge of an empty slatted-wood palette. "Little indiscretion?" Maggie shook her head. "Excuse me?" She just couldn't believe it. "Have you guys gotten sudden amnesia or something?"

"Not bloody likely," Darcy said. "It's in your best interests. That's all." She let out a heaved breath that crackled static. "So he cheated. But, good grief, do you know the circumstances, Maggie?"

Now they were making excuses for him? "No, I don't."

"You should," Kate advised her. "Maybe there are extenuating circumstances that warrant special consideration in his case?" Kate smacked her lips. "I don't know,

Maggie. I'm not feeling comfortable with your judgment. Things aren't looking so good for you on that front."

"I didn't *do* anything, Kate. And you're not remembering that has me seriously questioning *your* judgment." Maggie stepped out of the row into the center clearing. "Don't you guys get it? You trust someone with your best and your worst, and when they break that trust, it's just gone. You can't wish it back. You can't even order it back. It's been blown to hell, and it no longer exists."

"We get that," Amanda said. "Even Kate."

"Matter never dissipates, it merely changes form—and Justin didn't break your trust," Kate added.

Maggie ignored her and pushed Amanda. "If you get what I'm saying, then why are you telling me I should play ostrich and bury my head in the sand? So I can bust my ass to somehow get the courage together to try to trust again, and then put it in the hands of a man who has a history of blowing trust to hell and back? Come on, guys." She spun in a slow circle, sweeping the light from ceiling to floor, and caught a whiff of some scent.

Cologne. Subtle, too light to distinguish whether it was a man's or a woman's. She stepped off two steps in each direction, but lost the scent.

"I'm sorry," Darcy said. "I just don't understand you on this. You're usually reasonable, Maggie."

Now *she* was unreasonable? "Look, forget it. Just drop this." Maggie gritted her teeth. "Just drop it."

"No," Amanda said. "This is too important. Men like Justin really are rare, Maggie. How many have looked at you like he does? Or made you feel what he does?"

They were honestly on his side. A swift flood of betrayal

gushed through Maggie. Betrayal and abandonment. She stiffened against it. "Uh, Amanda. I'm the woman who burned the bed, boat, fence and storage building, and sent Jack out into the freezing night naked, riding on rims, if you'll recall. I live with that. How could you possibly think I'd ever again trust the way a man looks at me?" Anger at them for turning on her erupted. "How could any of you think it's wrong to hold being unfaithful against a man? How could you not understand how scared I am of it happening again?" She choked up.

"Oh, honey," Amanda said. "We're on your side. We just don't want you to miss out on a man who truly adores you."

"Yeah," Darcy said. "It's just a perspective thing. You know, being burned kind of tints the picture. You need to see it clearly."

"Look, Maggie," Kate said. "You get this right, you win. You screw up, we all lose. It's that simple. Now, we know you did all that stuff, and for some reason, it eats at you. But that was with Jack. Justin isn't Jack. And, frankly, Jack deserved every damn thing you did to him and then some. You know we all feel that way about it. You're just screwing up with Justin. We're saving you from yourself."

"Don't." She didn't need saving.

Finally she saw what she'd been looking for, and all other thoughts fled her mind. Her heart rate sped up a notch. "I've found the door."

She moved closer to the wall, dragged her fingertips over the fine joint. They registered barely a line. "Well, it's not actually a door," she amended. "It's a wide slat inserted in the wall."

"Check for trip wires," Kate suggested.

"Pressure-sensitive bombs," Amanda said on a rush. "Kunz is crazy about them. And laser. He loves laser."

"There's no light, Amanda," Maggie said a lot more calmly than she felt. "No laser. Ease up a bit. I'm checking every millimeter for everything." And she did. Twice. Then a third time, using a standard grid pattern, which she widened and went over a fourth time for extra caution.

"Maggie?" Justin's voice rang out. "Are you okay?"

He was back in the communications loop. That, too, comforted her—and irritated her because it comforted her. Refusing to wonder why, she said, "I'm fine," then finished the intense inspection. "There's nothing here. The area is barren."

Now why would anyone go to the trouble of putting in that window only to have an empty room? It didn't make sense. There had to be a reason. Uncomfortable, she tipped the flashlight to elevate its beam and checked the ceiling, then the floor, and then all points in between.

Still nothing.

Stranger and stranger. She again widened the grid to make sure the slat itself wasn't a lead that would act as a trigger for something else. "It's clean," she said, finally satisfied. "I'm going to pull the slat."

She grabbed the two-by-six and tested its weight. Lifting the bottom straight up, she swung it toward her, then pulled the slat out of the channel holding it in place at the ceiling. The slat broke free. Balancing its weight, she turned and stepped sideways, then leaned it against the wall.

"Slat's out." She moved to the center of the opening and peered inside. "I see the window."

Wiping gritty sawdust from her hands, she looked inside the narrow three-foot room, shining the light down to the left and then the right. "Estimate the room to measure three-by-sixty feet, maybe a little longer," she said, allowing for distortion by the lack of light. "Plywood walls, unpainted. Same concrete floor as the rest of the short-stack. The window is tinted to match the dome ceiling outside. It's roughly a square foot, actually a little larger than the visual observed from outside led us to believe."

"Any strange smells, sounds or other sensory input?" Darcy asked.

Obviously they were back to taping. "The wood smells new. It can't have been in here long. The three inner plywood walls all still have fuzzy fibers and curls of sawdust on the edges, same as those in the short-stack proper." She ran her fingers along the slat. "The edges of the slat haven't been sanded and they're not worn smooth. I see a few more wood shavings in here than outside. This secret room has been added recently." That fit with the photo Will had supplied dating it, as well. "No other scents, and no sounds at all. It's dead quiet in here."

"What's in the room?" Darcy asked. "Any contents?"

"Nothing. Not a single damn—wait." Something was at the far end of the narrow space. She moved toward it. "A fire hose." That made no sense, either. "It appears to be functional."

"Why would there be a functional fire hose there?" Kate asked. "And a window?"

"Stand by, Maggie," Darcy said. "Let me check something."

"Are you sure it's functional, the fire hose?" Amanda asked.

Maggie checked it, examined the wall connection. "It appears to be, yes."

Darcy returned. "I reviewed the plans again to be sure, Maggie. The short-stack has sprinklers, so the hose isn't needed for fire. Look out the window. What do you see?"

Maggie dragged the hose with her to the window, looked down. Hundreds of kids were playing in the snow. "I see the pit," she said. "And the fire hose is exactly the right length to reach the window. It reaches no further."

A pause, then Darcy added, "The hose is totally unnecessary. Sprinklers also circle the pit."

"You said they circle the pit. Does the spray cover what's in the pit?" Maggie asked, looking for an angle. There had to be a logical reason for this hose to be here.

"Other than today, there isn't anything in the pit that's vulnerable to fire and needs protection. Just a marble slab floor and steps leading down into it."

"Then why would someone fear fire enough to put a hose up here?" Kate asked, sounding as baffled as Maggie felt.

"Good question." One Maggie intended to put to Daniel Barone.

Maggie took one more look out the window, then stepped back. *You're missing something. You're missing something.* Her instincts hummed and an odd chill shot up her spine. A second later something scraped the floor behind her.

She spun around to confront it.

A swish of rushing air blew over her. Something hard cracked against her skull. Pain shot through her head, she staggered, spun, grabbing her skull, seeing stars. "Darcy!"

"What's wrong? No visual. It's too dark. Maggie? Maggie, talk to me!"

"Hold your positions." Her tongue went thick, her mind foggy. She stumbled, trying to get to the door. The flashlight fell from her hand. Its beam of light went out. She bumped into the wall, leaned into it, shaking her head to clear it.

Steadier now, she pushed off the wall and felt her way down it. The opening had to be close by.

"Someone…hit…me." She deliberately slurred her words, leading her attacker, she hoped, into believing she was more incapacitated by the blow than she actually was. "Hold…positions." She intended the instruction for Amanda, Kate and Mark at Center Court. They'd know by that she was luring her attacker.

A bare hand shot out to grab her.

She sensed the movement before she felt it, and threw a shot out, connecting with the armpit.

"Umph."

The grunt was too muffled to distinguish as male or female. Following the sound, she moved in, but met only air.

Retreating footsteps grinding on the concrete squeaked in the inky darkness. Footfalls quickly faded and then disappeared.

Maggie sucked in a sharp breath, felt her way to the door and stepped out of the hidden room into the long shadows of the short-stack. She looked for the attacker but, even straining, couldn't see through the deep shadows between the lights.

Just get out.

Yes, get out and lock down the damn thing with the attacker inside. Bring in a team to flush him or her out.

Counting her steps, she moved toward the exit door,

through a dark spot. Her shoe snagged on something and she twisted but lost her balance.

Crumpling, she braced. Her hands and knees collided with the concrete. Pain shot through her hands up her arms, through her knees and up her legs. The pain slammed through her bones, streaked to her shoulders and down to her feet. Sprawled on the concrete, she exhaled a heartfelt groan.

A strong hand closed around her ankle. "Maggie, it's me. It's me, Justin."

Justin? She crawled to her knees and tried to stand. "Why are you down on the floor?"

"I came in after you." He gained his feet with a few grunts and groans. "Someone hit me."

He helped her up and hugged her to him, his hands on her back trembling. "Are you okay?"

She gave in to the desire to comfort and be comforted, and rested her cheek against his chest. "I'm okay."

"Maggie, what the hell is going on in here?"

"Someone jumped me in the secret room. Hit me in the head. I heard him or her running away."

"Darcy?" Justin said. "Did you get that?"

"I got it."

"Darcy," Maggie said. "Get a SWAT team up here fast. Whoever attacked me might still be inside." Though with no guard on the exit door, he or she could also have left. "I want a CSI team in here as soon as SWAT clears it. If there's a print in this damn place, I want it identified." The person who'd hit her hadn't been wearing gloves. When she'd shot a jab to the armpit, she'd felt a brush of bare hand.

"Maggie, it's Will."

"Go ahead, Will," Maggie said into the walkie-talkie.

"Get the hell out of there," he said on a rush. "I've got the entrance covered—have had since Justin went in. No one has come out. The attacker is still inside."

"You're positive no one has come out."

"Damn straight, I am."

Justin tugged and Maggie followed, moving toward the exit door. "Darcy, there are no other short-stack exits, just the one door both Justin and I used, correct?"

"That's correct. Consistent with the plan."

"That's a freaking fire code violation," Amanda added.

"We'll deal with that later," Maggie promised. "For now, let's just get SWAT up here to flush out whoever attacked us, and see what else we find." She had a sneaking suspicion that the key to successfully halting any GRID attack lay in discovering the reason for that window and fire hose.

Closing the dark space between she and Justin and the exit, she accepted that, should they live, her head would pound for a week. "Why did you come in here, Justin?"

"I was worried. You were in here a long time with no contact."

He couldn't hear the private frequency.

"By the time I heard you, I was already inside. I was attacked seconds later."

He kept a hand at her waist and they moved back-to-back, so they had full circle view. Finally they reached the exit door out of the short-stack, and Maggie noticed that Justin was strongly favoring his left knee.

The door opened.

Light flooded in from the main thoroughfare outside. A relieved shiver raced up her back, and Maggie walked out to where Will stood waiting. "Did you see anyone?"

"No one came out, Maggie." Will looked her over, concerned. "You okay?"

She nodded. "Yes, thanks."

"Will's right," Darcy said. "No one has come out that door, Maggie. ETA on the SWAT team is two minutes, Maggie."

"Thanks." She looked at Justin. "Did you see your attacker?"

"No." He stepped to Maggie's side. "But I think it was a man."

"Why?" Maggie asked. She hadn't been able to determine whether the person had been female or male.

"Strength." Justin grimaced. "He whacked the hell out of my knee with a ball bat."

An intentional knee-shot. A professional. "A baseball bat?" Maggie turned around to look at him. "Or a nightstick." All the security guards had batons, but most people still called them nightsticks.

"It could have been either." Justin rubbed at his left leg. "All I know is I'm going to have a hell of a bruise and a lot of swelling. If he'd hit my head that hard, my brain would be mush right now."

Worry for him sliced through Maggie, cutting her deep. She stepped closer, touched his face and looked into his eyes. "But you are okay, right? You're sure?"

He inhaled, absorbing her concern, and covered her hand on his face. "I'm sure."

Relief washed over her. "Good." She caught a shaky breath, moved away and leaned against the banister next to Will. "So, who went in or out of the short-stack?"

"I didn't see any activity at all," Justin said.

Will nodded his agreement. "Me, either."

Darcy added. "I can confirm that on both counts."

Maggie looked at Justin. "If no one else was inside the short-stack with you and me, then who popped a home run on your kneecap and nailed me in the head?"

Justin could have caused his own injury and hers.

Justin's tone sharpened. He'd picked up on her suspicion and deeply resented it. "I can't answer that, Maggie. I don't know."

She let out a frustrated sigh. "Well, doesn't it strike you as odd?"

His jaw ticked. "Damned odd, but I was attacked, too, and I'm not pointing a finger at you."

He had been attacked, and in a way that was atypical for a self-inflicted injury. Maggie stopped, dragged in a calming breath and cooled her temper. "I'm sorry. I had to ask. It's my job. But I didn't believe you were the attacker, Justin."

"Well, thank you for believing the obvious." He stepped away from her, his jaw tight, his shoulders stiff. He stared into a store window at a mobile DVD player, obviously furious and trying to tamp his temper.

Maggie shot his back a glare meant to bend steel and raised her voice, hoping he'd catch it. "Obvious to you maybe, Justin. But not to me." Damn it, she'd had to consider him. She'd be a half-ass operative and a fool not to. Why couldn't he see that?

He stared back at her over his shoulder. A second's worth of pain, not anger, flickered in his eyes, then cool detachment replaced it, freezing her out. "There's something you're forgetting that you might want to remember,

Maggie. My ass is on the line here, too. And unlike you, I don't have to be here. I have a choice." A muscle in his jaw ticked. "I'm not saying losing my life would be a greater sacrifice than you losing yours, or anyone else losing theirs. But mine is as important as anyone else's, and it's damned important to me." Justin limped away, down the thoroughfare, clearly wanting to put some space and distance between him and her.

Damn it, she didn't need this right now. She called after him. "You'd better get Medical to take a look at that knee."

He didn't even look back.

Will said softly. "Aren't you going after him, Maggie?"

"No." She stiffened against wanting to do just that, shoved her hair back from her face and hit the sore spot on her head. Wincing, she flinched. "I'm not—"

"Maggie," Darcy cut in, claiming her attention. "Go to private frequency—now."

What could Darcy possibly have to say about this that needed to be relayed one-on-one? Maggie flipped over to it, her fingers shaking. "Yeah."

"For the record, Justin went down before you did. There's no way he could've attacked you. Someone else was already inside the short-stack, and is still inside it. I thought you'd want to know."

Damn it. Trust. Again with trust. Couldn't her freaking issues cut her a little slack even just once in a while? "Thanks." Spit. Now she felt like a skanky lowlife slug for doubting him—even if it was her job to doubt everyone. *Damn it. Damn it. Damn it.*

She'd apologize to him, of course. But it wouldn't be enough. It had never been enough.

"Heads up. Here we go again," Darcy said, then paused. When she came back, it was on a general frequency. "Unauthorized entry." Her tone hardened. "Level One, Door Two. Repeat. Unauthorized entry. Level One, Door Two. Two male suspects, both carrying handled Krane's shopping bags, and—oh, hell—both of them are wearing yellow jackets. These men are *not* valid mall employees, Security staff, HAZMAT personnel or members of the snow crew. Deduction—they are hostiles. Recommend immediate intercept. Repeat. Suspects are considered hostiles. Recommend immediate intercept."

Justin appeared from around the corner, hobbling to protect his bad knee. Maggie took off for the stairs in a wide-open run. Shoving past shoppers, she pushed her way down. "Excuse me." She sideswiped a man wearing a Santa hat. "So sorry. Excuse me."

She rounded the Level Two landing and grabbed the stairway banister. "Coming through. Coming through." She shouldered down the stairs, urged people to move aside with a sweep of her hand. "Excuse me. Excuse me. Coming through."

While Homeland Security and the Terrorist Threat Integration Center wouldn't consider the incidents occurring at Santa Bella today conclusive proof of a GRID attack and the evidence sufficient to warrant immediate and forced intervention, Maggie believed the incidents proved conclusively the realization of her deepest fears:

Kunz's henchmen had successfully invaded Santa Bella Mall and were now in position to launch their capabilities demonstration.

Chapter 9

Maggie circled Center Court. Level One, Door Two was to its northwest. She wound through the food court and spotted the two men.

"Suspects are at five o'clock, Maggie," Darcy said.

Both men were in their mid-forties, both dark-haired and skinned, and wearing yellow jackets. And they both carried the handled Krane's shopping bags. "I've got a visual," Maggie said softly.

"I'm picking them up on your pin as well as on the fixed monitor," Darcy said.

Maggie hung back. The men didn't appear suspicious, strolling along in no particular hurry, walking shoulder-to-shoulder and talking between themselves. "Darcy, I'm reluctant to intercept until we see what they have in mind. Does the colonel object to holding off?"

A moment lapsed, then, "No, unless they put someone else in jeopardy. Judgment call."

Justin arrived beside her. She was impressed he had caught up so quickly. "Justin, can you distract the guy on the left? I'll take the one on the right."

"You want to intercept them, then?" He sounded confused.

"No. I just want to see what they're carrying."

"Okay, but be careful," he said. "They could be armed."

Again, he forgot that she was the expert, and again, rather than annoying, she found his reminder endearing. She sidestepped a stroller of twin girls and circled a mom bent over wiping a runny nose with a tissue. "I doubt it. Kunz is never this obvious. He has a penchant for body doubles, subterfuge and subtlety. Torture aside, he never gets in your face with what he's doing."

"Your Dr. Morgan Cabot would applaud you pegging that behavioral note." Justin smiled. "Interesting."

"I missed a step. What's interesting?"

"Who," he corrected her. "Kunz. You, you're captivating. Kunz is merely interesting."

Captivating? Her? She tried the feeling on for a second and enjoyed it way too much to let it go. "Sorry to have to disagree with you—even in part—but Kunz isn't *merely* anything. He's way too sinister and dangerous for something that tame and mild."

"Even so, he's interesting."

A moment of sheer frustration leveled her. Twice, S.A.S.S. believed it had arrested Kunz and imprisoned him in Leavenworth only to find it had his doubles incarcerated instead. A third time, S.A.S.S. had killed one of his body doubles and had never even seen the real Kunz—and that had been on a major operation where they'd seized technology and weapons with a street value of $402 million. Kunz was freaking frustrating. "Okay, be interested in him later. For now, you take the guy on the left."

"I've got him." Justin fell into step behind the pair.

Maggie approached from the right and, when Justin stepped up behind and between the two men, she smacked into the right man's shoulder, knocking the shopping bag out of his hand.

It was empty.

"Excuse me," she said, giving the man a dopey smile, and then walked on. Out of earshot she whispered, "See anything, Justin?"

"Lefty's bag is empty, too." Justin walked past her, skimming their shoulders. "So do we take them down now?"

"For what?" Maggie asked. "Carrying Krane's shopping bags in a shopping mall or wearing yellow jackets?"

Darcy intervened. "Direct order, Maggie. Monitor, but do not intercept. Insufficient cause to detain."

"Darcy, relay to Will."

Will Stanton responded. "Security's monitoring."

Picking up her walkie-talkie, Maggie said, "Try to keep your distance, Will. If they notice you, they'll bail. I'd like to know where they're going and what they're going to do." Maggie paused near a small knot of people on the outer circle of the pit under the guise of watching the children play in the snow. "Darcy, where is the female shopper the FBI's tagging? Last report, she had left the hotel and was en route somewhere."

"She went to the grocery store, picked up cigarettes, two

cans of generic peas and a bag of potato chips, then returned to the hotel. She's parked in her room, Maggie."

"And the men?"

"Locals turned FBI onto the first one. They spotted him while watching the woman. He's in a room at the same hotel. I'm waiting for an updated report on the second male, Mr. Ponytail."

Justin came up beside her. "You look extremely tense, Maggie. Does your head hurt?"

It did. But she ignored acknowledging it for fear it'd just hurt more. "It's the willies," she admitted, bristling. "I hate it when I get the willies."

He didn't look or seem angry anymore, but he had been—justifiably so. "Justin, about before…" She risked a glance up at him. "I'm sorry." Now that she'd opened the door, she steeled herself for the recriminations sure to come. Unfortunately they always had. Now that she'd accepted guilt, he'd hold blame over her head for the duration.

"We're all wound up pretty tight." Justin squeezed her shoulder. "Let's just forget it."

Maggie didn't believe her ears. She looked up and over at him, sure she'd misheard him.

"Why are you looking at me like that?" He seemed confused. "Did I say something to tick you off again?"

"No. No, not at all."

"Well, what is it? I can't read you, Maggie, and I'm feeling like an alien."

The words tumbled out of her mouth before she thought to censor them. "I'm beginning to think that's exactly what you are."

He studied her a long moment, then his lip tipped a bit.

"I'm going to take that as a compliment," he said. "But only because you look completely stunned."

"I—I didn't expect…" She couldn't admit this. He wouldn't understand. How could a man who reacted as he did comprehend what she expected?

"What?" He waited, but she didn't say, and his expression softened. "You can tell me, Maggie. Whatever it is, it's okay."

Her mouth went dry. "I didn't expect your reaction." She glanced from his jaw to his eyes. "You surprise me, Justin. Often."

"One of the benefits of being considered scum. No way to go but up."

Her jaw dropped loose and Justin laughed.

"She wears surprise well, doesn't she, Justin?" Darcy said, an amused, indulgent lilt in her voice. "Sorry, I just couldn't restrain myself another second."

"She does," he agreed. "No apology necessary, Darcy. I'm learning fast that interest in one of you makes everything a man says or does fair game for all of you."

"Just about," Kate said, a slight warning in her tone that, gauging by his smile, didn't offend but amused Justin.

Her meaning wasn't lost on him. "You can relax, Kate. Only a fool would take on a pack of women who collectively know a thousand ways to kill a man."

Will Stanton's voice came through the walkie-talkie. "Stand down, Maggie. Justin. Suspects have exited the mall and gotten into a late-model white Ford van in the south parking garage. No distinct markings, Florida tag number M23PAD. Local police have intercepted."

"Darcy, run the tag and alert the FBI." Maybe these two

would beat a path to the same hotel as the first male and female shoppers, and then S.A.S.S. could start connecting some of the dots on this mission.

"In progress, Maggie."

"What is Kunz doing?" Justin asked. "These shoppers with the empty bags. It makes no sense."

"He's watching to see what we're doing," Maggie answered. "And monitoring how we respond to what he's doing. Over the past year, he's obtained substantial insights into our procedures and protocols. We're not the only ones who learn from experience. He's learned, too."

"Then what do you think this shopping bag business is about?" Justin persisted, fighting to make some kind of sense of this. "I'll be damned if I can grip this man's logic."

"I think he's baiting us," Maggie openly admitted. Unfortunately it was the only thing that fit. He'd probably gotten a couple good laughs at her expense, trying to determine if the bag drops were warnings or signals, guideposts or diversions. They were totally inconsistent, with the exception of all being Krane's bags. He was baiting her.

"It could still be coincidence, Maggie," Darcy said. "We haven't proven that there is a connection between these incidents, much less that they're indisputably connected to GRID. It wouldn't pay to jump to false conclusions."

"Two of them? Five empty bags in four separate incidents, during one shopping day? All five suspects enter the facility carrying handled shopping bags from the same store, abandon them and depart the mall. Not one of the five suspects buys a thing. And they do this nonshopping on the busiest shopping day of the year, when people who aren't forced by necessity to shop, steer clear of crowded stores?" Maggie harrumphed. "Coincidence? I don't think so, Darcy. Not even in fantasyland." Maggie sighed. "He's baiting us."

"Look, for the record, I don't think it's coincidence, either. But this isn't—and never has been—about what we think, Maggie. What we think is insignificant. This is about what we can prove."

Maggie's next order was obvious, but she hesitated at issuing it.

Colonel Drake could veto it, and she probably would. But if she did, then at least Maggie would have it on record. It needed to be on the official record.

Maggie squeezed her eyes shut and did it. "Darcy, add this latest incident and report it to the Threat Integration Center and up the chain of command. Include my personal opinion that the odds of these events being coincidental run about the same as odds that DNA is coincidental."

"That's a strong opinion, Maggie," Colonel Drake said.

"Yes, ma'am, it is, Colonel. But I believe it's true, so I have no choice but to report it."

Silence followed, and held. A long moment later the colonel finally responded. "Very well."

Maggie swallowed hard, feeling regretful and relieved. Regardless, she'd done what she had to do and she'd live with knowing that forever. If she turned out to be wrong on the judgment call, it'd wreck her career and her future with S.A.S.S.

If she proved wrong, then of course she'd take the hit. But she believed she was right, and to be right and silent would be a breach of ethics she wasn't willing to make.

She'd regret it every day for the rest of her life, and never be able to meet her own eyes in the mirror again. She already regretted plenty and would never willingly add more. "Report it, Darcy, and keep a sharp watch. I have the feeling we're about to find ourselves in the middle of a tempest."

"For what it's worth, Maggie, your instincts aren't working alone," Kate said. "I've got the bejeebers."

"Oh, hell." That, from Amanda. But it could just as well have been from any of them. When Kate got the bejeebers, hell was coming to call. Her personal warning system had never failed.

That reinforcement of Maggie's judgment was welcome, even if it incited dread.

"Right on cue," Darcy said, sounding resigned. "Heads up, people. Level One, Door One. The Olympians and Special Forces are arriving. Estimate? Two hundred. Makeup? Forty percent kids. Thirty percent parents. Thirty percent Special Forces and family."

"Criteria?" Maggie asked for clarity on how Darcy was defining them.

"Military haircuts, Maggie. Sorry, but it's the most obvious and specific trait avail—" She stopped suddenly and groaned. "Damn it, Maggie. They're all wearing yellow jackets!"

"What?" Surprise and annoyance ripped through her. "Why are they in yellow? I didn't order that."

"Colonel Gray," Darcy said. "Has to be that interfering, pain in the ass, issuing orders to stick his nose into Colonel Drake's business again."

Colonel Drake broke in. "Verify that directly with them and their boss, General Foster."

"I know it's him," Kate said. "Only Gray would be so unconscious. I'm on it."

"This one is going to cost him," Maggie vowed. "Are you wired to the Special Forces liaison, Darcy?"

"Yes, I am."

"Are we?"

"No, he's not on open communications with S.A.S.S."

"Ask him for verification that this jacket business was Gray's order, Darcy."

"Standby."

Furious, Maggie stood statue-still and Justin didn't utter a sound, though she knew he, too, was outraged. If he held his jaw any tighter, he'd crack a couple molars.

Kate answered first. "Colonel Gray issued the order for the yellow jackets. He said it was at the request of S.A.S.S.—and that's a direct quote, Maggie."

Darcy weighed in with the same response. "According to the liaison, Colonel Gray issued the order and he provided the parkas at our request, Maggie."

"Override it," Maggie said sharply, her temper engaged. "Notify General Shaw that I ordered the override and I'm seeking his endorsement. Also ask him to please have the MPs escort Colonel Gray to the OSI office for an immediate educational consultation with the general." Diplomatic way of asking the military police to deliver Colonel Gray to the Office of Special Investigations where the general could ream Colonel Gray a new one.

"Maggie, Colonel Gray *will* retaliate against you."

"Insignificant, Amanda. He's lucky I'm not arresting his ass. He lied about the orders he issued and deliberately jeopardized thousands of people for the sole purpose of insinuating himself into an operation totally outside the jurisdictional authority of his command. He'll take his hits, and I'll take mine. Let the chips fall."

"Hear, hear," Kate said.

"Yeah, well," Amanda said. "I warned you. When retribution comes, remember that your bitching rights have been revoked."

"Whatever." Maggie looked across the pit to where the Special Forces and Olympians had gathered and were depositing their things. Already the men were removing the yellow parkas. "Darcy, ask the liaison to secure those parkas and to forward us a full accounting on them." The last thing they needed was for them to fall into enemy hands.

"Done."

"Why would Gray do that?" Justin asked, his hands curled into fists and shoved into his pockets. "Doesn't he realize what he's doing?"

Maggie cupped her hand over her lapel pin mike so what she was about to say wouldn't transmit to the group. "He doesn't care if he complicates our job, so long as we have a tough time. It's all about punishing us."

"But he's putting others at risk. How can that not matter?"

"He doesn't care, Justin. Gray's a jealous bastard who so envies Colonel Drake and her job that he wants to create havoc to make her look bad more than he wants anything else—and that includes us successfully avoiding an attack. The jackass puts us in 'unintentional' jeopardy all the time, and he never fails to wheedle his way out of responsibility for it. That absolutely frosts my cookies."

"But surely he knows that this parka stunt of his could kill people." Justin looked suitably disgusted. "A lot of people."

"He should know it, but truthfully, he's probably not thinking in that direction, which goes a long way toward explaining why he didn't get Colonel Drake's job. The man wouldn't make a patch on Sally Drake's ass, and that's just the way it is." Maggie lifted her hand from her pin, signaling the topic was now closed. "Verify your medical personnel, inside and outside, are on their toes." The majority were stationed outside in unmarked vans.

That said, Maggie turned her attention elsewhere. "Amanda, is Mark back from dinner yet?"

"He will be in ten minutes."

"Rush him," Maggie said, turning toward the administrative wing. "Special Forces are now on-site. That definitely ratchets up the risks. Kunz is disciplined, but the opportunity to knock off fifty or so Special Forces and their families at one time is too much temptation to trust him to be able to resist." It would be unrelenting, gnawing at him, and likely overwhelm him. "Will, verify that your staff members are posted at all entrances and prepared to intercept on order." She brushed a strand of hair back from her face. "And make sure Donald Freeman is on that round on Level Three, and he's checked to make sure the new netting is in place and secure." When no one had returned to it by noon, Maggie had ordered the round renetted to free up security resources.

She passed the security office, cut into the alcove to run to the rest room and shoved the door open.

Two things knocked her back on her heels.

There was no attendant present. Every rest room and dressing room in the facility was supposed to be manned by a security guard, and this one was empty.

And on the floor near the first stall stood a Krane's handled shopping bag.

"Darcy?" Maggie moved toward the bag, looked inside. *Empty.* "Will?"

"Yeah?"

"I'm here, Maggie," Will said.

Her heart thumped hard against her ribs. "Level One, Administration Wing. Women's rest room in the alcove between Security and Medical. Who is the attendant on duty here, Will?"

"Judy Meyer," he said. "Why?"

"She's MIA."

"Meyer is missing in action?" Will sounded flummoxed.

"That's correct, yes," Maggie said. "And we have another abandoned Krane's bag in one of the stalls." Maggie had to pause to swallow a lump stuck in her throat.

The attendant's welfare was a major concern.

"Maggie, there's only one way Judy abandoned her post. Someone forced her, or killed her and removed her," Will said. "No drama intended, but that's Judy's nature."

"Darcy," Maggie said, "review the tapes and see what turns up on her."

"To get out of the alcove, she had to have gone through the camera's eye," Darcy said. "Colonel's reviewing the tapes now."

"This is the rest room located between *Security* and *Medical.*" Amanda sounded disgusted. "Damn it, Kunz is rubbing our noses in it."

Maggie inspected the bag. "For what it's worth, he wasn't as obvious with this as with the yellow-jacketed men. The bag's crinkled. Something was inside it." Could the virus have been set off here? There should be residue evidence and there was none visible.

But Kunz could have cut the virus loose in here, if he had wanted to do it.

And that was his message to Maggie. He was in control. He would pick and choose what he did and when he did it.

She curled her fingers into fists at her sides, galled by him, outraged, though logic and common sense told her that defending against an attack could be no other way. "My guess is whomever left it here wasn't wearing a jacket."

Moments later Darcy agreed and Colonel Drake verified it. No one on the tapes entered the alcove wearing a jacket.

"Will, is there any reason that Judy wouldn't be in here? Maybe someone was shorthanded and pulled her temporarily for other duty."

"Judy is supposed to still be posted there, Maggie."

A shot of dread mixed with fear and fired off inside her.

"That's verified," Will said. "No one pulled her and she wouldn't just walk. Someone removed her, Maggie. I'd bet on it."

"Put out an APB on her."

"Just within the facility?" Will asked.

"No, Will," Maggie answered. "Darcy, take it out, full-scale."

Maggie thought through this again, putting it in perspective, and then added it to the larger picture of events. One person had been conspicuously absent during every incident that had occurred in the last twenty-four hours—the person who initially had seemed most concerned about his facility, and always had been concerned with saving his own job and covering his own backside: Daniel Barone.

The man who knew nothing about anything and now seemed to want it that way, but at first had insisted on knowing everything about everything.

Behavior consistent only with that of a body double.

Someone rapped on the rest room door.

Maggie opened it to a tall, male, security staff member. "Oh, Marty. Good. Glad it's you." She was relieved to see someone she knew. "Stand guard right outside this door until Will gets down here."

"Yes, ma'am."

"No one, I mean no one, goes inside until HAZMAT arrives and removes the bag. When they give the all-clear, the rest room can be opened again, but you don't leave for any reason. Got it?"

"Yes, Captain."

Maggie strode through the thoroughfare to Barone's office, breezed right past a stunned Linda Diel and opened the door to Barone's private office. It was empty. She turned back to Linda. "Have you seen Judy Meyer?"

Seated at her desk, Linda sent Maggie a wide-eyed look. "She'd never be in Mr. Barone's office."

"I'm looking for him, too," Maggie said. "Judy?" she prodded.

"About a half hour ago, she was in the women's rest room, down the hall."

"But you haven't seen her since then?"

"No, I haven't. Why? What's wrong?" Linda straightened. "Oh, God. Has it started?"

"We're okay. Don't panic on me, Linda." Maggie ignored the question and nodded toward Barone's office door. Was he still hiding out under a do-not-disturb order? "Where is he?"

"You know, Captain, I don't have a clue." Linda set her jaw. "Can you believe it?"

Maggie walked over to the desk. Her feet were throbbing. To give them a break, she planted her hip on the corner of the desk, then leaned toward Linda. "No, I can't." His behavior seemed odd to Maggie, but was it to Linda? She knew him far better. "Does he always react oddly to danger?"

"I don't know." She shrugged. "We've never been in danger before." She rolled her eyes. "Maybe he's still at dinner. That was the last I heard anyway. He's not checking in today as he usually does, and he left over two hours ago. He could be anywhere now."

"Did he tell you where he was dining?"

"No, but he never does." Her elbow on her desk, she propped her chin on her hand. "He really values his privacy."

"Today, no one has privacy." A spike of anger stabbed into Maggie's stomach and spread through her chest.

"For what it's worth, I agree no one should, but apparently Mr. Barone does, even today." Linda clearly resented his not keeping her informed on his whereabouts.

"I'm sorry if I was abrasive earlier, Linda," Maggie said. "I've got my hands full and I'm in a hurry."

"It's okay. I'm used to it." She sighed. "People who come in here are always abrasive. I get the complaints Customer Service can't handle. Mr. Barone gets the praise." She added a knowing look. "Besides, everyone's out of sorts today. It's scary as hell, being here." Admiration burned in her eyes. "I don't know how you do this, Maggie."

Sometimes, when she thought about what it cost, neither did she. That's what confused her so much about Justin. She really liked his calmness. Just being with him soothed her. He was smart, quick, easy on the eye and calm—and if she got too close to him, she'd destroy that, too. Just as she had with Jack.

Her job was her job. It'd cost her Jack and, given the opportunity, it'd cost her Justin—or any other man she dared to find interesting. Though Justin was definitely worth the effort and the risks, she just didn't think she could live through another broken heart. "It's my job," she told Linda, then pointed to Barone's door. "Let me know as soon as he gets back, okay?"

"Sure. I'll notify you right away."

"Thanks." Maggie walked out of the office and heard Linda mutter, "God, please just let this day be over."

Maggie couldn't agree more.

Reports started pouring in from Justin, Will and the others. When enough reports had been received citing everything seemed all right, and everyone, except Judy Meyer, was in position and on alert, some of the strain ebbed out of Maggie's shoulders.

She honestly didn't know whether to hope Judy was found or to hope that she wasn't. All stations were searching their sectors and Will had dedicated two men to locating her. Locals and FBI were on watch. Maggie hoped hard and doubted seriously all of that would be enough to assure her safety. If Kunz was involved, Judy could have been removed from the facility and the local area. She could be dead or alive.

"Not to sound bitchy," Kate said to no one in particular, "but if we're all ready and watching and on high-alert, then why do these unexpected incidents keep happening to us?"

"Because we have to be right all the time," Maggie said. "They only have to be right once. Just once. And they already know what they intend to do. We have to figure it out."

Maggie took the corner by Macy's and headed up to check on the forensics team in the short-stack. "Darcy, the locals are in position, as well, correct?"

"Absolutely."

The snow pit was crammed with kids and grown men pretending they were kids. Under other conditions, Maggie would've stopped and just enjoyed watching them play. Instead she headed for the escalator. She scanned the whole way up, spotting Amanda and Kate. Mark Cross was back from dinner and in position near the stage. He was smiling, but anyone who knew him, knew he wasn't missing a thing going on in his sector. Hell, he'd know half the kids by name in fifteen minutes. That was S.A.S.S.'s blessing and likely often Mark's curse.

Maggie stepped off the escalator on Level Three and stopped to check on Donald Freeman. "Anything?"

He sipped from a steaming cup of coffee. "Not really, Captain Holt. Though, since the new netting's been put on, several people have tossed gum wrappers and trash into the round." He shrugged. "Have to expect it, I guess, with no trash cans around. The net has grabbed it all, so far." He hurriedly added, "I've watched it fall, ma'am, so I'm sure nothing has slipped through."

"Excellent. I appreciate your diligence, Donald."

"Yes, ma'am."

She nodded and grabbed her walkie-talkie. "Will, we need a special staff member from Maintenance at Donald's round." Donald lifted his chin, jutted his chest, clearly liking the "his round" reference.

"Specific instructions?"

Good. He hadn't missed her "special" staff request. Being certain Kunz's people were in the facility required them all to be a bit more cryptic in their transmissions, though not so much so that they sacrificed clarity. Odds were good that Kunz was intercepting all the walkie-talkie communications. Maybe some S.A.S.S. ones, too, though they would be significantly more difficult for him. "Yes," she said, considering specific instructions prudent. "Sterile." That would gain them gloves, a new plastic evidence bag, and assure them that nothing from anywhere else in the facility would be added to this evidence bag to contaminate what was gathered there.

"Suspicious, Maggie?"

He meant to determine if she suspected biological contamination. "No, but we can't take chances." Someone had removed the original netting for a specific reason. And until she determined why, she had to exercise extra caution.

"Got it."

She nodded at Donald. "Thanks."

"Yes, ma'am." His smile transformed his face.

Maggie went on to Level Three's short-stack.

A burly guard with a pit-bull face blocked the door. "No entry, ma'am. Sorry. Captain Holt's orders."

"I am Captain Holt, Sergeant," she said, reading his

rank and half expecting him to card her before accepting her identity as positive.

Surprise and then recognition crossed his face. "I'm sorry, ma'am. You look different out of uniform." He stepped aside. "Go ahead."

"No problem." She nodded. "Who's in charge?"

"Lieutenant Lester Pinnella, ma'am."

"Thanks." She walked inside. The short-stack looked totally different, and far less ominous, flooded with light. Halogen spotlights had been set up everywhere. A guy wearing a black jacket with CSI stamped on its back was bent double to the floor, dusting an area with white powder. "Lester Pinnella?" Maggie asked.

He looked up, then around. "Over there, Captain." Clearly recognizing her, he pointed to the center of three men standing near the slatted opening.

Hearing his name, Pinnella turned and watched Maggie approach. His hair was thin on top and graying, and his round face was clean-shaven. Pushing sixty, she figured, and judging by his weathered skin, he'd spent many of them out in the sun. Many men in the local area did. It was the lure of the Gulf of Mexico and fabulous fishing, Maggie guessed, and only in the last couple years had the sunscreen warnings kicked in and become real to them. She extended her hand. "Maggie Holt," she said. "How's it going?"

"I wish I had something positive to report, but we've been over nearly every inch of this place and we haven't found anything I can say definitively will help you."

"What about prints?" There should be a million of them.

"We've got a lot of them, particularly outside the secret

room. But damn few inside it, as you'd expect. We're running those first in the mobile unit outside. So far, no report of any unexpected ones turning up."

"Predictable, but disappointing," she admitted.

"For us, too," he said, well aware of what was at stake. "I'll keep you posted."

Maggie needed a fresh eye and mind. "Lester, walk through this with me, will you?"

"Sure."

"Two people were in here," Maggie said. "Both were attacked. Neither attacked the other—we know that for fact."

"Then there had to be a third person in here."

She nodded. "One did report hearing the retreating footfalls of a third person. The second was verified already down at that point. The two victims left the short-stack together. No one entered or exited between then and the time you arrived. And yet, when the short-stack was unsealed, you found no one inside." He hadn't told her that. "That supposition is correct, yes? The short-stack was empty when you and your team entered?"

"It was empty." Lester confirmed it with his voice and a nod.

"And there is no other way in or out, just the one secure door, correct?"

"That's all we've found," he said, scratching his neck. "But that slat grants me pause, Maggie. If it hadn't been specifically pointed out to us, we might not have found it."

"Same here," she admitted, appreciating his honesty. She'd picked up on its location from the dome because of the window. Not by anything she had seen on the inside. Even with her fingertips, that minute groove had been almost imperceptible. "It's a professional joint, all right."

"Yes, it is." His eyes turned serious. "Only a master craftsman could make a joint like that."

Maggie noted that observation, then shook her head. "Damn it, Lester. Someone else had to be in here. It's the only possible explanation."

"Where?" He looked around, not taking her doubt personally.

Maggie looked, too, but saw nothing except small, stacked boxes, light fixtures and sprinkler heads. "I don't know, damn it. I just don't know."

"Frustrating, to be sure." Lester reached into his pocket and pulled out a toothpick. "But it was just my team in here, Maggie," he insisted, and pulled the toothpick from his mouth. "And Ms. Diel, of course."

Surprise streaked up Maggie's back. "Linda Diel?"

He nodded. "She escorted us up and handled the security code to let us in."

Deflated, Maggie nodded. Of course Barone would insist a mall employee handle the codes. "Well, that's it, then. We're out of possibilities."

"Sorry."

"Me, too." There had to be something else. Had to be. She needed time alone to think. "Let me know if you hit on anything, Lester. And make sure only people on your team enter the short-stack."

"Sure thing," Lester said, turning to a man approaching him with an evidence bag. He took the bag and signed off on its seal. "Go ahead and take it down to the van," Lester told the man, then passed the bag back.

What Lester had said hit Maggie and she clasped his arm. "Lester."

He blinked hard. "Yes?"

"You said you wouldn't have found the slatted door if it hadn't been pointed out to you." Maggie tried not to hang too much hope on him. "Who pointed it out to you?" Linda Diel? If so, then she had to have known the door was there before today.

"Mr. Barone."

"Barone?" But he'd been missing in action for hours. "So he was with Linda when she opened the door for your team?"

"No, he wasn't."

"Then he came in later, after the team was already at work, preparing the scene?"

Lester shrugged. "Actually, I'm not sure exactly when he came in."

"It's okay." Darcy could verify that for Maggie. "Thanks, Lester." She walked away and made a mental note to ask Barone about the secret room. He certainly couldn't deny knowing it existed. Not under these circumstances.

"Darcy, any ideas? I'm tapped out."

"Nothing, Maggie."

"Barone had to already be inside when Linda opened the door for the CSI," Kate insisted. "Had to be."

"I'm with Kate," Amanda said. "Could he have been hiding inside the boxes?"

"They're way too small," Maggie said. "I didn't see one over a foot wide."

Maggie walked back toward the door, slowly studying everything around her.

One of Lester's men called out. "Is Mr. Barone still here?"

Still here? Maggie stopped. Barone was supposedly at dinner—and had been for the past two freaking hours. Maggie walked over to the man. "Excuse me. I'm—"

"I know, Captain Holt. I'm Arthur."

"When was Mr. Barone up here, Arthur?"

"Pretty much ever since we got here. He was waiting for us, and he's been in and out ever since."

"Where?" An icy chill crept up her backbone.

"Excuse me?" Arthur frowned, lost.

"Where was Mr. Barone waiting?" She clarified. "Was he inside or outside the short-stack?"

"I can't say for certain. I presumed he came in from outside, though I did first see him inside," Arthur said. "He declared the place empty and the door secure."

Maggie's blood pumped hard. "Darcy, did you get that?"

"Yeah, I did. But there's nothing on the tape, Maggie."

"Well, the bastard didn't just appear out of thin air."

"He didn't enter after the CSI team arrived, either. We're checking to see if there's any other explanation."

Maggie looked around with a fresh eye and settled on the boxes. Lester walked over and Maggie told him, "Have your people check through the boxes."

"What are we looking for?" He scribbled himself a note.

"Empties," she said. Small or not, the key to where the third person was had to be in them. "Look for ones taped together. Ones that could appear to be small from the outside, but could hide a man inside."

"Damn," he said on a breathy sigh. "You think—"

"It's possible." Maggie stayed noncommittal. "We need to confirm it or rule it out as impossible."

"It's going to take a little time to run the check. I'll get back with you as soon as we know anything."

"Either way," she said, then left the short-stack and headed to the stairs. "Will, talk to Linda and see if Barone's returned from dinner yet." Maggie could check herself, but Linda was scared stiff and seeing Maggie looking for Barone just made her worse. Or was she?

Barone might have returned and Linda might not have forgotten to let Maggie know. Throughout the day Linda had been helping everyone and deflecting those running to Barone with anything. Hell, she could be a player.

Will's voice came through Maggie's walkie-talkie. "Linda says he came back and she told him to contact you immediately, and then he left again. Now he's out, cruising the mall."

Icy claws sank into the back of Maggie's neck and she stepped aside, getting out of the way of a troop of Boy Scouts in a hurry to get downstairs to the snow. They passed her, excited and laughing, and she walked on, a sinking feeling pitting her stomach. A nasty suspicion had formed in her mind and her instincts hummed their agreement with persistent warnings. "Justin?"

"Yeah, Maggie?"

"Where are you?"

"In the administration wing corridor. Do you need something?"

"Your ears," she said, hoping she didn't come to regret not only relying on him but asking for his opinion. "Stay put."

"Oh, very good progress," Darcy teased. "She's needing body parts now."

"Yeah," Kate said. "Who knows? She may eventually work her way up to needing his—"

"Lips!" Amanda cut in quickly, derailing Kate.

"Shut up," Maggie groused. "You guys are never satisfied." She'd had to take more of their ribbing for going to Justin, but the women had run out of ideas on this attacker in the short-stack. She needed fresh insight.

When she rounded the corner at Macy's, she saw Justin.

He walked up to her. "What's up?"

"You know I've believed Kunz has someone working on the inside."

Justin nodded. "I'd say he'd have to, with the way things have been going around here."

"I think it's Barone. But if so, why was he genuinely surprised by the lockbox codes and the C-4?"

"His reaction on that did seem genuine," Justin agreed.

"So you think someone is helping him?"

"Yes, I do."

Maggie studied his face and interpreted what she saw there. "You think whoever is helping him may be doing even more than Barone knows or realizes?"

"If you consider Dr. Cabot's warnings on differentiating people from the doubles, you'd have very little wiggle room on deducing anything except that Barone is a double."

She had. But she liked the analytical way Justin's mind worked. How had he arrived at that conclusion? "Why?"

"Character inconsistencies, across the board."

"Logical." She looked into his eyes. "But there's someone else at work here, too."

"Who?" Justin lifted his shoulder. "Judy Meyer? Is that why she disappeared?"

"It's possible." Maggie spoke softly. "But my money is on Linda Diel."

"Linda?" He frowned. "But she brought in the Red Cross workers."

"Which proved her loyalty at helping us," Maggie said.

Justin chewed at his lip in worry. "I don't know, Maggie. Linda has been first in line to offer help to anyone who asks."

"Of course," Maggie said. "How better to stay informed and current on events?"

"That's true." He frowned. "She could be playing us."

"She opened the secure room and let the forensics team inside the short-stack. Our attacker had to be in there and Barone was, according to Lester, but Darcy saw no place on the film where he went in."

"So he was already there."

"I think he was. I can't prove it."

"And you think he attacked us."

"Yes, I do, but again, I can't prove it."

"And you think Linda is working with him, because if he was inside, then how did she open the coded lock on the short-stack door for the CSI? Only Barone could give her the authority or the code."

"Exactly." Maggie cringed. "Darcy, did you give her the code?"

"No, I didn't."

"There we have it, then."

Justin blew out a breath, reasoned through it. "So Linda sets Barone up as MIA, comes into the security office all harried, looking for him so we all know he's missing, and then while we're looking at him, we're not looking at her."

"Exactly."

"So is Barone working with her or not?"

"I thought, with her, until this chat with you," Maggie said. "Now I find myself thinking that's a good question, and unfortunately, it's one I can't yet answer." Maggie's instincts screamed and she heeded them. "If I'm wrong about Linda, I'll apologize. But if I'm right, she's going to be arrested."

"If you're right, she's lucky she'll be arrested and not shot." Justin shook his head. "Of course, she'll have to make it past Kate."

"Will? Darcy? I want a full staff watch on locating Daniel Barone immediately," Maggie said into the walkie-talkie. "Give it high priority." Should she tag Linda, too? *One bump at a time.* "Where's Linda, Darcy?"

Darcy coordinated and reported back. "In her office."

No harm done there. "If she leaves it, let me know."

Justin smiled at her.

"What?" At the moment Maggie certainly didn't see reason to smile.

"You asked for my opinion. You talked to me about this. Does this mean you've decided I'm not scum and I'm moving up from the bottom of the food chain?" He moved closer, his breath warm on her face. "Do I dare to think you trust me just a little?"

"Um, actually, the team was out of ideas and—"

"Oh, so you needed fresh meat and I just happened to be handy." Disappointment rippled off him. "I get it."

He was insulted, highly insulted, and who could blame him? "No, it wasn't like that." It hadn't been. "I wanted to know what you thought."

"Because?"

"Because I didn't know and...and I don't know exactly

why, Justin. Really." She shrugged. "I just wanted to know what you thought."

He clasped her arms and leaned forward, planted a quick kiss on her forehead. "For now, that's enough."

"Captain Holt." A man paged Maggie on the walkie-talkie. "Captain Holt, do you read me?"

"I read you. Go ahead," she responded, cursing the man's timing.

"It's Lester Pinnella."

"Yeah, Lester. What's up?"

"Hey, that was some hunch you had. We found it."

The boxes. "I'm on my way."

Chapter 10

Maggie shifted and wound through the heavy crowd. At the moment the stairs seemed like the least of all possible evils; everything was crowded. She took them up to Level Three.

Finally she got to the shortstack and, with a nod at Arthur, she cleared the door and went inside.

"Maggie, over here." Lester called, raising his hand and motioning her to the center right, midway to the secret room. The floodlights were on, but she ignored them and checked the bare-bulb fixtures then projected how much light they emitted and where it fell to gauge how clearly one would normally be able to see. The area Lester was in had been chosen as a hiding spot because even when the lights were on, it fell dead-center in the dark between two fixtures.

She walked around the far side of the stacked boxes, saw

a waist-high stack taped together on one side that swung open like a door. "Anything inside?"

"Nothing obvious," he said. "But we're moving it to the lab to do microscopic studies. If there's anything at all— a flake of skin, a strand of hair—we'll find it."

She nodded and motioned to the taped boxes. "Is this the only stack rigged to make a closet someone can get in?"

"Yes, it is. We've double-checked all of the boxes, and the others are normal."

Maggie nodded. "Thank you, Lester." Finally proof that someone could be in here and go undetected. The tape proved Barone hadn't come into the short-stack after forensics, but that he was here all along. So Barone had been here, had attacked Justin and Maggie, and then had hidden inside the boxes until Linda had let the forensics team into the short-stack. Once Forensics was inside and work was under way, Barone had simply stepped out of the boxes, and then out of the shadows—into plain sight.

Lester put his pen in his pocket. "It was a good hunch, Maggie."

"I got lucky," she said with a little smile.

His eyes burned bright. "I expect you get lucky a lot."

Not as often as she would like. "Hopefully, often enough to prevent a catastrophe here."

Lester looked down at the ground, then back at her. "Word gets around, Maggie, especially when the people walking in realize what they're likely walking into." He clasped her shoulder. "Regardless of what happens, no one could have given more or tried harder to stop this bastard."

Absolution. Reassurance. Both given by a man who had obviously had operations go south on him at some time in his past. His somber eyes turned earnest. "I've learned a thing or two over the years, Maggie, and one thing I know is guilt can eat you up inside. Failure haunts a person."

"Yes, it does." She knew that too well, personally and professionally.

"No matter how this turns out there is no reason for you to think you could've done more. You couldn't."

Touched by his compassion, Maggie nodded. Often contention between outsiders like her and the locals became a problem. But she'd seen none of that here. Barone aside, quite the opposite had been the case, and she was grateful for that. "Thank you, Lester." Her voice sounded thick and gravelly. She tried to suppress her emotional reaction but, hell, she was human and she couldn't. This mattered too much. The results of whatever happened would be with her forever, and there was no getting around that.

"Lester," a man shouted.

"On my way, Harvey." Lester smiled at her, then went over to consult with Harvey.

Maggie walked the short-stack again, more to absorb nuances than because she expected to find anything new, and to think through events and dissect them. As she did so, one thing already clear became more so, and that was the character inconsistency with Daniel Barone.

He'd been adamant about being briefed prior to any action being taken, about being intimately involved on every facet of the operation in the entire facility. He'd been an extreme micromanager. And yet after Maggie and Justin had returned from Regret late yesterday afternoon, Barone had been scarce, available only when summoned, and not always even then. Definitely dealing with two different people.

Certainty pounded through her, rolled over her in sickening waves, and Maggie stopped. Had to be a Kunz body double. In the past, he'd used them not just for himself, but as Colonel Drake had told Justin, Kunz had used them for key players in some of his high-level, high-stakes operations.

That had to be happening again. Historically the doubles were up close to the S.A.S.S. and involved, feeding Kunz inside information. But maybe in those cases, the doubles had required more extensive training for their missions. Maybe, due to time constraints, or to keep the need-to-know loop extra tight—which Kunz was always fastidious about doing—Barone's double hadn't gotten that training. Maybe Barone's double had Barone's physical attributes but not Barone's history, background or knowledge base down pat. Maybe there hadn't been time, or maybe Kunz thought the three-month absence would be too obvious or for whatever reason, Kunz planned this operation so that Barone's double just had to show up, to gain intel but not actively participate in the capabilities demonstration. Just show up, refuse to shut down the mall, then stay out of the way.

Was that possible?

Maggie thought it through, examining the situation from all sides and dissecting every aspect, every single incident. "Oh, God. It's possible," she murmured to herself, slightly dazed.

But is it feasible?

To make that call with a high degree of confidence, she needed more information. Yet she feared it was more than feasible.

She feared it was fact.

* * *

Justin met up with Maggie in the food court and they shared a cup of coffee needed more for the cover than because either needed to add a jolt of caffeine to spike their already elevated adrenaline levels.

Grateful that Colonel Drake had authorized full disclosure to Justin, Maggie quickly shared her deductions and suspicions, and with that discussion, also transmitted them to Darcy. "I believe Barone attacked us in the short-stack and then hid in the boxes until Lester and the forensics team showed up. That's the only way the facts add up and make sense."

"It's probable," Justin said, making a steeple with his fingers atop the table. "I don't remember seeing him during the time the short-stack was sealed. Did Darcy?"

Maggie smiled. Justin had forgotten that Darcy overheard every word spoken. "Darcy, did you spot Barone elsewhere at any time during the short-stack lockdown?" she asked.

"No, I didn't. The colonel and I have reviewed events and find Barone being the attacker plausible and troubling."

"You should," Amanda interjected. "We all should."

Maggie rimmed her cup with the tips of her fingers. "This sounds eerily familiar, doesn't it? Like one of Kunz's substitutions."

"We agree that it does, Maggie," Darcy said, speaking for her and Colonel Drake.

"Definitely," Kate added, though at that point, the possibility was pretty well regarded as a consensus.

"And he's still MIA?"

"So far," Darcy said.

Maggie sipped at her coffee then unclipped her walkie-talkie. "Will?"

"Yeah, Maggie?"

"Have you noticed any significant differences in Barone's behavior today?"

"To tell you the truth, I haven't seen him enough to be able to answer that with any certainty of being right, Maggie. We've given priority to locating him for over an hour and no one's caught so much as a glimpse of him. I can tell you that's not consistent with his typical behavior. Usually he's in everyone's face."

"Which precisely proves my point," Amanda said.

"Wasn't he in the security office when you discovered the codes had been changed?" Kate asked.

"That was later," Maggie said. "When you were disarming the lockbox."

"Well," Amanda said. "It doesn't really matter either way where he was then. It proves nothing. Kunz has pulled multiple simultaneous sightings on us several times. Remember that when he held me hostage, I saw my double in my own kitchen."

A double still at large.

Maggie remembered the event. That was when S.A.S.S. first learned that Kunz had created body doubles. God, what a firestorm that news had caused. And even after Amanda had successfully handled her mission, the news didn't get better.

Kunz had been apprehended and, *after* being tried and convicted of crimes, had supposedly been incarcerated in Leavenworth. Only S.A.S.S. discovered on its next mission that the prisoner it held hadn't been Kunz. It'd been a body double. Then, on a subsequent mission, Kunz had supposedly been killed in a GRID compound when it exploded. Only that man hadn't been Kunz, either. He'd been another body double. And on still another subsequent S.A.S.S. mission, Kunz supposedly had been in a Middle Eastern cave at the time it had been taken down by S.A.S.S. operatives. Only later, it turned out that the man there hadn't been Kunz, either. He'd been yet another body double.

If Kunz had created and inserted multiple body doubles for himself, then he damn well could do it for Barone. Kunz had also created doubles for several of his previous business partners. That, the S.A.S.S. knew for fact, having gone up against them. Darcy had been directly involved in such a case on a mission at the Mexico/Texas border where Kunz had an operation to bomb White House spectators gathered to watch the July Fourth celebration—an attack that Darcy had successfully prevented.

That Barone was likely one of Kunz's body doubles was but one of the many other possibilities they needed to factor into the situation until they could eliminate them. Maggie issued a new order. "Will, casually ask Linda if she has noticed anything abnormal in Barone's behavior."

"Sure, Maggie."

She switched to S.A.S.S. frequency, looked Justin right in the eye. "Darcy?"

"Yeah?" She seemed a little surprised at the frequency shift.

"When Will asks Linda about Barone, monitor her reaction."

Worry doubled in Justin's eyes and he reached across the table and clasped Maggie's hand. He understood the pressure she felt. It was bad enough having to fight outsiders, but the work became exponentially more difficult when you had to fight outsiders and enemies within.

Maggie gently squeezed his fingertips, swallowed her fear of her feelings for him, and held on tight.

"What exactly are you expecting from Linda?" Darcy asked.

Maggie swallowed the bitterness coating her tongue and throat. "A revelation."

Ten minutes later Lester gave Maggie an update, which was to say that his forensics team hadn't come up with anything else of consequence.

Donald Freeman at the round had more trash that needed to be collected, but nothing had gone through the net.

Mark Cross at the Center Court stage had caught two young women stealing coats from a troop of Cub Scouts playing in the snow and he turned them over to Marty from Security. The police were called in to handle them.

Justin checked in on his medical staff. The sound-off went down without a hitch. The prepositioned vials of antidote were verified safe by the undercover medical personnel. Local medical reinforcements were on standby status and gathered in the north and south parking garages. Local police were subsidizing the extra security staff Will had activated with the A-stores' blessings, reinforcing patrols of the open parking lots, watching for yellow-jacketed people carrying Krane's handled shopping bags and entering the mall.

The FBI reported that they'd followed the two men Maggie and Justin had intercepted earlier to an upscale restaurant on the dock in the harbor. They'd had no contact with anyone else, and it appeared that ditching the bag at the mall had been their entire assignment in the mission. The same seemed true of Mr. Ponytail and the first female bagger, who were still stashed in their hotel rooms, gorging on football games and a moviefest.

The Threat Integration Center reported there had been no activity whatsoever at any of the other potential targets, but it wasn't ready yet to declare Santa Bella an official GRID-attack target, due to insufficient evidence that directly linked GRID or Thomas Kunz to the incidents that had taken place.

Matt Elden also reported in to Maggie that he had four HAZMAT teams on-site in the parking lot, cooling their heels with all the other specialists. If biological contamination occurred, they were equipped and prepared to launch decontamination protocols.

And Judy Meyer, the guard assigned to monitor the rest room in the administration wing who'd disappeared without a trace, still hadn't been located.

In a corridor on Jewelry Row, Maggie stepped out of the heavy foot traffic, a steady thump pounding in her already-aching head. Juggling all the different aspects of the operation was a challenge, but she had a strong team. It was the waiting getting to her—knowing Kunz would strike, and that his window of opportunity was closing.

Maggie checked her watch. It was 7:45. In an hour and fifteen minutes, the Olympians and Special Forces would be leaving. Kunz would strike while they were here, which meant the launch clock was running down fast.

"Maggie." Darcy's voice split the moment of silence,

sounding tinny and brittle in Maggie's earpiece. "Linda told Will she had seen Barone within the last twenty or thirty minutes and she'd mentioned to Barone that Will needed to see him. Barone told her he'd handle Will, and he was going to visit the A-store owners. He's feeling too antsy to sit still. As soon as he left, she made a phone call. We're running down the trace to see to whom."

Maggie catalogued that information, adding it to the mix. "She's definitely placing Barone back in his office."

"She did, Maggie. She didn't parse words." Darcy let out a little moan of disappointment. "The problem is, Barone hasn't been to his office. Colonel Drake ran the surveillance tapes as soon as Linda made the claim. Barone doesn't appear anywhere on them."

"So is she covering for him? Or is she diverting attention to him?"

"She's playing both sides," Darcy said. "That's pretty clear. But whether she's doing it to protect him and thus protect her job, or because the two of them have a premeditated conspiracy going on, who knows? Those are, it seems, significant questions at this point."

"Some of them, absolutely." Unfortunately there were more questions and far too few answers. "Linda could be acting independently or in collusion with Kunz, Darcy."

"Yes, she could be."

"How long before we know who she called?" Heading back to Center Court, Maggie saw a teenager with spikes implanted in his head. He'd swear it was a fashion statement. She'd swear it was a cry for attention.

"A minute. Maybe, two."

In the food court, Justin stood and stretched. A guy

from the housekeeping staff was making the rounds, collecting trash left on tables and stuffing it in a plastic bag. Maggie watched him, watched Justin watching him, and wondered if much slipped past Justin.

"It's a rotator, Maggie," Darcy said. "We've been through seven countries, so far. She's dialed a freaking rotator."

"Damn it." Maggie couldn't believe it. They couldn't seem to catch a break with both hands.

"What does that mean?" Justin asked her.

"It means we won't be getting a trace. It means Linda Diel's definitely working against us." Maggie walked to the edge of the pit. She glanced at the Olympians and the Special Forces playing with them. The guys were laughing and goofing around, but they were aware and cutting questioning glances at Maggie.

Giving them reassuring nods, she unclipped her walkie-talkie. "Will?"

"I'm here, Maggie."

"I want constant observation on Linda. She goes nowhere, does nothing we don't know immediately. You get a feed on her and, Will, get it now."

"Sure thing. What about Barone?"

Barone? Hell, the real Barone couldn't even be involved. It could be just Linda, working with Kunz and a Barone body double. "What kind of car does Barone drive?"

"A black BMW," Will said. "He parks in the management lot, right outside the administration offices."

Maggie started walking. "What's the closest way to get there? Door Six?"

"That's right. Level One, Door Six," Will responded.

"Exit and then make an immediate right. His BMW should be directly in front of you."

Maggie moved in that direction behind three generations of women exchanging candid remarks about which male movie star had the cutest butt. Personally, of those mentioned, Maggie's vote went to Brad Pitt.

She stepped around the grandmother and cut down Men's Row, glancing into store windows as she passed by them. Sir Scot's was swarming with shoppers, but the checkout line for Handersham's extended out into the thoroughfare. Maggie arced around it and saw a gorgeous camelhair sweater in the window at Breck's. Two men standing outside were on Will's security team. She returned their nods and kept walking. The exit door was straight ahead.

She pushed through it.

Cool, crisp air rushed over her and chilled her skin. Shivering, she looked around. It was dark now, but the area was well-lighted. Hanging a right, she walked straight ahead to the parking slot marked Mall Administrator.

No black BMW was parked in it. The slot was empty.

Chapter 11

"I don't know, Darcy." Maggie walked back inside the mall and went up to Level Two, uncertain what to think. "Barone—the real one—could be innocent and have bugged out because he was afraid. I wouldn't cross that off as a possibility, considering he freaked about the lockbox codes being changed. Actually he's been hiding out since then." Anyone with sense would be afraid. He had to know that the clock was running out, too, which certainly wouldn't inspire him to hang around. "He might have been taken away, or lured away, or, hell, he might not have been here at all. We could've been dealing with a double ever since Justin and I returned from Regret to Santa Bella last night. That's when he began acting differently." Frustration raced through her, tightened her chest and left a bitter taste in her mouth. "There's just no way to be certain about this."

"We've been doing frame comparisons on him between yesterday and today, and we've noted a significant number of inconsistencies, Maggie. That was a hell of a catch," Darcy said. "Colonel Drake's called in Morgan to take a look."

Officially, Dr. Morgan Cabot was a psychologist and subject-matter expert affiliated with S.A.S.S. Confidential, a sister investigative unit also under Colonel Drake's command but tasked with very different missions. Maggie's S.A.S.S. unit had often relied on Morgan's expertise and training. Maggie had relied on her even more so. She'd been terrific at helping her work through this business with Jack, which oddly didn't seem as significant as it had for the past three years. "She's the reason I caught them—her training."

"I'll be sure to tell her. She'll be pleased staying awake has paid off."

Maggie remembered telling Morgan she'd attend the training and if she could stay awake, she'd be back for more. Morgan considered that fair enough. Maggie had stayed awake and often on the edge of her seat, and she'd been back as often as Morgan held training sessions. Everyone respected Morgan's opinion—even Kate—and God knew her respect was hard-won. "Has Morgan reported back to you yet with her opinion?"

"Coming in now," Darcy said. "She says Barone's verbiage isn't consistent—both word choices and phraseology—and even more telling, his innate expressions and body language are significantly different. Far outside the perimeters defined as normal."

"So we agree on all that. What's her professional, bottom line? Is Barone really Barone, or is he one of Kunz's body doubles?"

"We have no hard evidence that Barone was ever Barone. It's possible we've dealt with the real Barone or that we've dealt exclusively with a body double. We just don't know. But Morgan is certain that we've been dealing with two different men."

Knowing it and hearing it confirmed were two different things. For a second Maggie's legs went weak. She locked her knees and took in a sharp breath, her mind reeling. "You'd better compile a full-frame listing of every inch of tape we've got on him and get it to the Threat Integration Center STAT for high-priority review. Also, put out an APB on him, and personally alert the FBI agents working this case." Whether he was himself or a double didn't matter. Whether he was working for Kunz or he was Kunz's victim didn't matter at the moment so much as neutralizing the man. They needed him secured, not loose and able to create havoc.

"What about Linda Diel?" Kate asked.

Maggie weighed her options. "I want her secured, too."

"She might make a further move that would help us." Amanda added her opinion.

"No, I don't think so. She dialed a rotator, not a GRID operative or Kunz's operations base. That's likely all she's got. We all know that Kunz works in segments. He compartmentalizes assignments to keep even his own operatives working in the dark to secure his missions as much as possible. He wouldn't empower someone on the inside, much less someone like Linda, with much of anything on the off chance that we picked up on them."

"Maggie's right. That is the way he operates," Kate said. "He holds his cards close to the chest and never tells anyone anything they don't absolutely have to know."

Again Kate had surprised Maggie, backing her up. She rounded the corner by Macy's.

"Maggie," Justin interrupted. "I know you're up to your ears in Barone, but something's wrong here."

She stopped, not sure where she was needed. "Where's here, Justin?"

"Center Court, outer end. I'm with the Olympians and Special Forces, and I've spotted some trouble."

"What's wrong?"

"Poorly put. I *smell* trouble," he amended himself. "Scents at the pit have been pretty vague. Now, all of a sudden, I'm getting blasted with apples and cinnamon."

Maggie started running. "Kate?"

"Yeah, now I'm getting it, too."

"Amanda?"

"Ditto," she said. "I'm looking for a natural cause, but I'm damned if I see anything, Maggie. Mark, how about you?"

"No cause identified here. The scent is light near the stage, but it is discernable. Could be masked by all the smells coming from the food court."

Maggie called Will and told him what was happening.

Will muttered. "I'm on my way down there. Every stair, escalator and elevator is jammed."

"Where are you?"

"Freeman's round. He saw someone trying to shove something through the net and called a code."

"Why didn't I hear it?"

Darcy answered. "You were special frequency just then. It's not a problem. It's been checked out. Just a wad of chewing gum big enough to choke a horse. Male teen. He's been cleared and released."

"Now, I'm smelling lime," Justin said. "It's really strong."

"Me, too," Kate said.

Amanda and Mark reported the same thing, and again Mark reported the scent as faint while the others tagged it overpowering.

"Damn it," Maggie cut loose, hemmed in by shoppers slogging down the Level Two thoroughfare. "I can't get through."

"Stand by, Maggie," Will said. "I've got a visual on you. We'll take the shortcut."

"What shortcut?"

Seconds later Will stood beside her. "This way."

Maggie followed him in a run into the elevator.

They rode down and the door opened. He led her out, then shoved through the door marked No Exit she had seen several times earlier. Maggie recognized the little alcove between Security and Medical in the administration wing. On the plans, it was a shallow closet.

In reality the closet was an elevator. A small closet door was positioned beside it.

A chasm of fear cracked open in her. "Darcy, are you seeing this?"

"Yes, I am, damn it. It wasn't on the plan, Maggie. It was just a utility closet on the plan."

"That's the way I remembered it, too." Had this been the way Judy Meyer had been removed from the women's rest room? Not one word had surfaced on her; she was still missing without a trace.

"Barone had the elevator installed about a month ago. Only mall management and security staff have access to it."

Maggie walked back to it, looking for evidence Judy

Meyer had been in it. She glanced down at the floor inside the elevator. Something shiny caught her eye. Bending, she lifted the metal piece and examined it carefully.

"What is it?" Darcy asked.

"It looks like a valve off the snow machine." Maggie gnawed at her lip with her teeth, concentrating. "Now why would that be in here?" Harry and Phil Jensen, the snow company's owners, had no need for the elevator. They entered Santa Bella through Level One, Door One and walked straight to Center Court.

Will shrugged. "Maybe Mr. Barone insisted they be discreet and out of the way of shoppers, too."

"Discreet about what? They never left Level One. What would they do on any other level?"

"No idea. But Barone is the only one who can grant permission for anyone to use this elevator."

"Is he?" She recalled Linda and the Red Cross medical workers. "Darcy, is Linda in custody yet?"

"We're looking for her, Maggie. She went out on a break just before you issued the order."

"Outside the mall?"

"She said inside, but she's not at Emerald Bay or in the food court. We're still searching the restaurants for her."

Will frowned. "She could have let Phil and Harry on the elevator. Linda acts as an escort around here all the time."

She had escorted Lester Pinnella and his forensics team to the short-stack. Will paused a long moment, and Maggie saw the wheels in his mind turning in his eyes. "What's wrong, Will?"

"I think we've got bad trouble. But not with Barone. With Linda."

Maggie thought so, too. "It's complicated because she's in on the walkie-talkie communications with the security staff."

"Actually, she's not." Will waited for the door to open. "I pulled her equipment early on."

Maggie stepped off the elevator. "Why?"

He looked slightly uncomfortable. "Remember when she fixed up the Red Cross workers for us?"

"Yes."

"That didn't quite sit right. I figured if she worked for Barone and crossed him at the drop of a dime, she'd cross anyone else, too. If she'd needed convincing, I'd have felt better about it. But she suggested it right away, and that just didn't sit right, so I unplugged her."

"Well, thank God for your instincts, Will. I'm glad you followed them."

"Under the circumstances, me, too."

Maggie nodded at the door. "Put a guard on that elevator. No one uses it."

Will issued the order and a skinny, redheaded woman about thirty, named Cindy Pratt, took the post. Maggie recalled Donald Freeman telling her that Judy Meyer and Cindy Pratt had taken shifts at the round near Grimes and Stokes.

"Maggie," Justin said. "I'm smelling orange now. It's stronger than the other scents were."

"Darcy, get maintenance to check the heating filters."

"We just did. They're clear."

Maggie and Will ran, rounded the Macy's corner. A man stepped into Maggie's path, shot out his arm. It slammed against Maggie's throat. She flew backward, fell on the tile floor and skidded across its slick surface.

A barrel-chested man attacked Will, landed a powerful right cross to his jaw that lifted Will off his feet. He was out cold before he hit the floor.

"Will's down. Will's down. Two attackers." Maggie scrambled, spun—and got hosed full in the face with pepper spray. She gasped. "Darcy? Help me. I can't see!"

"Urgent assist. Urgent assist," Darcy put out an All-Call for help. "Corner of Macy's and Center Court, Level One. Will's out. Maggie's been pepper sprayed. Zero visibility," Darcy relayed, responding to anxious queries. "Urgent assist."

"Hold positions on Center Court." Kunz would use this opening to launch the DR-27. "Darcy!" Maggie cried.

"Forget rules," Colonel Drake insisted. "Go with your instincts, Maggie."

"Number One is at three o'clock—four feet out," Darcy said. "Number Two is hanging back—twelve feet at eight o'clock. Move right, thirty degrees and kick straight out, waist-high."

Maggie did exactly what Darcy said, felt her foot collide with his body, followed rushed instructions to feign left, fall back, move in, jab, hook, kick and duck.

He clipped her chin, jabbed her shoulder, but failed to land a solid punch.

"Back off, you son of a bitch!" Justin shouted, swooshing by her and slamming into the man.

Maggie had no idea what happened then; she couldn't see, couldn't distinguish the flurry of movements sensed. "Darcy? What's going on? What's going on?"

"They've hauled ass, Maggie. Just disappeared off the monitor. Justin, too. He's gone after them."

"God, I hope he doesn't catch them," Maggie said, her voice shaking. "They're pros." She fumbled in her fanny pack for her eye drops.

"You got your wish. They're outside, Darcy," Justin stated.

"Thanks, Dr. Crowe," Darcy said. "Relaying to locals."

A man rushed up to Maggie, breathing hard and heavy. "Are you okay?"

"Justin?" Relief washed over her. "No, I can't find my neutralizing solution. Help me."

"Describe the solution. What's it in?" He dug through the pack, his heaved breaths mixing with hers.

"Small, round, frosty-white. Green label."

"Got it." He pulled out the little bottle. "Tilt your head back."

She did, and he held her chin, put the drops in her eyes that would negate the effects of the spray. "Damn it, that hurts."

"I'm sorry. Any better?"

"Yes." She blinked hard several times and her eyes finally cleared. "Thank you, Justin." Her voice sounded ragged and raw.

"Thanks for trusting me." He seemed pleased about that, but then worry tensed his face again. "You really are okay, right?"

She nodded. "My throat hurts, but I'm okay." She rubbed at her neck, soothing the area clotheslined by that jerk, which would definitely be bruised, and looked around. Will was sprawled on the floor. A security guard bent over him. "Oh, God, Will!" She ran over, asked the guard, "Is he—"

"He's fine, ma'am. Just getting his wits back. He took a hard fall. Cracked his head."

"Does he need it checked out?" Maggie asked.

"Damn right, he does," Kate chimed in, sounding worried sick.

"I probably do." Will answered for himself. He grunted and grumbled and gained his feet. "But there's no reason to check it now. I'll do it later."

"Will, no," Kate's voice insisted through her walkie-talkie. "You get Medical to look you over."

"I'm okay, Katie. You've my word on it."

He looked charmed by her fussing over him, and Maggie imagined he was. Will was a widower and he had no children or other living relatives. But it seemed he now had a Katie—and a Katie now had him. Maggie smiled.

"Damn it." The befuddled expression left Will's face and he frowned. "They got away from us, didn't they?"

"Security picked them up outside," Darcy said. "FBI will be taking custody of them momentarily." Maggie relayed the message to Will.

"Do I dare hope we've gotten a break?" Maggie then asked.

"I wouldn't," Amanda said. "Thomas Kunz doesn't give breaks. His backup plan to his backup plan just kicks in."

Kate groaned her agreement, then added, "Mystery solved on the scents. The bakery near the food court busted the ban on adding scents to the vents positioned near their registers. We've been attacked by aromatherapy. Hot cinnamon buns and apple cider. Employee didn't get the word."

There was always that ten percent who didn't get the word, or who weren't paying attention when they had.

"What about the lime and orange?" Those were the scents that most worried Maggie. Citrus scents were often used to mask biological contaminates.

"Those, too," Kate said. "The filters have been removed, and the scents are fading fast."

"Good news is always welcome," Maggie said.

"Will?" Kate called him.

"Yes, Katie?"

"Don't damn scare me like that again."

"My most humble apologies, Katie girl."

"You're really okay, right?" Kate asked, sounding totally vulnerable in a way Maggie never before had heard her sound. "You're not just bullshitting me to get out of seeing a doc?"

"I'm fine. I gave you my word."

Concern and reassurance. So tender and touching, and humbling to receive. This was a rare privilege for a S.A.S.S. operative to see, much less experience. The secretive nature of their work made intimate relationships very difficult, and observing moments like this were so unique they were treasured. A little hitch settled in Maggie's heart.

Justin curled an arm around her waist. "Come on, Maggie."

Given what was sure to be a short moment without crises, Maggie and Justin walked to Center Court. Watching the Olympians pelt the Special Forces with hand-packed snowballs brought a smile even to the most cynical of faces. Maggie felt her lips curl and spread, and she risked a sideways glance at Justin, not at all surprised to see him smiling, too. She elbowed him lightly. "You're a soft touch."

He grunted and touched her face. "Only where you're concerned," he said. "Then, yeah, I guess, I am."

Far happier about that than she should be, Maggie bit back a smile. Her heart tripped over its own beat. A tingle started at the base of her spine and shot up through her shoulders. "That's a pretty strong statement to make to a woman, Justin." It would be if it was true. And God help her, she wanted it to be true. But he didn't keep promises to women, and this was no time to forget that.

"Strong or weak, what is just is," he said softly. "Sometimes, Maggie, we can't dictate what we feel. Smart or stupid, logical or insane, we just have to accept what we feel as real and valid."

"I'm not sure I find that flattering." She looked up into his eyes, risked saying out loud the fears deepest in her mind. So deep they left their imprint on her soul. "I trusted my heart and it betrayed me. I'm not sure even now that it's recovered. The head has to rule the heart, Justin. I learned that much. Emotions can turn on a dime."

"I know what you mean." He sent her a sympathetic look. "But life just doesn't work out that way. The sooner you accept it, the happier you'll be."

She swallowed hard, inspired to believe him, tempted to act. She opened her mouth to tell him, but fear bit her hard. "I—I can't live any other way."

"Because you choose not to, Maggie," he said. "It is your choice to make."

"Control is power. Don't you see that I can't ever again relinquish control?"

"You sound as if you did, you'd be lining yourself up for an execution."

"More or less." Her throat hurt. "I don't want to be crushed again."

"Neither do I, and I well might be." He shrugged. "I've been clear about my interest. I care about you, Maggie. The only clues I've had about your feelings for me are that you asked for my opinion, and you allowed me to put drops in your eyes. That's not a lot for a man to hang his heart on."

He'd hung his heart? He'd thought about hanging his heart? Her own heart beat hard and fast, thumping against her ribs. She didn't know how to respond to that. Wasn't sure she wanted to think about that just now, much less talk about it. The thing was, she had to be honest with herself, and what she was feeling. Boy, was she feeling. He'd released a whole barrage in her, and her emotions ran full spectrum from fabulous to frightening.

"Be brave, Maggie. It's your nature."

With her life, yes, maybe. But this was her heart. She stared hard at him, blinked. "I think this talk would be best saved for later."

"Coward."

She had been, and she deserved better from herself. He deserved better from her, too. Her mouth turned as dry as dust. She pulled up her courage and faced him. "It seems as if we're a team, Crowe. I haven't figured out why, or what that means yet. Maybe you've got it all sorted out."

He let out a shuddery sigh and the tension in his face turned to relief. "Later, when every word isn't being heard by half the county, I'm going to do what I've wanted to do every time you get that look on your face."

"Damn," Kate said. "Inquiring minds want to know."

"Shut up, Kate," Darcy said. "This is private."

Private? Maggie doubted they knew the meaning of the word.

"Hell, it's all been private, Darcy," Kate came back at her. "This is the good part."

"Maybe so, Kate," Colonel Drake said. "But we've been officially excluded. Accept it."

"Hardly seems fair, Colonel," Mark Cross, who'd had the good sense to keep his mouth shut until now, chimed in.

"Mark?" Justin sounded shocked. "You've been listening in, too?"

"Yeah, sure," Mark said. "I just have enough smarts to keep my mouth closed—so I don't get shut out of the good parts."

"Careful, Cross," Amanda said. "You're treading on dangerous territory with those kinds of remarks."

Totally exasperated, Maggie had to control herself to keep from screaming. "Will you guys shut up and butt out?"

"We apologize," Kate said. "Everyone means it but me. I'd be lying, so I'm holding out."

"Whatever, Kate." Maggie turned her focus to Justin. "What look was that you were talking about, Justin?"

He let out a little chuckle. "The adorable one that says you have plenty to say but are too afraid to let yourself say it." A twinkle lighted his eyes.

That was true about at least half her professional work and about nearly everything in personal life. "I look forward to exploring that…later."

Disappointed groans from the others tied up the radio.

Almost shy, Justin smiled, checked his watch, then ordered a sound-off from all the undercover medical personnel.

"Dr. Crowe," a man said in a rushed voice.

"Yes?" Justin said.

"Dr. Crowe, this is Mike Mapleton on Level Three. It's gone, sir. I don't know how, but it's gone. I haven't left my station—but it's all gone."

Justin tensed. "What's gone, Mike?"

"The antidote, sir." Mike sounded panicked. "It's gone, sir. Every vial of the antidote is gone. All that's left are the empty boxes."

Chapter 12

"Justin?" Maggie stood at Center Court. Hundreds of people were crammed in and around the pit, and the noise level was deafening, the mood light and gay, in stark contrast to that of those in the need-to-know loop. They were hyperalert. "Run a full verification on the antidote vials," Maggie said "Do it now."

He immediately called for a sound-off, adding, "Check the boxes. I want an eyes-on the actual vials."

"Level Three, Station One. Oh, no. It's gone. All of it is gone!"

Maggie's stomach knotted. She looked across the pit. Amanda, Kate and Mark were at their posts, scanning for signs of trouble, certainly as disturbed by the findings as Maggie.

"Level Three, Station Two. Gone, sir."

"Level Three, Station Three. I—I can't believe it. Gone, sir. Every single vial. Dr. Crowe, I haven't moved from this station. I swear it. How could this happen?"

"Later, Three-Three," Justin said. "Right now, we need to focus on total status. What's your report, Three-Four?" Justin sounded as impatient and stunned as Maggie felt.

"Empty, Dr. Crowe. I haven't taken my eyes off these boxes but every damn one of them is empty."

And so it went, from the top of the facility all the way down to Level One, Station Six.

Maggie turned clammy cold. "Justin, do you know what the hell happened?"

"Give me two minutes, Maggie." He then went back to the sound-off general frequency he'd been using since his first status report check.

In ninety seconds he reported back. "The last eyes-on vial check was before dinner, Maggie. None of the undercover medical personnel checked the actual vials on returning from their dinner breaks. They just counted boxes."

Maggie silently cursed, the taste in her mouth bitter. "And the substitutes covering for the undercover medical personnel during dinner had been arranged by the same person who had arranged for the Red Cross volunteer medical staff in the first place."

"That's right, Maggie," Justin said. "Linda Diel."

"Damn it." Kate let out a heartfelt huff. "She took it out during the changeover."

Darcy piped in. "No one walked out of the facility with vial boxes, Maggie. I'm positive of it."

"No, the boxes are all still here," Justin said.

"We pulled the handled Krane's shopping bags off the

sales floor when the baggers started bringing them inside empty."

That would have been nice for Maggie to know. "Who pulled them, Amanda?"

"Officially, the Krane's store manager, but Linda actually secured the bags."

"Which means she had access to them to give them to the medical subs to package and remove the vials. But how did she get the bags to them?" Maggie asked. "She's been missing since right before I issued the order to secure and detain her."

"Maggie," Justin piped in. "I've just been told by one of the medical personnel that Linda has been making courtesy calls on every station all afternoon, checking to see if the volunteers need anything."

"Yet she's avoided all of security looking for her?" Kate asked.

"Easily," Maggie said. "It's a madhouse in here."

"True," Darcy said. "If she didn't want to be seen, she could arrange it."

"So she visited each of the stations during the time the subs were manning them," Kate said. "How did she get the vials out?"

Maggie covered every potential scenario and landed on a probable explanation. "What about the private elevator?" She could have moved them using it.

"Definite possibility," Darcy said. "We didn't know about that elevator at that time, Maggie. There's no monitor there. It was wide open until you posted Cynthia Pratt on it."

Judy Meyer knew the elevator was there. Had she gotten in Linda's way? Is that what had happened to her?

"Will," Maggie said into her walkie-talkie. "Get Cynthia Pratt, STAT."

He paged her, but got no response and then tried her again.

Still no response.

Terrified she knew what had happened, Maggie broke through the dense crowd, rushed to the administration wing's alcove. "That elevator has to be it, Darcy."

"Judy could've gotten in Linda's way," Darcy said.

"I've been thinking the same thing. I'm on my way there now."

"Colonel Drake's reviewing tapes, Maggie. She's seeing a pattern form."

Cutting through Macy's, Maggie exited right down the thoroughfare from the security office. "What pattern?"

"After the dinner breaks for our regulars, the substitutes filling in for them left the stations with handled shopping bags. All of them had made purchases, so the bags did hold merchandise. I dismissed them as unimportant." Recrimination filled her voice. "But all of the subs converged at that damn elevator, Maggie. *All* of them."

"Linda delivered the shopping bags to them at the time they made their purchases. The subs put the vials in the bags and after the regulars returned, the subs delivered the bags to Linda." Oh, man. This was bad. Really, really bad.

"That's highly probable. We don't have full three-sixty vision on these stations. Being familiar with Santa Bella's cameras limitations, Linda knows that." Darcy cursed. "Damn it, I shouldn't have dismissed that." Something cracked, as if she'd slammed a fist to her desk. "She had the subs walk right out with the freaking antidote vials."

"It's not your fault, Darcy. Let's focus and go forward from where we are now." Frustration and fear mingled in Maggie. The entire mall—everyone in it—was wide open to attack with no defense. "Contact the Threat Integration Center and General Shaw. I want to close the mall immediately." They were just too vulnerable without the antidote on-site.

A scant few minutes later Darcy returned. "Colonel Drake's requesting permission, Maggie."

She waited, knowing the longer it took for a response, the less the odds were for agreement.

"Denied." Darcy sounded as frustrated as Maggie felt.

Kate erupted. "What do they want, a frontal assault, full-scale attack before they'll make a freaking commitment?"

She'd override it.

"We've also been told that they'll override any national security order, should you choose to use it to countermand their decision on this."

Outrage roiled in Maggie. "Why?"

"Similar events have occurred in three states. Right down to the C-4. But nothing proves conclusively GRID is involved or that the incidents are irrefutably connected. Until such time as we, or Intel, conclusively make those connections, locals have ultimate authority. That's Barone."

"Who is MIA," Maggie said, not adding that even if he weren't missing in action, he wouldn't have the balls to do anything about this.

"Missing or not, only he can shut the place down. The owners each are free to make their own choices."

"They have." Frustration flowed through Maggie and

erupted. "HQ's tied my damn hands," she said, referencing headquarters. "Maybe they need to get their asses down here to counter Kunz, then."

"Maggie," Colonel Drake said. "Remember what I told you about the rules."

To break the rules to do what she needed to do. Maggie sighed. "Got it, Colonel."

"Things are what they are," Kate said. "We suggested, they said no, and that's that."

"Considering the administration's in hiding, and we have no authority to go back to the owners, that sucks, Kate," Maggie said, hell-bent on doing what she could to comply, but if they got to the wire and it warned her to close the mall, she would close the mall.

"Hey, I never said it was smart, only fact."

"Will?"

"Yeah, Maggie?"

"Survey the twenty-six on shutting down."

"I'm all over it."

Maggie cut the alcove corner and slipped past the line of people waiting for the rest room, then looked inside.

Cynthia Pratt wasn't at her post.

Oh, no. No, no, no. "Has anyone seen a woman in here wearing a jacket like mine?"

They all nodded no.

Maggie backed out, went down to the end of the hall and shoved at the door marked Private—No Exit. Her stomach flipped at knowing now there was an elevator behind it as well as a closet.

Still no Cindy.

"Will, where are you?"

"Level Two, Station One, Maggie."

"Where is Cindy?" Maggie asked, but innately she knew Will hadn't moved Cindy. Innately, Maggie knew that Cindy was as gone as Judy Meyer.

"Guarding the private elev—"

"No, Will," Maggie cut in. "I'm here and Cindy is nowhere in sight."

A long pause and then Will said, "She's not answering her page, Maggie. Something's wrong, like with Judy. Cindy has been with me over three years. I know her. She'd never walk off a post."

Maggie's throat went tight. "You think someone forcibly removed her?" Maggie scanned the floor and walls, looking for any clue.

"I'd bet my life on it," Will said. "Kicking and screaming is the *only* way anyone would get Cindy to abandon her post."

Gouges on the wall.

Maggie crimped her fingers, followed the path scratched through the paint. Kicking and screaming is exactly what it appeared Cindy had done. "It looks like she fought hard, Will. Nail marks are through the paint and into the wallboard." On the left wall was a locked door. Rattled, Maggie mentally scanned the floor plan, trying to remember for certain what was on the other side of it. "Closet. It's a closet, right, Darcy?" Maggie was shaking, inside and out.

"It's a utility closet," Darcy said. "Yes."

"Thanks." Maggie talked into the walkie-talkie. "I need a key down here for this utility closet, Will."

Dread laced Will's voice. "I'm, um, on my way, Maggie."

She went back into the alcove, talked to the fifteen or

so women in line. "Did anyone see a skinny redhead wearing a yellow jacket like mine come through here?"

Again, no one had.

"She didn't leave via the alcove, Maggie. Tape verifies that."

Maggie made her way to Exit Six, walked outside into the crisp night air and turned right. Barone's BMW was back in its parking slot. "Will, APB on Barone. His car's back, so he's bound to be around somewhere. I want him found and detained immediately."

Will disbursed the order.

"Maggie?"

Damn it, she didn't want to look inside that closet. The wind burned her eyes, had the tip of her nose cold and tingling. "Go ahead, Justin."

"I've been to every station on every level. There isn't one vial of antidote in this entire facility, and there was a sub at every station for dinner. What do you want me to do?"

"Get as detailed descriptions as you can on the substitutes." They could be GRID members, or just temporary mall employees Linda or Barone had hired. Either way, they needed to be checked out. Likely, they had no idea they'd done anything wrong.

Maggie went back inside, headed to the alcove. She got back to the utility closet. Just looking at the door had her stomach totally in knots. And Will still hadn't made it down. "Where are you, Will?"

"Had to bust up a fight on Level Three. I'm on my way down. It's going to take a while. Everything's jammed."

With people crammed to the rafters, it could take him fifteen minutes to get down to her. Maggie reached into her fanny pack and pulled out a flat file, then went to work to pry the hinges from the door. She couldn't pull the lock as quickly as she could just unhinge the door.

The hinge pins popped up. She pulled them out and stuffed them into her parka pocket. Jiggling the door, the hinges separated and the door broke loose from its frame.

And a woman's blood-soaked arm fell through the opening.

"Darcy, get me some help down here right away. Clear the rest rooms and seal the alcove between Security and Medical. Get everyone on their toes."

"Judy Meyer?" Darcy asked.

"No." Maggie looked at the skinny redhead's battered, bloody face, and shuddered. "Cynthia Pratt." She swallowed hard. *There was too much blood.* "Call in the coroner. We have a fatality."

The alcove was sealed off and two guards stood at its mouth in the thoroughfare corridor. Maggie was at the end of the hallway, near the utility closet. She'd gently placed Cynthia Pratt's body on the floor, rather than allowing her to tumble out.

The entire front of her parka was covered in blood. "Darcy, get someone to bring me a parka. Not Will."

"Marty's on the way with one, Maggie."

She shrugged out of it, then removed the halo pin and put it on her blouse collar.

"Captain Holt?"

It was Marty. She walked to the end of the alcove, took the parka. He looked devastated. "I'm sorry, Marty."

He blinked hard. "Can I do anything?"

"No." No way would she put him through that. "I'll take good care of her." Maggie patted his shoulder.

"I'm, um, better get back, then."

Maggie nodded, watched him walk away and then went back to Cindy's body.

Daniel Barone arrived at the scene first.

"Where the hell have you been?" Maggie asked him, feeling that same sense of revulsion that the child had felt, recoiling from his touch.

"Level Three, mostly. Rotating between the A-stores."

"Mr. Barone," Maggie said through clenched teeth. "Do not test my patience. I promise you, I have none right now. I know you left the building—I've had everyone in it looking for you for hours—and for a long time, your BMW wasn't in the parking lot."

Justin and Will arrived, both surprised to see Barone there.

"Can I do anything to help, Maggie?" Justin asked.

"It's too late," she said softly, positioning herself to block Will's view of Cindy's body. "I'm sorry, Will."

Pain settled over him like a shroud. "Did she suffer?"

"I don't know." She'd fought like a hellion. That was clear from her jagged bloody nails. "The coroner will be able to tell you that. I know she fought hard."

"She was in the utility closet?" Will asked.

Maggie nodded, gently stroked his upper arm and kept him from stepping around her. "Don't look, Will. Cindy wouldn't want you to remember her like this."

He stopped, looked deeply into Maggie's eyes and a tear rolled down his cheek.

"Will?" It was Kate. "You okay?"

He sniffed hard and his voice came out thick. "I'm okay, Katie. It's just...."

"You've never lost a member of your staff like this, and you cared about her."

His Adam's apple rippled the length of his throat. "Yeah."

"When you've got a second," Kate told Will, "come buy me a cup of coffee."

"Will," Maggie said. "Go on and make Kate take a break. She hasn't had one in nine hours. She can't stay as sharp as she needs to be without taking a break now and then."

His huge body shuddered and Justin patted his shoulder. "I'm sorry, Will."

Barone rolled his eyes. "This is a public relations nightmare. The damage will be horrific."

Maggie glared at him. "A woman is dead, Mr. Barone. Show a little respect, even if you have to fake it."

"Don't be melodramatic, Captain."

At that moment she hated him. "Darcy?"

"Yes, Maggie."

"I'm placing Mr. Barone under arrest. Get me a uniform to pick him up—and tell them to hustle. I want this soulless ass out of my sight as soon as possible."

"Me? Under arrest?" Surprise and fury pounded off him. "Have you lost your mind, Captain Holt? You can't arrest me."

"I can and have, Mr. Barone," she insisted, ignoring his snotty comment about her sanity.

"On what grounds?"

"Assault, first of all. I'm considering adding suspicion of treason, conspiracy, undermining a federal investigation—and maybe even murder."

His jaw fell open.

Two MPs arrived. Darcy had summoned them rather than locals. "Excellent," Maggie said, considering she couldn't be sure if he was Barone or a Barone body double. "Gentlemen, if you'd escort Mr. Barone to Providence, I'd appreciate it. Paperwork will be waiting for you when you arrive. Oh, do read him his rights."

"Yes, ma'am."

"Holt, you're going to regret this for the rest of your life."

"Don't threaten me, Barone." She bared her teeth. "I'm not afraid of you, and if provoked, you have no idea what I can do." She nodded at the MPs. "Get him out of here."

They led him out of the alcove, then out of the facility.

Franklin Walker reported in. "Captain Holt, Will asked me to check with the twenty-six. They voted eighteen to eight to stay open."

Figured. "They know we've had a fatality?"

"Yes, ma'am."

"Okay, then. Thanks, Franklin."

"Can you believe it?" Darcy said.

"No, I can't." Maggie had Fred from Security come down from Level Two and take over for Maggie—he hadn't known Cindy—and Maggie and Justin walked out of the alcove.

He stuck a hand in his pocket. "Was the Barone arrested *the* Daniel Barone or was he a body double?"

"I don't know," Maggie said. "That's why he was taken to Providence, where Dr. Joan Foster, one of our experts, can make that determination." Joan, who had once been forced by Kunz to prepare doubles, had a process for revealing true identities.

"Best to take him out of play either way, I suppose," Justin said.

"That was my thinking." Maggie took in a steadying breath. "Especially since the jerk attacked us in the short-stack."

"My lab is bringing over more antidote. It should be here in twenty minutes, maybe a little sooner."

Maggie checked her watch. Eight o'clock. "We've got one hour to go." Kunz had to move soon. Had to. She unclipped her walkie-talkie. "Will?"

"What do you need, Maggie?"

His voice sounded steadier, more normal. The coffee break with Kate had done him good. She'd calmed him down. "You finished with that coffee?"

"Yeah, I am. Katie had to get back to work."

Maggie still had trouble reconciling anyone calling Kate, Katie, and surviving it. But with Will, Kate had granted latitude.

"Meet me at Center Court, left of the stage." Maggie waited for verification from him, then returned the walkie-talkie to its clip at the waist of her slacks. "Justin, you'd better check on the vans outside and make sure the antidote is still in them."

"Is that why the honchos wouldn't close the mall? Because we've got antidote out there?"

She nodded. "That's likely one of the reasons. For all that's happened, they're not indisputably attributing any of the incidents to GRID. That's another."

"Are you okay, Maggie?" He frowned. "Finding Cynthia had to be hard on you."

It was. "It happens in my job."

"That doesn't mean it doesn't affect you."

"It does. But I'm okay." She'd have nightmares of Cynthia's hand falling out of the closet for a month.

He nodded, paused and bent forward. "I'm sorry about Cindy."

Maggie's eyes stung. "Me, too." And she sure wished she had word on Judy Meyer. After finding Cindy, the most godawful images of Judy were running around in her head, and Maggie would really appreciate being able to ban them. But a facility-wide search had turned up nothing. She didn't know whether to be grateful or terrified that Kunz had taken Judy.

Maggie called Will for an update on Judy Meyer and Barone. She discovered nothing new of note. Her eyes felt gritty, as if they were full of sawdust, and the balls of her feet were throbbing. Finding Cindy Pratt had seriously drained Maggie's energy reserves. She shifted her weight from her left foot to the right and pinched her halo pin to shut down communications temporarily. "Justin, I didn't want this going out over the radio."

"You know GRID's here and, because of Cindy, you think they're listening in?" He looked horrified.

That was exactly what she thought. "It's probable. The GRID organization is very resourceful." And the man running GRID was even more so. She'd run into a lot of twisted people in her career, but never had she met anyone more twisted or more ruthless than Thomas Kunz. "I want you to check out Daniel Barone's car before I have it impounded."

"It's probably locked." Justin masked any emotion from showing on his face.

"Probably is." She looked him level in the eyes.

"Okay, no problem." The silent message to pop the lock had been received and accepted. "What am I looking for?"

"Anything. Everything." She pulled a mint out of her fanny pack, gave one to Justin, then squirted a few more eye drops into her eyes. "I need insight on the man. I need to know if we've been dealing with him or a double. The man we've got says he hasn't been outside today, but his car wasn't here. Someone had to be driving it."

"Maybe…?" Justin prodded her to reveal her thoughts on who.

"Maybe him. Maybe his double. Or maybe Linda Diel."

Justin tinkered with the volume control on his walkie-talkie. "Linda is still missing. She could've had his car. She damn sure doesn't have her own. It hasn't moved out of the parking lot."

"Do you know that for fact?"

"Yes, I do." He shrugged. "I stole her battery."

Shock rippled through Maggie. "You stole her battery?"

He nodded. "I figured a lot of people were going MIA— Barone, Judy Meyer—and if Linda joined them, it'd be after she sounded an alarm on her car battery being stolen. We'd know she intended to report."

"You do surprise me, Dr. Crowe."

He smiled. "Given the chance, I could do far more…" The look in his eyes made it clear that *more* was very personal.

"Ah, together we'd be passionate and crazy," she predicted. "And then just crazy." She shrugged. "Job perk."

"More like a hazard."

"Depends on your perspective." Maggie smiled, appreciating Justin's foresight in pulling that battery. "Maybe Linda did have Barone's car when it was missing. Darcy's reviewing the tapes, but so far there's nothing that shows anyone taking the car. In one frame, it's there in its slot. In the next frame, it's gone."

"There's nothing in between?"

"No," Maggie said.

"The camera has a delay, then?"

She nodded.

"Does GRID have the ability to doctor the tapes?"

"Very astute, Justin," she said, again impressed. "Kunz has done that before, run a loop feed and removed a segment from a tape that would have given us helpful information. So it's possible."

"But I thought these communications between you and your headquarters were secure."

"Secure means reasonably secure. No communications are fail-safe."

"If I find anything in the car, I'll let you know right away."

"Thanks," she said, watching Justin head for Exit Six. Women watched him walk past. Jealousy, strong and nasty as it always is, coursed through her.

"Hey, Maggie."

Justin. "What?"

"Just got a report. The vials in the vans are secure and the backup supplies have arrived. Do you want them inside?"

She checked her watch. Forty minutes until closing. "We can't risk a second interception. I'll handle it. You press on with what you're doing."

"You're cute."

"You, too, Crowe. Now get the hell off my radio."

Picking up her walkie-talkie, she pressed the button. "Will?"

"Right here."

"Have the locals guard the vans and the supply truck. Position it right outside the main entrance, Level One, Door One. And make sure there's sufficient medical staff ready to converge on any area that needs assistance quickly."

"Got it."

Maggie moved to Center Court and checked in with Kate, then with Amanda and Mark. All three claimed their sectors were fine, and appearances bore that out.

Maggie moved on, around the pit to the food court. The Olympians were having a great time, building a snowman four feet in diameter. The Special Forces members were wary and watchful, but they hadn't reported the first anomaly, much less anything ranking abnormal.

Maggie wished she could agree. She tried and tried and still couldn't peg specifics, but God, she knew something was seriously wrong on the virus. She sensed it, felt it, could almost smell it. She couldn't yet identify the exact challenge, but it *was* there.

Digging in her fanny pack for another mint, she pulled out the valve she'd found in the elevator. The two owners of the company handling the Winter Wonderland, Harry and Phil Jensen, were down in the pit in the thick of things. Harry saw her and waved. Phil noticed, and nodded her way.

She nodded back, fingering the valve, and a sharp, stabbing warning went off inside her head.

"Maggie?" Donald Freeman paged her on the walkie-talkie.

"Go ahead, Donald."

He sounded skeptical and disbelieving. "Did you cut Mr. Barone loose?"

"Why?"

"He's up here on Level Three, cruising. Marty is with me and he says Barone just tried the code to get into the short-stack, but he couldn't open it."

Level Three was never crowded. Clearing the shoppers wouldn't be difficult. Maggie weighed all her options and decided that was safest. "Secure all the shoppers on Three inside the stores, Donald. Tell employers not to let anyone out. Say there's a felon in the thoroughfare about to be arrested, and they'll be able to leave just as soon as authorities grab him. Keep them in the back of the stores, as far away from the thoroughfares as possible. Be as discreet as you can, so Barone stays unaware," Maggie said. "Do it now, and let me know when you're done." She turned to Darcy. "I need two SWAT teams prepositioned on Level Two. Have them use the secret elevator."

"Issuing the order now."

Minutes later Maggie was still trying to get to an escalator or staircase that didn't have a mile-long line, when Donald radioed back. "Maggie."

"Yes?"

"Level Three is secure."

"Barone is still up there, correct?"

"Yes, ma'am. He's walking the thoroughfares."

"If he tries to leave the floor, you and Marty work together to keep him up there. Backup is coming to take him down."

"Yes, ma'am."

"Exercise caution." If he was a double and not Barone, he was definitely more dangerous. "He could be armed."

"Yes, ma'am."

"Darcy, have the SWAT teams move in."

"SWAT teams are ascending from Level Two."

Less than two minutes later Will radioed Maggie. "Dr. Crowe hasn't answered a page, Maggie." Worry riddled his voice. "His company truck driver wants his personal authorization to allow medical staff to guard the antidote vials in his truck. Otherwise, he's not letting anyone get close."

Justin should have reported back to her by now. Fearful, she headed for Exit Six. "I'm checking on him now, Will."

"Shots fired on Level Three," Darcy reported. "Repeat. Shots fired on Level Three."

A breathless minute passed. Stairs, escalator and elevators were jammed. No way could Maggie get up there in time to help.

Another minute, then Darcy added, "Two men down. Daniel Barone has been apprehended and is in custody."

"Who's down, Darcy?" Maggie wound through the crowd toward the Exit Six door.

"Freeman and a SWAT team member, Maggie."

"Donald?" Maggie stopped. She couldn't breathe. "Is he—"

"Both have minor injuries. They'll be fine."

Thank God. She let out a relieved groan, went outside and then turned right. Barone's BMW was in his parking slot and Justin was sitting in the driver's seat.

The hair on her neck stood on end. Cautiously, she approached the car. "Justin?" She tapped her nails on the window.

No answer. He didn't move.

"Oh, no. No, no, no." She jerked open the door.

Justin tumbled out of the car onto the concrete.

In his fist he held an antidote vial.

Chapter 13

"Justin is down," Maggie transmitted, shaking all over. "Justin is down!"

She squatted beside him on the concrete, searching for injury, pressed her fingertips at his throat. "He has a pulse. Repeat." Immense relief washed through her. "He has a pulse."

"Cover for me, Amanda," Kate shouted, and the vibration in her tone proved she was already running.

"He has a vial of the antidote in his fist."

"Where are you, Maggie?"

"He was in Daniel Barone's car. He's now on the ground beside it," she said, hearing him groan. Relief flooded through her. "Justin? Justin, talk to me. Who did this to you?"

He was coming around more fully now, blinking, trying to orient himself. "Maggie." His eyes closed.

Kate burst through the door and ran over to them, her chest heaving, her blond curls tossing in the wind. She collapsed on the concrete beside Maggie. "You okay?"

She was shaking all over. "Fine." Maggie scooted in, cupped his face in her hands. "Justin? Damn it, Justin, you look at me right now. You're scaring the hell out of me." Tears burned her eyes, the back of her nose. "Please, God, please don't scare me like this."

Justin opened his eyes, lifted a shaky hand to her face. "Shh, it's okay, Maggie." He comforted her. "I'm all right."

"You're on the fricking concrete barely conscious with a vial in your hand. You were out cold in Barone's fricking car. Don't damn tell me it's okay and you're all right. You are *not* okay, and it's *not* all right."

"I am…now," he insisted. "You're here now."

A tear leaked out and dropped to Maggie's cheek. "As soon as I know you're okay, I'm going to kick your ass for this. Who did you let get the drop on you?"

"Linda," he said, his throat scratchy. "It was Linda Diel."

Maggie looked over at Kate and she nodded, then stepped away. "Darcy, did you get that?"

She took a second to respond. "Yeah. Security staff is on it."

Maggie barked out the order. "Activate twelve of the Special Forces and two additional SWAT teams. Have them sweep the facility."

"Got it," Darcy said. "Does Justin need an ambulance?"

"God, I hope not," Kate said on a groan. "But Maggie might. She's the color of an ice cube."

"I'm fine."

"Does Justin need an ambulance?" Kate repeated Darcy's question.

Maggie lifted a finger, signaling Kate to wait. "Justin, other than your pride, what's hurt?"

"Nothing. She shoved something over my face, strong chemical smell, probably chloroform. But other than a headache, the effects are gone now."

"We should get you checked out," Maggie said. "And when you're okay and this is over, I'm putting you in training."

"Getting checked is a waste of time and money, but I'll take that training. This proves I've been in the lab too much." He sniffed. "My head's clearing. If you'll let go of me, I think I can even get up."

Maggie scooted back, but kept a hand on his arm. She couldn't bear to break contact just yet. Logically she understood it. From his first look at her, Justin had taken her into his heart. She'd fought it, not wanting to be attracted to him, but she just was, and she cared about him. That was it, and, while she'd have to work on accepting it, obviously what she felt wasn't going to go away.

Darcy asked again. "Does he need medical attention?"

"Probably." Maggie exaggerated a sigh. "But he's too pigheaded to get it. I'm watching him."

And Maggie would be even more pigheaded, if she felt the need—and no doubt, she would win.

"Justin?" Maggie asked. "Did you see where Linda went?"

"No, I didn't. Is the car still full of antidote vials?"

"Just the one vial that was in your hand."

He grunted and groaned and got to his feet. Maggie clung to him. "You okay?"

"I'm fine, Maggie." He patted her hand on this arm and his eyes softened. "There were hundreds of vials in the car, in Krane's shopping bags."

"Darcy, put out an APB on Linda Diel." Maggie radioed Will. "What kind of car does Linda drive?"

Will and Justin answered simultaneously. "A 2005 green Honda Pilot." Justin added, "Battery for it's in Will's SUV."

"Okay," Maggie said. "Darcy, run the car down."

"Dispatching the orders now, Maggie," Darcy said.

"Kate, thanks for the backup. I'll be with Justin until I'm sure he's totally stable." It was just as well that Maggie assume the duty officially. She wasn't leaving him until the fear in her for him died, and gauging by her stomach knots and shaking hands, that could take a while.

If it were anyone else reacting this way, it'd be quite touching. But it wasn't. It was about her, and because it was, stark terror tightened the knots.

Maggie and Justin walked back into the building and she checked her watch. Fifteen minutes. Linda had to be GRID's trigger. Kunz's point person. And, it scared Maggie to death to admit it, but the odds were high she'd already released the virus. Probably right after putting Justin's lights out. "Justin, we need to get to Center Court to see if anyone there is exhibiting symptoms."

That little window. It had to be significant. Had to be.

"Are you really okay?" she asked him.

"I am. Honest." His eyes shown warmth, appreciation. "Thanks for being there for me, Maggie."

"It looks like that's the way it's going to be, doesn't it?"

He nodded.

"God help us both."

"I need to go up to Three. You watch for symptoms here."

He nodded.

Maggie switched to a private frequency. "Guys?"

Kate, Amanda, Mark and Darcy all responded.

"Keep an eye on Justin for me. He's watching for symptoms in Center Court. If you see anything, any signs he's unwell, yell."

"We will," Kate answered for the group, and for once, without sarcasm in her voice.

Certain he was covered, Maggie took the private elevator up to Level Three, then walked to the short-stack's door. Forensics was done and the door had been locked, sealed and coded. But was the short-stack empty? "Darcy, did someone change the code on the short-stack door?"

"I did. After Lester Pinnella and his forensics team left. What's going on up there?"

"Maybe, nothing. But—" The warning niggle hit Maggie again. "I need to get inside to check it out."

"Go to the secure frequency."

Maggie flipped over to it and then waited.

"Three, three, three, nine, seven, eight, three, one." Darcy relayed the new sequence to Maggie.

"Thanks." She keyed in the code. "Have we heard anything from the FBI on our outsiders?" The first female and male shoppers who'd left empty bags in the mall.

"Report's just in. The men all boarded a plane about ten minutes ago for New York. They're slated to fly on to Jordan. We don't have enough to detain them. The woman is still in her hotel room watching movies."

They'd satisfied their assignments. Kunz was running

true to form, compartmentalizing. "Justin?" Maggie asked for an update on his observations. "Anything noteworthy?"

"No, Maggie. I'm not seeing any of the symptoms that would signal DR-27 exposure."

She breathed a little easier and stepped inside the short-stack, wondering how many on the security staff had been compromised and were on Kunz's payroll. Barone had been doubled, that was a fact. With both of the men in custody, Intel and Special Investigations officers, aided by Dr. Joan Foster, would settle out who was real and who was a double. She'd do her thing with both the Barones, and the truth about their identities would be revealed.

"Maggie! Get down to Level One—now!"

"What's going on, Darcy?"

"Yellow jackets with shopping bags. They're swarming every entrance. Dozens and dozens of them."

A walkie-talkie alert came through. "Abandoned shopping bag, Level Two, Station One."

"I've got one on Three at Station Four."

"Level Two, Station Five. Two abandoned bags."

"Darcy, sound the bomb alert. I want this building emptied—now!"

Sirens wailed and the public address system boomed, drowning out the Christmas music that had been playing nonstop since opening. "Please exit the mall immediately. Use the nearest stairs to exit the mall immediately. Do not use the elevators. Repeat. Please exit the mall immediately. Use the nearest stairs. Do not use the elevators. Repeat…"

Pandemonium erupted. People screamed and shoved and ran, pouring into the thoroughfares, emptying out the stores, storming down the staircases.

"Maggie," Justin said. "Something is happening at the pit. The ice machine has shut down. Phil and Harry are freaking out. They didn't do it and can't get it up and running again."

"Code Red, Priority One," Darcy said. "Level One, Kid's Row. Code Red, Priority One."

There was a fire on the main floor. Maggie looked for a way down from Level Three that wouldn't take her forever. At the glass-wall banister, she glanced down onto Center Court, shifting to see past the giant plastic flags that read Winter Wonderland, Happy Holidays and North Pole.

The sprinkler heads caught her eye, and what Justin had said in the auditorium when meeting with the store owners about water activating the virus rushed through Maggie's mind. She looked at the snow. Fire triggered the sprinklers and water melted snow. *The snow.* The snow was Kunz's delivery system!

And if that snow melted... "Oh, God!"

She pushed away from the banister. "Darcy, Will, lock down the sprinklers," Maggie shouted, shoving her way between, around people, trying to get down there. "Do *not* allow the sprinklers to come on. No exceptions!"

"Barone and I have the only keys to lock them down, Maggie," Will said, then immediately followed up with, "Oh, no. It's gone. My damn key is gone off my key ring."

The clothesline incident replayed in Maggie's head. The key could have been swiped from him then. It would explain why the incident occurred. Until now, there'd been no discernable reason.

One bump at a time. She inhaled a sharp breath, blew it out slowly. *Think, Maggie. Think.*

Secret room. Window. Fire hose. Water.

Window above the pit.

"Oh, God." The pieces fell into place. "Justin. Justin, the snow!" Maggie shouted. "It's the damn snow!"

"What? Sorry, Maggie. It's nuts down here. I can't hear you."

"The DR-27 is in the snow!" She gasped. "Darcy, Justin, keep the water off the snow!"

A tall man bumped into Maggie's arm. She darted a look up at him and beyond him saw the little window—and a face.

Linda Diel.

Chapter 14

Maggie pulled her .38 from her fanny pack, then punched in the security code on the short-stack door.

A knot formed in her throat. She could hardly breathe around it. She should get Donald Freeman to act as backup before going in—he'd returned to work after sustaining that minor injury in capturing the second Barone—but there just wasn't time.

Maggie eased the door open. It was pitch-dark inside. Feeling beside the door for a switch, she turned on the lights.

Something sizzled, the lights flashed, blowing out the bulbs. Glass shattered and sprayed on the concrete, then darkness again swallowed everything in sight. Her heart racing, Maggie reached for her flashlight. "Darcy?"

No response.

"Darcy, if you can hear me, take over as Primary. I'm in the short-stack. Going in after Linda Diel. I saw her from the stairs through the little window. She's got to be going for the fire hose to wet the snow. She's got to be Kunz's inside contact—or at least his primary one, if Barone is on his payroll, too. I'm convinced she's the trigger. Water on the snow. That's all it's going to take to launch the DR-27 attack for Kunz's capabilities demonstration."

In a cold sweat, Maggie dragged in a shuddery breath. "Darcy? Darcy, can you hear me? Can anyone hear me?"

She waited, but no one responded.

Torn, Maggie paused and squeezed her eyes shut. She should wait for backup, but that could give Linda the precious time she needed to wet the snow. Maggie had to go it alone. The costs were too high to risk going back.

Keeping her back flush to the wall, she edged her way through the inky darkness, circling the short-stack perimeter until her shoulder bumped the wall near the outer edge of the dome. "Darcy, please get everyone out of this place," she whispered, hoping to be heard. "Please get the pit emptied. Please answer me."

But Darcy didn't answer.

And worse, no transmissions were feeding in through the satellite system or the walkie-talkie. Why, Maggie couldn't be sure, but it was as if someone had activated a communications-blocking device. Probably Linda. Kunz damn sure could have provided her with one.

Terrifying thought. One that meant every person on Maggie's team was acting solo, without any coordination from Home Base or any backup from outside the facility—or within it.

God help them all.

Her mouth dry, her throat raw, she inched her fingers over the rough plywood, sliding…sliding…sliding blindly along the short-stack wall.

Her fingers met with air. She'd run out of wall. Imagining where she was in her mind, she stopped. Fourteen steps and she'd be at the inside wall of the secret room. Then she could slide along it to the slatted opening.

She silently counted off three steps and then tried communicating again. "Darcy? Justin? Anyone?" Who would have thought she'd need night-vision gear on this assignment? But, man, she wished she had it now.

No answer.

Four, five, six. She unclipped the walkie-talkie, praying that while she wasn't currently receiving messages, she could transmit one. That there would be a hole in the block, as sometimes happened. That's why multiple blockers and systems were used at Regret in the conference room and operations center. Layered coverage equaled added protection. "Will? Will, I need help in the short-stack. STAT."

No answer.

Damn it. *Seven, eight, nine, ten—*

A fist slammed into her jaw then sliced at her arm, catching her just above the wrist. Pain shot up to her shoulder. The gun flew from her hand. The flashlight crashed on the concrete and the light went out. Knocked back to the wall, she twisted and caught her balance, then charged with a series of rabbit punches, aiming for Linda's throat, followed with a kicked gut-shot to her midsection. Her foot connected.

"Awww!" Linda went down hard.

Maggie went after her. They tumbled on the concrete, wrestling for control, banged into boxes that flew off their stacks, spilled and tumbled on the floor. And then a dreaded sound echoed through the short-stack and through the chambers of Maggie's mind and heart: a trigger being cocked.

She went statue still.

Linda stood. "Move one inch and I'll blow your freaking head off, Maggie."

"Okay. Okay." Maggie didn't move. Linda's voice quavered. She was high on an adrenaline rush and not totally in control. "Just calm down."

"Stand up." Linda sucked in squealed, sharp breaths. "Slowly, and get your hands up."

"What are you going to do, Linda?" Maggie gained her feet, her hands raised. "Are you going to kill me now, like you did Cynthia Pratt and Judy Meyer?" If she believed Maggie already knew, maybe Linda would reveal what really had happened to Judy. "Or are you going to just attack me again, like you did Justin?"

"You know it all, don't you?"

"Damn right, I do. We all do." Linda believing that the truth wouldn't die with Maggie could save her life. "If the sprinklers circling the pit come on, they wet the snow. That releases the DR-27 virus."

"Oh, it's a miracle." Linda's voice dripped sarcasm. "Give the captain a medal. She's finally gotten that she should fear the snow." Linda guffawed. "They warned me to be very careful around you, but I have to say, you're much slower on the uptake than they think."

"I'm fast enough to know you saw that the sprinkler

heads skirted the pit, so you needed the secret room and the fire hose to get sufficient water down to the pit fast— before everyone could evacuate." Maggie kept talking, giving Linda time to calm down, to get rational and realize she wasn't going to walk away. She would be held accountable. "Without the additional water, too many would get out. That would seriously reduce the number of people killed and maimed, which would totally screw up Kunz's capabilities demonstration showing huge numbers of fatalities."

"He'll get them," Linda swore. "By, God, he'll get them."

Maggie ignored her and talked on. "And that would devalue the DR-27 virus on the black market. Naturally, Kunz wants maximum dollars, and for that he needs maximum fatalities."

"I told you, he'll get them!"

"Yes, indeed you did," Maggie agreed with her. She was listening; that was a good sign. "So your assignment was to get the kill numbers as high as possible. To do that, you had to spray additional water through the window get water on the snow quickly to activate the virus while chaos reigned and people weren't yet thinking about a mass exodus. But you failed."

"No, I haven't."

"The mall's being evacuated, Linda. It's too late."

Linda looked outraged. Even in the diffused light, her face twisted and looked red-hot, and her eyes stretched open overly wide. "You're wrong, Maggie."

"No, Linda. I'm not."

Linda stopped, grunted and sloughed off her anger. "You're slow, but overall, very good. You almost had me. Almost." Linda held the gun aimed at Maggie's chest. The tip of the barrel shone in the beam from her flashlight. The damn gun was shaking so hard, if Linda fired it, only God knew where it'd hit. "I suppose your ability to deduce his plans explains why Mr. Kunz doesn't want you dead."

Now that was useful information to know, even if it conjured horrible visions of torture.

"He wants the pleasure of your company, too, though I doubt you'll be as gently treated." Linda tilted her head. "Actually, I'd bet on that."

Too? "So that's where Judy Meyer is. Kunz has her."

"That's right." Linda smirked. "You thought she was dead."

Oh, God. Poor Judy probably wished she was dead. Hell, she likely was praying for it. Kunz was a sadistic son of a bitch, a monster, and she was facing him as a novice without any training whatsoever to help her endure it. "What could he possibly want with Judy?"

"I didn't ask," Linda said. "But he did like her an awful lot."

Surprise streaked up Maggie's back. "They met?"

"Oh, yes. About a year ago." Linda let out a little giggle. "When he was here, he and Judy spent a lot of time together."

Maggie couldn't believe it. Kunz had been *this* close. This damn close, and the S.A.S.S. had no idea. "Are you saying Thomas Kunz has a romantic interest in Judy?"

"Most definitely," Linda said, a purr in her voice. "But not in you. And from all I hear, that's not good news for you. Actually, I'm told he quite hates you."

Maggie's insides curdled. Every awful, horrifying image she'd ever seen of Kunz's victims flashed through her mind in vivid color—mostly red from blood—and she went weak all over. He'd be even more vicious with her.

"You look ill, Maggie." Linda baited her. "I suppose you've heard stories about him, too. He did say I should tell you that there's been nothing personal in his actions."

Nothing personal? Kunz was a bastard who loved torture and hated S.A.S.S. operatives. If he got his hands on her, it'd be very personal. He hated all of S.A.S.S. as much as he hated Special Forces. No way was Maggie going to become his prisoner. She'd die first—after she disarmed Linda and stopped the attack.

"You've done all this dirty work for Thomas Kunz." Maggie couldn't wrap her mind around it. But Linda's reasoning certainly hadn't been a romantic interest, not with what she had said about him and Judy Meyer.

Linda nodded, gleeful and clearly aware of his reputation. "Oh, I was absolutely happy to do it—and would gladly have done more."

Appalled, Maggie asked, "Why? How can you kill innocent people just for the sake of killing them?"

"These people mean less than nothing to me. They're strangers." She grunted. "Why should I care what happens to them? They don't care about me. None of them care a thing about me." Her face twisted in the shadow from the flashlight. "They come in here day after day and abuse things. They steal and complain and they're never satisfied. No matter how hard you try, or what you do for them, it's never enough. They're all takers. Every damn one of them. Takers and users, and I'm sick of them."

"For God's sake, they're human beings, Linda. They have lives and families and they care about things just like you."

She stiffened her shoulders. "Takers and users—ones who have money and use it to do whatever they want." Her eyes narrowed. "I hate the people who shop here."

Did she realize how crazy she sounded? "If you feel this way, then why didn't you just quit?"

"And do what?" she asked. "This is what I know."

"But this is just a business. One that provides goods and services to customers. That's what your job is. You're paid to listen to them complain and to deal with their abuses. You chose it, Linda, and when they come here and spend their money, they pay for the service you give them."

"Shut up. Just shut up. You don't understand."

"Well, explain it to me, then."

Linda hesitated, her jaw clamped tight. "Never. Not once in my whole life, have I had money. Not for what I *need*, much less for what I *want*. For *anything* I want. For a second, I thought you might understand, but you don't. You have to live poor to get it. Making do, doing without. So just shut up!" Linda tossed her a cloth. "Cover your nose and mouth—and don't bother trying to fake it. I'll know, and I'll shoot you."

She wouldn't kill her. Kunz had ordered Linda to bring Maggie to him. Maggie caught the cloth and felt a little spray come halfway up her arm. It was soaked, all right. Chloroform. Taking advantage of the poor lighting, she pressed her hand to her nose and mouth, kept it between her face and the rag, then held her breath.

Linda stood and stared at her, the gun barrel wavering, just waiting for Maggie to fall.

Maggie had to breathe. When her pulse thrummed in her temples and her chest ached for air, she crumpled to the floor, letting the cloth fall loose from her hand.

Linda waited a long moment, then cautiously approached Maggie, picked up the rag, and stooped to cover her face and mouth with it, clearly wanting to take no chances that Maggie wasn't out, or that she came around before Linda wanted.

Maggie didn't breathe. She lay still as long as she could, giving Linda time to relax and get comfortable—and hopefully, complacent. Finally, Linda let out whistling breath.

That was the signal Maggie had awaited. She reared and attacked, shoving the gun from Linda's hand. In a flurry of punches, jabs and kicks, Maggie gained control and kept it.

Squaring off, she landed a solid blow to Linda's jaw, swept at her knees and knocked her off her feet. Sprawled on the concrete, she moaned and didn't move.

Breathing hard and heavy, more from nerves than exertion, Maggie jerked her handcuffs from her center back belt loop, dropped her knee to the small of Linda's back and jerked her arms behind her, then locked the cuffs on her wrists.

Blowing calming breaths, Maggie retrieved her gun and the working flashlight off the floor, then pulled Linda to her feet. "Let's go." Maggie pushed her toward the short-stack door and followed her out into the thoroughfare.

"You're too late, Maggie." Linda laughed. "The fire will make the sprinklers go on automatically and the water will hit the pit. It'll take a little longer to release an impressive amount of DR-27 than it would have if aided by the fire hose, but it will happen."

"In your dreams, bitch." Maggie shoved at Linda's shoulder.

The Level Three thoroughfare was now deserted. Maggie looked around, but saw no one. She handcuffed Linda to a stabilizer pole that went through all three floors. The only way it was coming out was if the damn building went down. "Darcy?"

Still no answer. She pulled out her earpiece and saw the wire was severed. *Well, that explained it.*

She grabbed the walkie-talkie. The problem had to be in the damn batteries. Nothing else made sense. Who was closest? Maybe still around? An image of Donald Freeman, his pride in his round, in her trust of him, filled her mind. "Hey, Freeman, do you hear me?"

"Yeah, Maggie."

Relief washed through her, head to toe. "Get your ass to Level Three, now!"

"I'm on Three, guarding the round. Where do you want me?"

Guarding the round? With a fire burning on Level One below him. God love his dedicated heart. "At the short-stack door. Hurry." She had to get downstairs, get those sprinklers locked down.

Donald came from around the corner in a dead run. "I'm here. I'm here."

"Can you contact Will?"

"Hadn't tried."

"Try."

He pulled his walkie-talkie. "Will?"

But only static came back. It wasn't the batteries. It was certain channels.

Maggie shoved her gun into Freeman's hand. "She's the enemy." Maggie pointed to Linda Diel. "If she moves, shoot to kill."

"Shoot to kill? Linda?" Stark shock registered on his face. "Are you sure?"

"Yeah, I'm sure. Linda is most definitely the enemy," Maggie repeated. "Can you shoot her, Donald? I need to know, and I need to know now."

"She did all this to us." Anger replaced his shock. "Hell, yes, I can shoot her."

"Good. You release her only to the FBI. No one else. Got it?"

He nodded, and Maggie turned and ran toward the escalator, then rode and ran down the steps, shoving past people still heading down. Cutting the corner, she headed down from Level Two to Center Court.

"Justin!" She shouted above the screaming, scurrying, push of people cramming the exits and backed up into Center Court. Everything was logjammed—and some were trapped with no way out of the snow. "Justin!"

Hearing her, he swiveled around, searching faces, looking for her. "Maggie?"

"Two o'clock!" she told him, now that he'd honed in on her voice.

He saw her, started toward her.

"It's in the snow. Tell Darcy, it's in the snow!"

Justin repeated what she'd told him. She saw it from his lip movements, and heard Darcy confirm it a moment later in a message she delivered over the PA system.

It boomed through the half-empty mall. "Get out of the snow. Everyone immediately get out of the snow and exit the building."

Maggie wound through throngs of people and met up with Justin. "My earpiece died. No communications. Tell Darcy that Kunz's primary point person is Linda Diel. I've got her handcuffed to a pole up on Level Three. Donald

Freeman is guarding her at gunpoint under orders to shoot to kill. Get the FBI up there. The DR-27 virus is—"

"In the snow!" Justin said, running for the nearest store.

Maggie followed. "Where the hell are you going?"

"Plastic bags," he answered, speaking not to her but to a startled clerk. "Give me the biggest ones you've got, and all the little ones."

Maggie grabbed them by the armfuls, passing instructions through him to relay. Darcy had visual but audio was out. She needed verifications.

"Kate, Amanda, Mark—keep the water off the snow. Darcy," he repeated all Maggie had told him and then added, "did you lock down the sprinklers?"

"There's a fire," Darcy said. "I can't shut them down."

"Can't Will manually lock them down?" Justin asked. "Water breaks the capsules and releases the virus, Darcy. We've got to stop any water from hitting that pit."

Darcy relayed to Maggie through Justin. "Barone's key is lost and someone stole Will's."

"It wasn't on Linda," Maggie said. "Consider the keys gone and go to backup protocol. Darcy, shut off all the water to the facility."

Justin shifted a huge load of plastic bags to his left arm, pulled out his earpiece and stuck it in Maggie's ear. "I've got to get these shields on the kids in the pit." He ran with the bags out of the store and into Center Court.

Carrying more, Maggie headed for the other side, telling everyone she saw to get out of the building. People were panicked. Shoving. Screaming. Crying. Dropping packages and dragging bellowing, terrified kids.

"Maggie, the main shutoff is outside and only the water department—"

"Get them on it, then," Maggie interrupted Darcy. "Now." She looked down the corridor toward Men's Row. The smoke was gathering, growing thick. The sprinklers could go on at any time. Guessing, they had five to seven minutes. "Talk to the fire department, too. Maybe they have emergency access."

"Will do."

Maggie tripped over a fallen woman well into her sixties. She bent to help her up, then told her to leave right away.

"But I need to exchange—"

"The damn building's on fire," Maggie said, losing it. "Get out!"

"Well, all right, then." The woman left in a huff, swinging her handbag and muttering.

Maggie found Justin down on his knees, showing a small group how to fashion waterproof vests out of the bags. She dumped the extra bags at his feet.

She straightened and pulled a quick visual assessment. People poured out through the exit, but there were so many more yet to go. "Darcy, run that directive to have people exit away from Center Court nonstop, until the stampede thins out, and then get some medical staff outside the other exits to check those injured coming out."

A man was swinging his cane, clearing a path. Justin spotted him, had words with him, and the guy took a swing at him. Catching the cane midair, Justin snatched it and tossed it up onto the empty stage.

About twenty people went down like a row of dominoes. He and Mark headed in that direction to help get folks moving again.

Maggie looked at the sprinkler heads above her, at the wall of smoke pushing toward Center Court. Thank God the fire was still small. It would activate the sprinklers—she checked her watch—in less than five minutes. Five minutes, and there were still thousands to get out of the building. The fire and water departments were working on cutting water to the building, but if they didn't make it...

"Justin," Maggie called. "We've got to stop the sprinklers." She pointed to the heads circling the pit.

Justin looked down the thoroughfare, estimated when the sprinklers would engage. "We've got less than three minutes. No one can shut down the water main before they engage. We need a miracle."

The pit was empty on the back end. The front end was jammed with an overflow of people trying to get out through the exit. Spotting the Happy Holidays banner, Maggie yanked it down. "Grab that end of the sign, Justin."

He caught on to what she was doing. "Amanda, Kate, Mark, get the other banners. Tarp the people on this side of the exit. The pit, too, if we can extend that far."

Justin and Maggie stretched the banner above the heads of those trying to get out the door. Those farthest away were making vests of the plastic bags, using the small bags to cover their shoes. Justin's idea had caught on and now the panicked people waiting to get out were fashioning their own vests and shoe covers, taking action. Special Forces members darted in and out of the stores; rounding up more bags and helping those farthest from the exits get covered.

The smoke inched closer and closer. It was at Macy's, creeping into the far edges of Center Court. A minute at most and it would cover them.

Maggie gave Justin the earpiece back and then grabbed a food court chair, positioned it on the far right of the exit and stepped up on it. Justin did the same on the left side of the exit doors, and they held the plastic banner stretched above the shoppers' heads. "Go, go, go." Maggie rushed the people out. Covering the pit wouldn't prevent the problems. The shoppers had snow clinging to their clothes. They were contaminated. "Go, go, go!" She looked down. The smoke was curling at her feet. "Oh, God, hurry!"

People poured out of the building. Shoved, trying to get under the tarp. They had no idea why it was important, but reacting to the panic, they innately knew that being under its cover was critical to them.

"Justin," Maggie shouted across to him. "Tell Darcy to get the HAZMAT crews working outside to decontaminate them as they come out."

He nodded, then relayed, paused and then shouted back to Maggie. "They're working it, Maggie."

Good. Good.

Amanda and Mark stretched a second banner behind the first, copied Justin and Maggie, extending the tarp further back, into the pit.

And Kate and Will stretched a third behind the second.

"Justin, what about the sprinklers?"

"Will couldn't override the system, that's why he's now with Kate. If he had shut the system down without the key, all the sprinklers throughout the entire facility would have engaged. It's an added safety measure. Fire and water departments are working it from the water main outside."

God, they were going to be too late. And there was still a third of the people in the pit that weren't under tarps.

In the crush of people getting out, several teams of Special Forces broke ranks, picking up on what Maggie and the others were doing. In short order, they ripped down more of the huge plastic banners and filled in behind Kate and Will.

The smoke thickened, crept up to Maggie's waist in roiling whirls. At least they didn't have to worry about flames reaching the people. But the smoke was choking some farthest from the exit.

Her arms aching, her shoulders throbbing, she looked back. The entire pit was covered by tarps. Everyone was under the flags. A knot of gratitude and relief swelled in her throat. Her nose tingled, her eyes burned and tears blurred her vision.

The sprinkler heads came to life.

Water sprayed down, splattering on the marble in the thoroughfares, misting the outer edges of the tarps.

"Get away from the edges!" Maggie shouted. "Get away from the edges!"

The crowd began to chant it to each other and the warning worked its way through them as they huddled toward the center, still pouring out the exit doors.

Panic seized the shoppers. Frantic, they started to stampede, trying to get outside. More Special Forces members lined the way, directed and kept them from trampling anyone and further choking up the exits. Firemen and police intercepted the shoppers on the other side of the doors, shuffled them to the medical staff set up in huge numbers in the parking lot. Once injected with antidote, HAZMAT team members put the shoppers through decontamination chambers.

Maggie watched it all happening above the heads of those exiting through the glass doors. She scanned hungrily, anxiously, praying that no one would die, that the water and fire departments would shut off the water at the main soon, that the makeshift flag-tarps would hold until the last person was out. If the water touched the snow, melted it, the encapsulated DR-27 virus would be released and the two-minute window for administering antidote would trigger.

The mist was gathering at the edges of the tarp.

Fifteen seconds later Darcy sounded the extreme-hazard alarm.

It blared through the mall, piercing ears, setting them to aching. Panic tripled. Shoppers shoved at each other, at the exit door, screaming, swearing, pushing, punching, crying, keening, and Maggie stood helpless. All she could do was stand with her aching arms extended, the smoke burning her eyes, holding the flag above their heads.

And then the sprinklers suddenly stopped.

"Water department got to the main," Kate shouted.

A tear slid down onto Maggie's cheek. She and Justin locked gazes through the smoky haze and smiled.

Chapter 15

Chaos finally gave way to order.

The fire was out and Santa Bella stood empty of shoppers and nearly all its employees.

For the past hour, security staff and Maggie's team had been verifying stores empty and locking them down with the heavy steel grates that served as doors and sealed them from the mall's common areas.

Maggie appropriated a new earpiece and was back up running communications. Additional HAZMAT teams had been called in and were working inside, decontaminating the mall, hauling snow out of the pit in sealed biohazard boxes. Phil and Harry Jensen were dazed by their part in Kunz's capabilities demonstration and giving statements to FBI agents. It was clear within the first five minutes of interrogations that neither of the owners had a clue what they had on their hands, or that the valve Maggie had found in the elevator had been replaced by a crew member working for Kunz with one designed to release the encapsulated virus only at the appointed time into the already frozen snow. Darcy ran a comparison check between the snow crew members and nonattributed intel file photos, and came up with a match, moving yet another man from the Persons of Interest list to the Known GRID Operatives list. That greatly enhanced their odds of catching him, and greatly hampered his ability to move freely inside the U.S. or to cross its border.

Colonel Drake had driven down from Regret and was running interference, keeping the press focused on the locals, specifically working through the Providence police department's Information Officer, and keeping all mentions of any S.A.S.S. member out of the media.

"Maggie? Justin?" Colonel Drake paged them. "Meet me at the food court."

They walked over and saw her waiting for them at a table near the Wee Bit O' Pub entrance.

"Have a seat." She dropped onto a chair and waited for Maggie and Justin to sit. When they had, she began. "Keeping that fire hose in the secret room out of Linda Diel's hands and the waterproof canopy with those flags prevented a major disaster here tonight."

"I'm just glad I saw her," Maggie said.

"Me, too," the colonel agreed. "HAZMAT's verified what you'd already told us, Justin, that the mist getting on the shoppers, who had any snow whatsoever clinging to their clothes, would have released the virus."

He nodded.

"We were lucky the DR-27 wasn't disbursed until just before closing. I just wanted to make sure you knew it hadn't been, and you two doing your jobs so well saved a lot of lives."

"It took a lot of people doing a lot right to prevent this disaster." Justin wasn't playing at being modest; he was being honest and blunt.

"That's right, Colonel."

"True. But even with all those right things, when crunch time came, it was the absence of that hose and the presence of those tarps that prevented a tragedy and an epidemic."

Seeing a flash of movement, Maggie swerved her glance. Two men and a woman wearing FBI jackets were leading Linda Diel out in handcuffs. Donald Freeman was walking three paces behind them. Maggie smiled at him and he saluted her. "Diel intended to take me to Kunz," Maggie said.

"I heard." Colonel Drake shuddered. "I'm glad we avoided that."

"We all are," Justin said.

"He's got Judy Meyer," Maggie said. "He has a romantic interest in her. She was apparently working with Linda—and has been for the entire year Kunz has been planning this operation. That's according to Linda. She says Kunz was at Santa Bella a year ago, and that's when he and Judy got close. I doubt the real Barone knows anything about anything."

Colonel Drake dragged a hand through her hair. "I was in on most of the operation, but we've got a gap—when you went into the short-stack after Diel and your communications equipment went down. Are you up for debriefing?"

"Sure," Maggie said, then launched into it.

Justin added his comments, they answered Colonel Drake's questions, and then Maggie disclosed her supposition on the yellow jackets with the handled shopping bags. "I think their purpose was twofold. To enter the mall as decoys to divert our attention from the snow machine, and to remove the antidote from the premises, which Kunz obviously hoped would go unnoticed by leaving the empty boxes. The missing antidote vials might have gone unnoticed, if Justin hadn't been positively anal about checking up on them every few minutes." She smiled at him to let him know that his being anal on this was a very good thing and she was grateful for it.

The queries and answers went back and forth for another half hour and then the briefing was done.

"Maggie, you did a hell of a job under very difficult circumstances." Colonel Drake's pride shone in her eyes. "It's dawn now, and you've been going full-out for two days straight, Darcy tells me, without even power naps." A small chastisement laced with concern thread through the colonel's voice. "Overt forces—local authorities and FBI—can take it all from here." She looked back and forth between Maggie and Justin. "I want you both to go home, rest and have a wonderful Christmas."

Christmas. It was Christmas. And while Cynthia Pratt's family and friends mourned, a nation had been spared. "Merry Christmas, Colonel." Maggie stood, seeking solace in that, but finding little. Those who loved Cindy were grieving. And grief and loss, Maggie Holt understood too well to minimize.

Justin stood, too, a light stubble shadowing his chin.

"Merry Christmas, Colonel." He extended his hand. "It's been a privilege."

"All mine, Dr. Crowe," she said, shaking warmly. "Thank you. Both of you."

Maggie and Justin walked outside together, then wound through knots of people and around the decontamination equipment area to the section of parking lot where Maggie had left her Jeep. She glanced up at the sky, at the tinges of pink and lavender streaking all the way to the horizon. "Merry Christmas, Justin," Maggie said, feeling as if tons of weight had been lifted off her shoulders.

He eased his arm around her, pulled her close and dipped his head until his lips brushed against hers. "Merry Christmas, Maggie," he whispered against her mouth, then kissed her soundly.

When he parted their mouths, he almost smiled, and swept her hair back from her face. "Magical."

"Yeah." She smiled up at him.

They got into the Jeep and she cranked the engine. "How can I be dead on my feet but still feel wired for sound?"

"Adrenaline's still pumping." Justin clamped his seat belt. "How about some breakfast before the sleepfest?"

"Sounds good to me." The sleepfest was hours away, at least, hours away. She just couldn't change gears and drop off high alert any more quickly. "What's open on Christmas?"

"I don't know. Let's ride until we find something."

Maggie eased the car into reverse, backed out, then took off. "Don't you have plans for today with someone?"

"Um, actually, no, I don't. I'm on my own."

"Me, too." She said it and felt that inescapable sadness that came on every holiday she spent alone while everyone else spent it surrounded by family.

"I hate being on my own on Christmas. Let's be on our own together," he suggested.

Maggie chuckled and looked over at him. Charming. Totally. Her feelings for him had changed so much since she'd first seen him in the S.A.S.S. bunker at Regret. He wasn't the man she'd thought, and the man she'd seen him to be intrigued her. Infinitely pleased, she adjusted her rearview mirror and bit a smile from her lips.

On Highway 98, she spotted a shiny aluminum diner. "Lights are on. They must be open."

"Two cars in the lot," he said. "Appears they are."

Maggie whipped into the parking lot, gathered her keys and purse and they went in. It was warm and dry and friendly inside, pleasant and, thankfully, quiet.

Maggie slid into a booth on the outside wall and Justin sat across from her. A waitress in pink and white and a ponytail that hit her mid-back walked over with plastic-coated menus and a coffeepot.

"Merry Christmas." She filled their cups, cracking her chewing gum.

They repeated it back to her and took the menus she extended to them.

"I'm going to be really bad," Justin warned her. "Double stack of pancakes, strawberries, sausage and the biggest glass of orange juice you have."

Maggie laughed. "I'm going to have to roll you out of here."

"Probably." He grinned.

"I'll have two eggs over easy, bacon, grits and blueberries. Oh, and whole wheat toast. And juice."

She jotted down their orders on a little thick pad. "There was a big ruckus going on down at the mall all night," she said, passing along the latest gossip.

"Really?"

The waitress nodded again. "Some shopper got bored, waiting in line, and started a fire. They had to evacuate everybody. I heard all the stuff in the whole place got wrecked." The gum cracked. "Smoke damage."

"Goodness," Maggie said. "Guess we should turn on the news now and then, right, honey?" She looked at Justin.

"I guess we should." His eyes twinkled.

"Food'll be out in just a minute." The waitress went to the kitchen, turned their order in. "Hey, Frankie. Order's in."

In a few minutes the food arrived. Smelling it had Maggie's stomach growling and her mouth watering.

They ate and chatted through half their meal, about everything, about nothing, starting the mental and emotional transition of coming out of crisis.

Justin poured more syrup on his pancakes. "May I ask you something, Maggie?"

"Sure." She dabbed at her mouth with her napkin, then took a bite of blueberries.

"Well." The look in his eyes warmed. "Actually, I guess it's a comment I want to make more than a question I want to ask."

"Go ahead. But remember, it's been a long two days and I'm a little punchy and short-fused."

"You're armed, too." He smiled. "Maybe I'd better wait until another time." Justin set down his fork, looked at her over the edge of his chilled water glass as he took a drink, then set it down. "What the hell? What's life without risks?"

"Safe."

"Ah, yes, but you miss so many opportunities. Some that are so rare you never have a second chance. They're lost forever." The ice clinked against the sides of the glass. "There will be another time, right?" His voice, both hopeful and uncertain, wasn't quite steady.

Her heart rocketed into overdrive and her own hopefulness and uncertainty surfaced. "You mean, for us to get together on a personal basis?"

"Yes, I do." He dragged his thumb down his glass, leaving a streak on it. "I'm going to leave myself wide open here and hope I don't regret it." He dragged his teeth over his lip. "Hell, I can't regret it. It's honest."

How did she feel about that? She had no idea what to think about an opening like that, much less any idea what to feel.

He reached across the table, lifted her fingers and placed his under them, then curled his fingertips around hers. "The truth is that there's something about you that just does it for me. The way you look, the way you talk, the way you say what you think even when it's not politically correct or it'd be easier on you to just say nothing at all. Even the way you eat—just watching you, makes me feel good."

"The way I eat?"

He nodded. "You eat all of your eggs before touching your toast. All of your toast before touching your berries. You eat the outside of a sandwich, all the crust on the bread, before you eat the center of it. And when you eat a slice of pie, you start at the point and eat your way to the crust. It fascinates me to watch you eat. It appeals to me, Maggie. Everything about you speaks directly to me—" he touched his free hand to his chest "—and something so deep inside me I don't even know where it is, or what it is, answers." The look in his eyes turned tender. "I knew it the first time I saw you, and I feel it every time I see you. You do it for me, Maggie. All of it. Everything."

Humbled, awed, honored and stunned, she couldn't find the words to share all she was feeling. Her emotions were in riot, tumbling one on the other, and a joy so sweet and unexpected welled in her chest. The back of her eyes burned, her nose tingled and she blinked hard to not let a tear fall. "Justin, you awe me. You…awe me." Never, not in her wildest dreams, had she believed for a second that a man would come into her life and feel about her as Justin clearly did. Never, not in her most secret fantasies, did she dare to dream for even a sliver of all he had shared.

The confusion about him disappeared and her feelings suddenly seemed so clear. The past, their histories, were insignificant. They were no longer the people they had been then. Experience had changed them. They were wiser now about their own parts in creating the challenges of their pasts, and because of that, they were more aware, more invested in creating their futures. Better futures.

"Will there be other times for us, Maggie?" he asked again.

She brought his hand to her lips, kissed his fingertips. "Absolutely."

He smiled, then turned serious. "I know you have concerns."

She'd had concerns. Looking at him, she didn't have

them any longer. Still, she would like to understand the past so she could finally put it to bed and move on with her life without thinking of it again. Yet she couldn't ask and be delicate, wasn't sure she even should be delicate. "Justin, I'm not judging you now, but I need to understand."

"You want to know why men cheat?"

She nodded. "Can you answer that for me?"

"I swore that after the divorce from Andrea was final, I'd never speak of this again. But for you, I'll try, Maggie." He paused and thought a moment, then went on. "I can't answer for all men, but I can and will answer for myself." Justin stopped, gathered his thoughts and then finally continued. "It wasn't deliberate, or something I went out with the intention to do. Things between Andrea and I were really good until she got mixed up in that garden club." He took a drink of juice, as if washing a bitter taste of out his mouth. "Going there changed her. She got darker and, well, 'kinky' is the only way to describe it. Sexually, I mean." He gave himself a little shake. "This is totally embarrassing."

"If you'd rather not, I understand," Maggie said.

"No. No, we need to be open about everything." He pulled in a steadying breath. "Let's just say, I came to hate being with her."

The truth dawned on her. "The garden club has nothing to do with gardening, does it?" Damn, she felt like an idiot. Of course, it didn't.

"It's a sex club, Maggie." His face flushed red. "Anyway, that's how it all started. She was worse, the nights she went there. I didn't know where she was going, then. Fool that I was, I thought she was faithful. On the nights she went out with the girls, I thought they were doing chat sessions or whatever women do when they get together. I had no idea what she was really doing. But I learned quickly to stay away from her on those nights."

"How did you avoid her?"

"I'd drive around and not come home until I knew she'd be asleep. The next morning, she'd be furious, of course, but dealing with her when she was furious was nothing compared to dealing with her when I was home. She was twisted."

"So you just made sure you weren't there."

He nodded. "I didn't know what else to do. I didn't believe in divorce, she refused to see a marriage counselor and she wouldn't take no for an answer. I didn't want things to get violent, but she was heading in that direction fast. I just didn't know what else to do, so I stayed away from her."

Maggie wasn't sure she would've known what to do in that situation, either. Short of leaving, what was left? He could've stayed, let her get violent and called in the police, but would they believe this from a man? Without emasculating him? Probably now, yes. But it still would have been hard to stomach doing that. All in all, getting out seemed the best option.

"One night while I was driving, I found this park. The one on Oak and 47th streets with the Oriental garden and foot bridge."

"I'm familiar with it," she said.

"I like the feeling of that park. It's peaceful and quiet."

"It usually is." Maggie had run there often.

"Everything home wasn't anymore. So I stopped and stayed there awhile. There's a bench on 47th, not far from the corner. A woman was already sitting there."

"Is she the one?"

He nodded. "The first three or four times I saw her there, we just exchanged polite hellos. Then, one night, we started talking. Her name was Melanie."

"And the more you talked, the more you liked her, and before you knew it, you were in an affair."

"That's pretty much it, Maggie. Melanie was kind and gentle and decent—everything Andrea had ceased being."

Maggie tried to imagine, to see this situation through his eyes. "And seeing those things in Melanie reminded you of all that no longer existed in Andrea?"

"Yes. The contrast was stark. Like darkness and light, good and evil." Justin shrugged. "I wanted goodness and light, so I divorced Andrea."

He divorced *her?* Maggie sat too stunned to speak. She just stared at him for the longest time, trying to let all he'd told her sink in. "I thought Andrea divorced you for being unfaithful."

"No, I left her." He shook his head, his gaze fixed on the table. "I was so naive, Maggie. It wasn't until after I filed for the divorce and she came to me begging me not to expose her membership in the garden club during the legal proceedings that I discovered the garden club—and, as you put it—that it had nothing to do with gardening. Damn, but I felt stupid. Stupid and used."

Maggie knew exactly how he felt on that front. She reached across the table, covered his hand with hers. "I'm sorry, Justin."

"But you still think I'm scum for being unfaithful to her?"

"No, I don't," Maggie said. "I think it was wrong, and

I won't say it wasn't. You could've left her first. But I can definitely see now how, being in your situation, you'd be vulnerable to a gentle woman like Melanie." That wasn't all Maggie saw, and she, too, had to be honest. "I shouldn't have painted all men with the same brush." That was a serious understatement, considering the circumstances. "I was wrong to do that."

"I should've respected marriage and myself, even if I couldn't respect my spouse anymore. And I should've divorced her before getting involved with someone else. I see all of that now, of course. But back then, when I was in the middle of it all, I didn't realize how bad things had become with Andrea until Melanie came along. The change happened by degrees, you know? And all of a sudden one day I found myself in hell, and I wasn't sure how I got there, or exactly when it happened."

"One of those situations where you can't see the forest for the trees," Maggie said.

"Exactly." He nodded. "I didn't intend to hurt anyone. It just happened. But I swear, Maggie, it will never happen again."

She believed him. "What about Melanie?"

"She went home." He took a bite of sausage, chewed and swallowed. "She had an apartment by the park and spent a lot of time there because it reminded her of home."

"Where was she from?"

"Barth, Mississippi," he said. "From her description, it's a beautiful little town with moss-draped oaks and wide front porches."

"Sounds quaint."

"It does, doesn't it?" He smiled. "Melanie still loved her

husband—we talked about him a lot—and she decided to go home to try to work things out."

He helped her find her way back to her husband? How very charming. "I wonder if she did."

"I don't know. She called me once, as soon as she arrived, to let me know she was safely there, but I haven't heard from her since then. I hope she and her husband worked everything out. I hope she's happy."

"Did you love her, Justin?"

"No, I didn't. She didn't love me, either." He looked Maggie straight in the eye. "But I respected her, and I'll always be grateful to her. She helped me see the truth about Andrea and how destructive that relationship had become." He gave Maggie a sweet smile. "Melanie helped me find the light in my life again. That was quite a gift."

It was. "And now you've helped me see things in a different light." Maggie tilted her head, humbled by the way things ripple out and are passed on to those who need them. "Thank you, for being so open about all this."

His expression sobered. "It's important to me that you know the truth. You know why, Maggie. You know exactly how I feel about you."

She did. "Yes." And she felt the same way about him, but before she could tell him, a large group of people entered the diner. So many that they were lined up, waiting for tables.

"We should go," Justin said.

Maggie gathered her things and they left. Outside, walking down the sidewalk to the parking area, Justin offered Maggie his hand.

Her heart full, she clasped it. "So what are we going to do for the rest of the day?"

"Something very special," Justin said.

"Very special." Maggie hummed. "Whatever will that be?"

Maggie and Justin sat in Justin's den, sprawled on the floor against the sofa, in front of a roaring fire. "Are you really upset that you didn't get Kunz, Maggie?"

"No." She wasn't accustomed to drinking early in the morning, but it felt more like the end of a very long night and it was Christmas, so what the hell? In a compromise, they'd decided on eggnog. "I wish we'd gotten him, but the truth is, you've got to be realistic about these kinds of people. Even if we had gotten him, he still has a legion of GRID members behind him. So if he's out of the picture, one of his henchmen just takes over."

"He went to a lot of trouble to double Barone." Justin shook his head. "I have a hard time wrapping my mind around that."

"He had no choice. Barone held authority on closing the mall. As long as I couldn't conclusively prove GRID was attacking Santa Bella—and Kunz made sure I couldn't by having events occur at other potential targets and rumors of more attacks—Barone had the last word. The real Barone would've shut down after the C-4 was found. Kunz had to double him so his double could replace him and refuse to close the mall."

"But the real culprit," Justin said, "was Linda. How did Kunz get to her?"

"He's very good at playing people, and he can be extremely sympathetic and charming. Linda was bitter about being poor and serving others. Kunz played on that and gave her a way to be wealthy. He showed her a world she'd dreamed of all her life. One where only a few thousand insignificant users-and-takers would die, and Linda would be served and treated like a queen forever. She couldn't resist."

"It's sick. Playing people's vulnerabilities."

"Yeah, and he's made it an art form." Maggie paused. "You know, the Krane's bag shoppers bug me. It's just.... Damn. He was using them as decoys!" The truth slammed into Maggie. "That's all there was to them. So our people would be tied up with busywork and become complacent before Linda's people removed the antidote."

"But he had to be after something else—besides the virus," Justin said. "It's the only way what he did makes sense."

Maggie turned to Justin. "Listen, let's make a pact. If ever you're the victim of a three-month absence, you'll let me know. And if ever I am, I must let you know."

"And then what?" he asked.

"You, me, we go to Colonel Drake."

"Agreed."

"Great." Maggie turned her thoughts. "He had to be studying one of us, Justin. Maybe all of us. Who knows? He's done that with Amanda, Kate and Darcy over successive missions. It had to have been you or me this time."

"Or Colonel Drake," Justin added.

Maggie agreed. "Or Colonel Drake."

"We have to brief her on this, our concerns, I mean," Justin said. "She needs to be aware."

"Yes, she does." Maggie sighed. "I'll tell her tomorrow."

"So *you are* disappointed about not getting Kunz."

"No, acceptance comes with the job on these terrorist cases." She'd reconciled herself to less than a hundred percent resolutions a long time ago. "We can't lose sight of the goal, and that's to intercede, interrupt and intercept him and his business. That's realistic, and it makes us all safer. So, no, I'm not upset that we didn't get him, though I wish we had—and one day, we will."

Justin touched a hand to her face. "I'm so glad you're here with me."

"Me, too." Her heart skipped a little beat. "You're a special man."

"I dare you to stay with me and tell me that again next Christmas."

"Do you really think there'll be a next Christmas for us?" She hoped there would, so much it could be frightening, if she'd let it. Instead she was going to enjoy it.

"Absolutely." His promise carried over from his mouth and shone in his eyes. "I told you, Maggie. You just do it for me."

"Then, yes, Justin." Maggie smiled and breathed next to his lips. "I'll take that dare and double it. Because you do it for me, too."

He curled his arms around her and pulled her close. "I think I'm going to like Christmas from here on out. Me and you, on our own, together."

"On our own, together," she said with him.

Laughing, they kissed deeply and settled in to dream by the fire.

Epilogue

On a remote island in the South Pacific, Thomas Kunz sat in his operations center, drinking a glass of milk and watching the mopping up going on at Santa Bella Mall. Judy Meyer sat beside him and three women stood behind them that bore striking resemblances to Amanda West, Kate Kane and Darcy Clark.

"Well, that was a lot of work and planning for nothing," his Amanda double said. "The virus wasn't activated—or was it?"

"No, it wasn't." With his arm around Judy's shoulder, Thomas rubbed small circles on her upper arm.

"Nearly a year of planning, down the drain."

"No," he told Darcy's double. "We got exactly what I was after."

"How's that?" Kate sat on the edge of his desk. "There was *no* capabilities demonstration, Thomas."

"Oh, but there was, my dear Kate." He smiled.

"Not on the DR-27 virus," Amanda said, then halted suddenly and gasped. "Oh, you clever, clever man!"

"What?" Kate's double asked, clearly irritated.

"Thomas, resident genius and millionaire-maker extraordinaire's objective wasn't to demonstrate the capabilities of the virus, Kate," Amanda said. "It was to determine the capabilities of Maggie Holt!"

"Very good, Amanda." Thomas Kunz laughed deeply. "The three-month absences have become obvious to our counterparts at S.A.S.S. I needed a process that would give me all I need to know quickly. This event was that process." He smiled, clearly pleased with the way things had worked out. "I know now how she thinks, how she reacts in crises, and her vulnerabilities when it comes to relationships. In two days of high-pressure observations, we gained all the information needed to double her—though only for limited exposure, I confess. Still, it's been a very enlightening two days. And, since Kate, Darcy and Amanda were active on this mission, as well, I also received current status information vital to you ladies."

"A winner all around." Kate's double groaned. "I should have known."

"Yes, my dear," he answered honestly, admonishing her. "You should have."

Darcy chewed at her lip, worrying. "They think you failed."

"Of course, Darcy." Thomas looked at Judy, curled contentedly beside him. "They always do."

"And you've got the Threat Integration Center half convinced you're dead."

"That's true, too." Thomas finished his milk and stood, his shadow falling across the tiled floor.

"How long will you let them believe it?" Judy stood, too, stroking his shoulder lovingly.

"Oh, for a time." He sent her an enigmatic smile. "For a time...."

A man passed the glass, short, fat and dressed in a dirty blue-jean jacket. Shaved head. He hesitated at the door, then opened it and came in. He looked nervous, but that might have been the natural tentativeness of a man ill-suited to high-end suits coming in to browse....

No. It wasn't.

In the mirror, his eyes focused on Lucia. Not in the way that a man normally examined her, either—this was a pattern-recognition way, as if he'd been given her description. Or a photo.

She carefully put the shirt back on the table and positioned her hand close to her hip, a split second from going for the gun concealed by the tailored leather jacket she was wearing. She automatically swept the store for collateral victims. The clerk was positioned safely behind a counter;

he'd surely duck if gunplay started. Odds were good he'd survive, unless her newcomer was carrying an Uzi or was an incredibly poor shot. No other customers, unless they were in the dressing rooms.

She balanced her weight lightly around her center, ready to shift at a moment's notice, ready for anything, as the man made his way closer, one hand in his jacket pocket.

She turned and the world slowed to a crawl. *Tick*, and his eyes were rounding in surprise. *Tick*, and her hand moved the small distance inside her own coat and her fingers touched the cool grip of her gun.

Tick, and his right hand emerged with nightmare slowness from his pocket...

...carrying a red envelope.

Time fell back into a normal rush of color and noise, and Lucia felt her heart hammering, knew there was color flooding her cheeks. Adrenaline was an earthquake in her veins for the second time in an hour.

The courier silently held out the red envelope to her. "Here you go, lady. No signature required." He sounded spooked. She wondered how she had looked to him, in that instant when she was making the decision whether or not to kill him.

"Thank you," she said, and took it. Automatic courtesy; she certainly wasn't feeling grateful at the moment. He backed up, turned and hurried out the store fast enough to make the discreet, mellow bell hung about it clatter like a fire alarm.

She turned the envelope over in her hands, frowning down at it. The size and shape of a greeting card envelope. One sheet of paper inside, it felt like. Her name was block-printed on the outside; the courier had, no doubt, been told exactly when and where to find her, even though her choice of this store had been on impulse.

No point in delaying the inevitable. She reached in her pocket and took out a slender pocketknife, flipped it open and slit the side of the envelope, very carefully. Preserving what evidence there might be. She slid out the paper using a pair of tweezers from her purse and moved shirts to lay it flat on the table.

It didn't require much scrutiny. It read, "One of you has made a mistake," and it was on the letterhead of Eidolon Corporation. No signature. She held it up to the light. No watermark. No secret messages. No hints as to its meaning. *One of you?* Meaning her? Jazz? McCarthy? Impossible to tell. It was a meaningless taunt of a message, designed to unnerve; showy, like the delivery by courier. Designed to show that they could literally find her anywhere.

She could just imagine what Jazz would have said to that. It would have been something like, *Bring it on, you bastards,* only more unprintable. The thought made her smile.

Jazz.

Her smile faded as she flipped open her cell phone and speed-dialed James Borden's number. He picked up on the second ring, sounding lazy and sleep-soaked, but he sobered up fast when she said, "It's Lucia."

"Hey. Um, good morning. What time—crap. It's late."

"Is Jazz with you?" she asked.

There was a short pause and then the tenor of the call changed; she heard the rustle of sheets, a sleepy murmur, the quiet closing of a door. He'd stepped out into the bathroom or the hall. "She's asleep," he said. "I don't want to wake her up if I don't have to. Do I? Have to wake her up?"

"Soon," Lucia said. "Eidolon just delivered a note to me. Did she get one?"

"No deliveries—oh. Hang on." The phone rattled, set down on a counter, she guessed. He was back in less than ten seconds. "Yeah. Somebody slid it under the door."

"Open it."

"You're sure?"

"Yes."

Rattle, pause… "It says, 'One of you has made a mistake.' On Eidolon Corporation letterhead."

"Same thing I got. Have you ever received one from Eidolon before?" She realized that she was pacing, a habit when she was nervous. The store clerk was watching her. Not, she was relieved to see, in any way that implied he was a conspirator; no, this was the plain, unvarnished interest she was used to attracting. She gave him a small smile and he found something to be busy with that took him out of her eyeline.

"Look, *I* don't get messages from anybody. I'm not a Lead."

"Any idea what it might mean?"

"Not a clue. Unless—"

"Unless?"

He cleared his throat. "Well, Jazz and I—maybe it has to do with us."

"You think falling in love with her is a mistake?"

"I never said…" He gave up on the reflexive denial, to his credit. "No, I don't. I hope she doesn't, either."

"Then it's entirely possible it might be referring to this morning. To me helping McCarthy get released."

"Then why not just send it to you? Why send it to you *and* Jazz?"

"McCarthy's connected to both of us now. I think the better question is, why would Eidolon warn us? Wouldn't they *want* us to be making mistakes?"

"I have no idea what Eidolon wants." Borden sighed. "Look, I barely know what my boss wants half the time. So far as figuring out motives, good luck. You want me to wake Jazz?"

"Yes, you'd better get her back to Manny's. Better get yourself booked somewhere else, too, or see if Manny has a spare sofa you can rent. They know where you're staying."

"You're talking like a cop," Borden said. "If Eidolon wants us, they can always find us. Well, me, anyway. You and Jazz, it's tougher, since you're leads. They can only predict you through the effects you have, not your exact location."

"Then how did they just deliver me a note?"

A rattling sigh. "It's too freaking early for philosophy and physics, Lucia. But Leads blip on and off the radar. You're a blue most of the time, but sometimes they can see you clearly. It's like somebody who usually drives really fast having car trouble."

Interesting. "All right. We'll need to have a war meeting later at the office. One o'clock? Bring Jazz in through the garage entrance, it's the most defensible. I'll have someone meet you."

"Someone who? You're not giving Manny a gun, are you?"

She laughed. "Not that Manny would need one of mine, he has plenty of his own…but no. I've hired a friend of

mine to help us out. His name is Omar. He'll meet you in
the parking garage."

"We'll be there."

* * * * *

Who has made a mistake? How will Lucia fix it?
And what will the next red letter bring?
Find out in DEVIL'S DUE,
available in January 2006!

Silhouette® BOMBSHELL™

THE IT GIRLS

Rich, fabulous...and dangerously underestimated.

They're heiresses with connections, glamour girls with the inside track.

And they're going undercover to fight high-society crime in high style.

Catch The It Girls in these six books by some of your favorite Bombshell authors:

THE GOLDEN GIRL by Erica Orloff, September 2005

FLAWLESS by Michele Hauf, October 2005

LETHALLY BLONDE by Nancy Bartholomew, November 2005

MS. LONGSHOT by Sylvie Kurtz, December 2005

A MODEL SPY by Natalie Dunbar, January 2006

BULLETPROOF PRINCESS by Vicki Hinze, February 2006

Available at your favorite retail outlet.

Lucia Garza suspected she'd made
a deal with the devil when she opened her
detective agency. And the red envelopes
containing tricky assignments kept coming
from her shadowy bankroller. Now Lucia was
an unwilling pawn—in a battle to control
the future of the world.

RED LETTER DAYS:
YOU'LL NEVER BELIEVE
WHAT'S INSIDE

DEVIL'S DUE
by Rachel Caine

Available January wherever books are sold.

eHARLEQUIN.com

The Ultimate Destination for Women's Fiction

For **FREE online reading,** visit
www.eHarlequin.com now and enjoy:

Online Reads
Read **Daily** and **Weekly** chapters from
our Internet-exclusive stories by your
favorite authors.

Interactive Novels
Cast your vote to help decide how these
stories unfold...then stay tuned!

Quick Reads
For shorter romantic reads, try our
collection of Poems, Toasts, & More!

Online Read Library
Miss one of our online reads?
Come here to catch up!

Reading Groups
Discuss, share and rave with other
community members!

For great reading online,
visit www.eHarlequin.com today!

If you enjoyed what you just read,
then we've got an offer you can't resist!

Take 2 bestselling love stories FREE!

Plus get a FREE surprise gift!

COMING NEXT MONTH

#73 DEVIL'S DUE—Rachel Caine
Red Letter Days

Lucia Garza suspected she'd made a deal with the devil when she opened her detective agency. And the red envelopes containing tricky assignments kept coming from her shadowy bankroller. Every order Lucia followed—or disobeyed—could mean someone's life or death. But as she made her move to get out, Lucia learned that her backer and his enemy were using Lucia and her team as pawns in a battle to control the future of the world. And if she left, there might not be a future at all....

#74 A MODEL SPY—Natalie Dunbar
The It Girls

As a former supermodel from a wealthy family, Vanessa Dawson was the perfect fit for the Gotham Roses's latest society crime-fighting mission. Two Miami models were dead, and all signs pointed to a drug ring operating from high fashion's highest precincts. Was hip-hop mogul Hot T involved? Vanessa went undercover as a swimsuit model to find out, but soon shoot-outs replaced fashion shoots as the order of the day....

#75 TRACE OF INNOCENCE—Erica Orloff
A Billie Quinn Case

For criminologist Billie Quinn, using DNA evidence to nail the bad guys was a personal crusade—after all, her own mother had been murdered by a serial killer. But sometimes DNA proved innocence, and Billie knew—in her *heart*—that the wrong man was in prison for the infamous Suicide King killings. When her ex-lover fought to keep the wrong man behind bars, Billie had to ask herself—who was the real Suicide King?

#76 THE BIG BURN—Terry Watkins

After a daring California wildfire rescue, smoke jumper Anna Quick was a little burned-out. But fire waits on no woman, and Special Ops team leader John Brock needed her—now!— for a dangerous secret mission in Malaysia. Anna expected the "routine" challenges of fighting a big blaze. Instead, she discovered deception, smoke screens...and incendiary revelations about the war on terror and her own family.

SBCNM1205